The Great Cause

Book 5 *in the* Lord Edward's Archer *series*

The GREAT CAUSE

GRIFF HOSKER

LUME BOOKS

LUME BOOKS

Published in 2022 by Lume Books

ISBN 978-1-83901-474-1

Typeset using Atomik ePublisher from Easypress Technologies

www.lumebooks.co.uk

Quhen Alexander our kynge was dede,
  That Scotlande lede in lauche and le,
  Away was sons of alle and brede,
  Off wyne and wax, of gamyn and gle.
  Our golde was changit into lede.
  Crist, borne in virgynyte,
  Succoure Scotlande, and ramede,
  That is stade in perplexite.
  Andrew of Wyntoun

Orygynale Cronykil of Scotland (History of Scotland)

Real Characters Mentioned in the Novel

King Edward, King of England and Lord of Aquitaine and Gascony
Queen Eleanor of England
King Alexander of Scotland
Edmund Crouchback, 1st Earl of Lancaster (and King Edward's brother)
Thomas, 2nd Earl of Lancaster, son of Edmund Crouchback
Henry Lacy, Earl of Lincoln and Constable of Chester
Sir Reginald Grey, 1st Baron Grey of Wilton, Lord of Castell Rhuthun (Ruthin)
William de Beauchamp, 9th Earl of Warwick
Madog ap Llywelyn, rebel and pretender to the Welsh crown
Robert de Brus, 5th Lord of Annandale
Robert de Brus, 6th Lord of Annandale
John Balliol, Lord of Galloway and Barnard Castle and, latterly, King of Scotland
Antony Bek, Bishop of Durham
Sir John de Warenne, Earl of Surrey and John Balliol's father-in-law

Glossary

Centenar – a commander of one hundred men

Familia – household knights of a great lord

Glanogwen – Bethesda

Llanfihangel-yng-Ngwynfa – Llanfihangel-nant-Melan

Pencraig – Old Radnor

Vintenar – a commander of twenty men

Y Trallwng – Welshpool

Prologue

Kinghorn, Fife, Scotland, 1286

The two men who landed from the Norwegian boat were dressed as merchants, but had there been any watching who was in the least bit observant, they would have recognised them for what they were – soldiers or hired swords. A few would have spotted that they were more than that; they were killers. They would have seen the clues and recognised the thin-bladed knife known in Italy as the *misericorde* and in England as the bodkin blade. They would have seen that their swords were made from the finest Spanish steel and without adornments. Killers did not need beautiful weapons, they wanted weapons that they could rely upon, that would kill. Such observers would have wondered at the tanned skin and the dark hair, which did not suggest a Norwegian.

All of those were to be clearly seen but Kinghorn, despite the fact that there was a royal residence in the town, was too quiet and sleepy for such clues to be identified. Even though the Queen of Scotland was there, expecting her new child, there were few soldiers. Queens were not murdered. It was their husbands whose lives were threatened.

So it was not surprising that few noticed them, for the small fishing port had been invaded by the new Queen of Scotland, Yolande de Dreux. The influx of visitors were all attending on the queen: ladies, physicians, cooks and the like augmented the small population of the Fife port. To them, the men landing from the ship were invisible. The pregnant queen was there to have a peaceful confinement in the pleasant port which, as its name suggested, was a Royal burgh and castle that Scottish kings favoured for its peace. The fact that it had been some years since the Scottish royal family had visited explained why all was being done to make the queen – and when he arrived from Edinburgh, the king – welcome.

The two killers simply slipped in and met the Scotsman who waited with two horses for them. The three were gone before the crew had begun to unload the cargo. The captain had been grateful for the extra income and the two, almost silent, passengers were forgotten before they had covered a mile. Had that captain been questioned after the event, he would have struggled to describe them. They had huddled beneath their cloaks and kept away from the crew on the voyage from Norway.

Despite the fact their destination was a mere ten miles from Kinghorn, and they could easily reach it in less than two hours, the three men rode slowly. The Scot with them pointed out various features on the road. He was the local whose expertise would allow them to do their job. There were no cliffs, as such, but there were some escarpments and the whole coast had dragon-like teeth close to the sea. It was not a place where people sought seafood and shellfish from the rocks.

When they passed the abbey at Burntisland and the church at Dalgety Bay they rode quickly, for these were not their final destination – but the two places were identified and would be important in their plan. Once they reached their destination, the quiet town of

Inverkeithing, they entered their Scottish guide's mean dwelling to formulate their plans properly.

The two killers, Jean and Konrad, had learned their trade in Germany and the Holy Land. There were assassins in the Holy Land who were very efficient, but Christians found the hard to hire. The two Germans found that there were many Christians who wished to have other Christians killed, and they soon discovered this was an easier way to make money than fighting the Turk.

Jean and Konrad were expensive because they always succeeded. The Scotsman who had hired them had done so through an intermediary, Bergil Petrsson, a Swede. The identity of the man who had paid them two hundred florins was unknown. Even Jamie Kirkpatrick, the Scot who met them, did not know the identity of the men's employer, just that he was an important Scottish lord and that Jamie ought to ask no questions. Having lost his family fortune through a gambling addiction and been reduced to living in what amounted to a hovel, he was happy to serve the killers for the fifty florins he would be paid.

Jean's voice was barely accented, for the men had learned to disguise everything that might identify them. "Can you be sure, Scotsman, that he will seek local guides? From what I have observed the road to Kinghorn would be well known to all."

"Aye, it will be as we said. The work will need to be at night and the journey from Edinburgh to Kinghorn, in March, is a treacherous one. Queen Yolande's birthday determines the day. It will be the night of the nineteenth. I know this land well." He shook his head, bitterly. "Indeed, I had a castle, not ten miles from where we sit. It is I who will be asked to guide them, but I will become unwell and my two cousins," he waved his hand at both of them, "will have to do it."

Konrad nodded. "And the horses you have are the equal of the king's. He is a good rider and a fast one. You will be able to keep up with him."

Jean shook his head. He was the one who made all decisions for the killers and he was not happy. "How will you explain our skin and our accents? We cannot speak Gaelic."

"It matters not, for the lords who will be coming prefer French or English. Speak French and they will be grateful. If you spoke English, then they might be suspicious, but Scottish lords like to speak French."

Konrad put down the goblet he had just drained. "And after?"

"When you have disposed of the horses you have a short walk, less than two miles to Dunearn Castle."

Jean seemed surprised. "A castle?"

"It is not occupied, for it is an old hill fort that has been empty since the Roman times. There will be two horses, food and water there. How you leave the country is up to you, but I suggest you avoid Kinghorn and Edinburgh."

Jean snorted. "Do you think us fools? This is not the first time we have done this sort of thing. We have our route planned, but it is *here*." He tapped his head. The two had learned to survive as long as they had by keeping secrets both theirs and others.

Jamie shrugged. "I care not. So long as you are never found, then I am safe."

King Alexander had always been a hard worker. The death of his first wife, Margaret, had made him look at his life again. It had reinvigorated his ambitions and those of his country. He had not done enough in the north of his land, where there were enemies like the Norsemen as well as lords who disliked the rule of what was, to them, a Norman. King Alexander now planned to remedy that by showing his power in the Western Isles. He had sent a summons for his lords to meet in Edinburgh, and he would take an army and make the north of his realm as peaceful as the south. He and King

4

Edward understood each other well. The King of England would not threaten Scotland, as King Alexander was an ally as well as a brother-in-law.

King Alexander made the plans based on a safe south of his realm. It was late when he finished, but he was determined to be with his new wife for her birthday. Despite the awful weather, he and a handful of the nobles who were closest to him mounted horses and rode for Dalmeny on the River Forth, where they would take the ferry to Inverkeithing. His lords were not happy, for they liked the life in Edinburgh and did not relish a night ride to Kinghorn. Even more importantly, a spring storm threatened to prevent them crossing the Forth – and none wished a ride to the river, a wet wait and then a return to the castle. King Alexander laughed at their misgivings.

"Gentlemen, if you fear to cross the river then I shall go alone! I am sure we shall make the crossing without harm, but I will not ask any to unman themselves. If you fear for your lives, then stay here!"

Of course, such words only served to ensure that he boarded the ferry with all his nobles. Whilst a wild crossing, it was not a long one and the ferrymen knew their business. They also knew that the shape of the estuary prevented the full force of the storm from being felt. Of course, the road from Inverkeithing to Kinghorn was a different matter and there, riders braving the elements would be subject to the full force of the storm. It did not concern them, for by the time the king was on that road, they would be safe in their homes counting the coins they had gained from carrying him!

The burgesses of Dalmeny had seen the king board the ferry and when he landed, he and his nobles were taken to the home of the richest of them, Lord David Dalmeny. His cook had previously worked for King Alexander, and Lord David hoped to gain favour by having his king's former cook prepare food. He also hoped to

5

induce King Alexander to stay for the night. This was how men increased their power. The crumbs that fell from the king's table were valuable ones!

"My lord, I am humbled by your visit."

"Lord David, we cannot stay long, but the smell of food is enticing. We will eat before I travel on to join my wife."

Lord David led them to his hastily-prepared feast. The cook, Alexander Le Saucier, was there, ladling the stew into bowls as his cooks cut the bread into manageable pieces.

When he recognised the cook, the king said, "Alexander! I wondered where you went when you left my service! How goes it with you?"

"Well, my lord. I was sorry to hear of Queen Margaret's death. She was a lovely lady."

The king took the proffered bowl and spoon. "Aye well, she was too good for me and, like all of my children, God took her." He said to no one in particular; "Perhaps I am cursed."

Lord David hastily reassured his liege lord. "No King Alexander! We have enjoyed many years of peace under your rule. It is just ill luck."

The king nodded. "But I shall take no chances with my new queen and unborn heir. I have made all the plans required and now I shall join her, and stay with her during her confinement."

The cook, satisfied that all had eaten, wiped his hands on his apron. "I hope that you will stay here this night, my lord. I have a fine breakfast planned!"

The king was a fast eater and, having finished the stew, wiped his hands on the cloth over his left shoulder and then emptied his goblet. He shook his head. "I have to get to Kinghorn this night, for tomorrow is my queen's birthday."

The cook, who knew the king better than the nobles with him, spoke plainly. "My lord, what are you doing out in such weather and darkness? How many times have I tried to persuade you that midnight travelling will do you no good?"

King Alexander laughed. "Many times, my friend – and when did your advice ever do any good?"

Lord David was disappointed, but still saw a way to ingratiate himself. "The road is dangerous. At least let me find you a guide, for the road is a desolate one."

"I will brook no further delay. Have you a horseman who can be my guide?"

Lord David nodded. "Yes, my lord, Sir James Kirkpatrick has fallen on hard times but he knows the road and he is a good rider."

"Then take me to him."

The heavily-bandaged arm sported by Jamie Kirkpatrick made Lord David frown. "Sir James, I thought to have you escort the king to Kinghorn. You are injured?"

"Yes, my lord, but I have two cousins staying with me who know the road well."

"So *they* are to escort the king?"

"Do not worry, Lord David, the king will be as safe with them as he would be with me and there are two of them. They are both good riders and have good horses."

King Alexander had heard none of this, however, and when the two men emerged from the stables with two coursers, he was delighted. "Dalmeny, I am in your debt. With those horses, we will not have to keep to the tardy pace of the men with whom I ride! Mount, gentlemen. The night is fearful, and I would be with my wife rather than here!"

The two men did not have to say a word. They mounted, and the two killers set off at a fast pace. The king gave a loud cheer as he dug his spurs into his horse's flanks, and before they had gone half a mile there was already a huge gap developing between the king and his nobles.

King Alexander thought it good sport and kept his horse close to the rumps of the two horsemen, who seemed to know the road well. They were his equal, and that was a rare thing. He smiled as thought of the foolish advice from his former cook and Lord David. He had often taken midnight rides, and this would see another successful conclusion.

He was already anticipating his arrival as they passed the abbey. Another half hour and he would be with his wife and before a warm fire. He would enjoy his wife's birthday and they would stay at Kinghorn until the child was born.

The storm had been fiercer than he anticipated, but the two men were good at their job. One had gone ahead and the other stayed to his left. They had found the right path and, despite the wind and the rain, he had been in no danger of falling.

But even as that thought entered his mind, the rider on his left suddenly wheeled to his right. King Alexander was a good enough horseman to recognise the potential danger of putting his horse's leg into a hole and he instinctively veered right. The other rider had been directly in front of him and when he too veered, King Alexander tried to do the same. There was simply no ground before him.

All the king could see was the dark sea and the white flecks of wild waves. He was suddenly falling, and he could do nothing about it.

Horse and rider made not a sound until their bodies crashed and cracked on the waiting rocks.

The two killers dismounted and led their horses to the edge of the escarpment, and they watched King Alexander strike the rocks first, before his horse fell on top of him. If the fall had not killed him, then the crashing horse would have. The two men wasted no time, for they knew that the nobles would be soon on their tails. They drew their swords and slit their horses' throats. The horses' weight took the animals over the escarpment.

Waiting only to ensure that the carcasses were visible, they turned and headed through the dark on foot to the distant hill fort. They had covered barely one hundred paces when they heard the nobles gallop along what passed for a road. There was not even a pause in their gait. They hurried on, passing the body of Alexander with no sense that Scotland was now without a king..

The killers found the waiting horses and headed south to England. They would take a ship to France and await their next commission; there were always nobles willing to pay for their services. Jean had heard that Edmund Crouchback, the brother of the King of England, might be their next target. The two men did not mind whom they killed, so long as the pay was commensurate with the risk.

It was mid-morning when the men searching for the king and his guides found the monarch's body and the three dead horses. Now, all of Scotland's hopes lay with the unborn child in Queen Yolande's womb, and a three-year-old child in Norway.

Chapter 1

Yarpole, 1290 (four years later)

I am Gerald Warbow, and I am still known to many as Lord Edward's Archer, even though Lord Edward is now King Edward of England. My name is well known by the archers who fight for England and it is feared by England's enemies. I have fought for King Edward in lands as far dispersed as the lands of the Mongols to the east, and the Welsh borders to the west. My life began as a humble archer in Wales, but my association with King Edward means that great lords like the Earl of Warwick know my name. I have risen far.

The last time I fought for the king was when we defeated Prince Llewellyn; that was the last real threat to English dominance, and Wales was subdued. I remained a warrior, but I was now a warrior without wars to fight. England was at peace.

I had thought, three years earlier, that I might be going on another crusade. I was not happy at the prospect, for I knew they were doomed to failure, but King Edward wanted his captain of archers and the men he led. Fortunately, it came to nothing and we stayed at Yarpole, close to the Welsh border. That I was not at war did not stop me from training every day. My men and I would spend at least an hour a day loosing arrows at targets in the field. When we were not aiming at the butts then we would be training young boys to follow in our footsteps.

I was happy there. I had my archers still and each Sunday we practised with the men of Yarpole and Luston, for the king wished every man in England to be able to fight for him. My archers would use their expertise to make the yeoman archers better. Most were now, like me, older men with sons –in some cases grandsons – of their own. Those sons and at least one grandson came with us to the archery field each day. While we practised, they would watch and then fetch our spent arrows. Then, we would watch them with a critical eye as they drew back their shorter bows. We made small adjustments to their hands, arms and legs, for we wanted them to be better than we were. They would be the new archers, whom I would lead should I ever be called upon again to go to war. I was happy at the thought.

My eldest son, Hamo, trained with them. I had ensured that he was trained well from an early age. Alan of the Woods had not gone to war against the Welsh, and so he began my son's training. Alan was a master archer and Hamo had learned well. Alan could not find fault with him, and that was rare. The difference with the training I had received was that I also trained with a sword. That skill had saved my life on more than one occasion: I had a good sword and I knew how to use it. Many a knight had been surprised when the archer put down his bow and fought them with his sword.

Hamo and I sometimes had amusement when we trained, for occasionally I would mount one of my horses, take the bow and arrows given to me in the land of the Mongols and then I would ride and loose an arrow at the targets. I did not delude myself; I was worse than the poorest Mongol archer I had ever seen, but still better than any English archer, for we could not use our longbows from the back of a horse. I enjoyed the experience, but when it was over the bow and the arrows were placed back in the chest. I would never use the Mongol bow in war.

My eldest daughter, Margaret, was growing too and within a year or so would be ready to begin a family. Already her stunning looks had attracted the attention not only of the young men of the manor, but also the sons of the lords. I might not be a knight, but I had a title – I was a gentleman – and therefore Margaret would be a good catch; but my wife and I were determined that when she wed, it would be for love. I was a rich man and she would have a fine dowry when she chose a husband.

That was something else Mary and I agreed upon. Mary had been a slave at the court of the Mongol khan and although well treated, she had been an object that was sold and used. When we wed, it was because we each found joy in the other and we would have the same for our children. Joan, my third child, was still just that, a child, and for that I was happy. The problem was that Margaret thought we were isolated at Yarpole. She was right, but that was the way Mary and I liked it.

My life was full, and the two manors of Yarpole and Luston kept me occupied. Of course, I had drawn my bow and sword in anger, but that had not been on either King Edward's or Sir Roger's behalf, but for my manor. There were still brigands and thieves. There were those who were too lazy to work and sought to take from those that were hard-working. My justice was swift, and the last hanging had been two years since. Bandits liked the forests and woods. My men and I had learned how to see their signs and we hunted them well. Those who merely passed through, having fallen on hard times, we did not bother. In fact, my wife often fed them and gave them discarded garments. We knew the difference, and when livestock disappeared, or travellers were attacked, *then* we began our hunt. The fact that we had not hunted for two years showed how effective we were.

I thought this would be my life until the royal pursuivant, Sir Godfrey, came to see me.

Dressed in his royal finery, Sir Godfrey looked like a gilded peacock, but this was an illusion, for he was a soldier. King Edward chose his men well. His unannounced arrival, accompanied by just two servants, made the hairs on the back of my neck prickle. Did King Edward need me again? The thought worried me, for King Edward only used me for the most dangerous of tasks. I had thought, indeed I had *hoped*, that he had found another, younger man to do his bidding.

However, I smiled at Sir Godfrey when he arrived; not only because it was the polite thing to do but because I liked him. We had fought together and there was honesty between us. John, my steward, brought him to the large room we used during the day. It was sunny and light. Mary was sewing, as were our two daughters. Hamo was with the other young men. They would be practising and gambling; archers liked the edge of winning and losing. Gambling provided that, even on a dull training day. Hamo's skill meant that he won money more often than he lost.

"It is good to see you again, Sir Godfrey. The years have been kind to you."

He smiled and bowed to Mary, who, whilst not having the title of a lady was a lady in every other sense of the word. "And you, Gerald, have done even better. You have an idyll here, which I envy."

John poured the wine and put food on the table.

I tasted the wine. John had chosen well. It was a Gascon wine from Bordeaux and one of my favourites. "And I do not think, Sir Godfrey, that you have ridden from wherever the king is housed, merely to pass pleasantries and compliment me."

He laughed. "I do enjoy speaking with you, Gerald. You are

refreshingly honest and cut to the heart of the matter. Forgive me, Mistress Mary, but I require a conference with your husband. I will not keep him long."

My wife was quick thinking, and she said, "Then will you be taking him from us immediately, or should I have chambers prepared?"

He bowed. "Tomorrow morning will suffice, so I thank you for the offer of a chamber." Once outside, he said, "It is not the king who summoned you, but the queen. She is travelling north to visit her manors and to arrange the marriage of her son, Prince Edward, to Margaret of Norway, the heiress to the Scottish throne. Since the death of her father, the child is the most valuable person in Scotland. A marriage to England means peace on the northern border for another generation. She wished you and some of your archers to be part of her escort."

I cocked a questioning eye. He shrugged. "I would be lying if I said that Queen Eleanor is popular. She is not hated, but she has enemies and she would feel safer travelling through the great forests of the north with you at her side. She is very fond of you, you know."

I was relieved and it showed in my smile. "Then I am more than happy to do so."

"You may be away from home until the end of summer."

I nodded. "I will take my son as one of the archers, and my wife is also very fond of the queen. It will not be a problem." I could tell that Sir Godfrey was not telling me everything. "Come, Sir Godfrey, we have fought alongside each other. No secrets!"

He nodded. "Aye, you are right, but what I have to tell you is for your ears and your ears alone." I nodded and, taking out my dagger, kissed the hilt. "Thank you for that. The queen is ill. When she was in Gascony, she was bitten by a mosquito and suffered double quartan fever. She recovered – or at least, she did not die – but she is still weak. If I tell you that King Edward will also be with her for part of the journey, then you will understand the seriousness of the illness."

I remembered when Queen Eleanor procured the medicine that saved King Edward's life in the Holy Land, and how much the couple loved each other. "And there is no cure?"

He shook his head. "There are medicines that she takes, which alleviate the symptoms, but each day sees her just a little weaker. It is not a question of *if* she worsens, but *when*."

"Then she is dying?"

Silence hung between us. Sir Godfrey nodded. "It is not something spoken of, but I have looked into the queen's eyes and I know that she knows."

"Thank you for your confidence, my lord, and it will remain a secret, although I will tell my wife." His eyes widened. "You are a bachelor still and do not understand such matters, but Mary and the queen were close and I could not in all conscience keep such news from her. It will not go beyond Mary."

"I trust you Gerald, and I pray that my trust is not misplaced."

When I told my wife, I thought her heart would break. She had served Queen Eleanor before she had become queen, as a lady in waiting. The queen had encouraged us to wed. That her death was not imminent did nothing to ease the blow.

I confess that I was not able to give her my shoulder to weep upon for long. I had decisions to make about the archers I would take. Sir Godfrey had asked for me and seven others. In the past, that choice would have been easy, but the fact I considered taking Hamo told me how long it was since I had led my stalwarts. I needed young men, for they would have an edge and would be keen to impress. I doubted we would need to draw a bow and fight, for it was unheard of for a member of the royal family to be attacked, although King Alexander of Scotland's death four years earlier had made me, for one, suspicious. The king had been riding in a storm and became separated from his companions. He was found dead, with a broken neck. I had been the protector of a king and knew that such things should never have happened. There was no real proof that he had been murdered – but I had suspicions and so I intended the men I took to be the most alert of any.

The decision was almost made for me. More than thirty archers followed my banner, but many had farms and homes some way from my hall. I had but ten who lived close and would not be missed if we were away for months. They were largely unmarried. John, son of John, was an obvious one. His father had the farm closest to the hall. Richard of Culcheth's son, Robin, was probably my most experienced young archer and he was a second. He lived with his mother and father on a farm in the village. David's son, Gwillim, had shown me that he was as good a man as his father. He and the others lived in the warrior hall. Dick of Luston had helped defend our land against the Welsh and had been with me since his father died. He was not only a good archer but, like Gwillim, also a highly-skilled scout. When we hunted bandits, those two usually found them. They seemed to have the ability to sniff out those who were a danger. Harry of Chester had been a wanderer and came to serve me just two years earlier, but he had fought against the Welsh and was as good an archer as I had met. The last archer I would take was Ralph the fletcher. He had a wife and a young son and had come to me, seeking work. Fletchers were vital and I took him on happily. He had not been with me for long, but he had impressed me and he wanted to show me that his family would not be an encumbrance.

I also chose to take Hamo. There were many reasons for this.

Firstly, it was to give him the experience of mixing with warriors and to further his training. I had done the same when I was his age and it made me the archer I was. Secondly, it gave us a horse holder. We would ride, but English archers were not Mongols and did not fight from the backs of horses. Hamo was strong and could manage our eight horses easily.

I sought out the men and told them, in the barest of terms, that they would be following me for the next few months. The married men, all three of them, would have to explain to their wives but the younger ones were happy to be riding abroad. The last man I spoke with, as I washed up for the meal, was Hamo. Each time I saw him I saw myself before I met Lord Edward. He had been well fed as a bairn and had as broad a chest as any. He still had some growing to do, but the constant drawing of a bow would merely add to his size. It would not be long before he was drawing my bow – and that would be a measure of his prowess. My wife was speaking with Sir Godfrey and we were alone when we spoke.

"Hamo, I would have you ride with me and my archers on the morrow. We have been asked to protect the queen."

He was young enough to have difficulty controlling his feelings. His face lit up like a sunrise. I did not wish to disappoint him later, and so I gave him the bad news straight away: "You are there to tend to our needs and hold the horses."

The smile left and his face fell as he dried his hands. "I do not take my bow?"

I laughed. "Of course you take your bow. You are an archer. But I doubt that you will need it. I doubt if any of us will need them, and they may well spend the whole trip in their cases. However, it is as well to be prepared and if there is trouble then you will hold the horses while our men and I defend the queen."

As he grew up, Mary had often chastised me for the way I spoke to our son. I used the same tone as I did for the men under my command. It was my way, but I knew it made Mary think I was colder than was really the case. The result was that Hamo never questioned me, and now his nod told me that he accepted my decision.

When we ate, I learned much from Sir Godfrey. He was not an ordinary pursuivant. He was a good warrior and a clever man. As such, King Edward used him to gather information. He told us of the discord north of the vague border between England and Scotland. The future queen of Scotland was just seven years old; King Alexander's children had all died and his granddaughter was the only one left to inherit, so she was important beyond her years. She was called the Maid of Norway, for she was the daughter of the King of Norway. Sir Godfrey told us that there were as many as seventeen other Scots who thought they had a claim to the throne.

"That is why Queen Eleanor's visit is so important. If Prince Edward is married to the Queen of Scotland, then England can ensure peace on our northern border."

"And is Wales quiet now? Have the castles worked?"

King Edward had built and repaired many castles in the north of Wales to keep a tight grip on the heartland of discontent.

He shrugged. "That is a good question, Gerald, and I wish I knew the answer. Much of my work has been in Gascony and Scotland. You are closer to the Welsh than any. What do you think?"

I laughed. "That they are not done yet. We had strong walls around my hall, and we are vigilant still. Sir Roger also keeps an eye on the border."

Mary shook her head. "Why must you always talk of war? There is peace, let us keep it that way."

Sir Godfrey looked at me. We were both of the same opinion and it was I, as host, who voiced it. "The way you keep the peace is to be

18

prepared for war. Since I returned there has been no war, but if war comes, then I have more than thirty bowmen who would make any of England's enemies pay. You keep the peace by preparing for war and letting your enemies know that you do so. Those who beat their swords into ploughshares delude themselves."

I saw Hamo taking in the fact that Sir Godfrey nodded his agreement. Margaret had been silent up to that point and as the conversation ended and we ate she asked, "Does this mean that Hamo will be riding with the queen?"

I nodded.

"I should like to see the ladies of the court. It is dull around here."

I looked at Mary; this was her area. She smiled and said, "I am sorry, young lady, that we have kept you safe from harm. How could we have enlivened your life?"

"I would visit lords and ladies in great castles."

I saw the narrowing of Mary's eyes. She had lived at court, both the Mongol court and Queen Eleanor's. She knew the dangers of such places, but more pertinently, she did not enjoy the implied criticism. "Young lady, when I deem you ready for that world then you will enter it. However, you must learn to appreciate what you have!"

I saw the smirk on young Joan's face as Margaret scowled, knowing that she had been beaten. Children!

We rode to Lincoln. All of my men wore my livery, for the sight of it would tell any would-be attackers that we were the best of archers. Our bows were in leather cases attached to our saddles and our arrow bags were made of hide; this was not usual, but it protected our arrows and we had learned that just one damaged arrow in an arrow bag or belt could spell disaster. The hoods we wore when riding would keep us warm while our oiled cloaks would keep us dry and doubled

19

as tents. Hamo led the sumpter with the tent, spare arrowheads and food. When we were with the queen we would be accommodated in monasteries and castles, but we liked to be prepared. I rode with Gerald at the fore and Hamo brought up the rear. For this task, he would be an archer and not my son.

As we rode, I found out more about the world of King Edward. Before the last Welsh war I would have been the one to give out information, but I now lived in a backwater and was not privy to the machinations of one of the strongest kings England had enjoyed. One had to go back to the second King Henry to find a king of the same magnitude. I had fought in Gascony for Lord Edward, but that had been when his father was king. King Edward had now taken more French land and, Sir Godfrey told me, now ruled as much of France as the French king. Wales was a vassal of England and with the marriage of Margaret to the Prince of Wales, Scotland would be his, too. So, I saw the importance of this ride north and it explained why King Edward would risk his wife.

We met the queen at the royal palace of Eltham. It was not a fortress, but a home close enough to London to be convenient when King Edward needed to conduct royal business. The queen was reclining on a settle when I entered and bowed. She looked ill and I saw that Sir Godfrey had not exaggerated; this was not the same woman who had nursed her husband back to life in Acre.

She beamed when she saw me. "You came!"

"I could not do other, my lady."

"And how is Mary, she is well? And your children?"

"They are all well and I have Hamo with me. He will act as a servant on the ride."

She clapped her hands together. "Then fetch him. I would like to see him!" There was genuine joy in her voice.

The archers had been whisked to their quarters when we arrived. Sir Godfrey said, "I will find him."

There were just two ladies and a male servant in the small chamber. Queen Eleanor said, "Robert, serve Gerald some wine."

As he poured, she said, "Godfrey has confided in you?" I nodded and she sighed. "I have ever been active, and the worst part of this ailment is that I tire easily. This journey will take longer than it should."

I sipped the wine, nodded my approval, and said, "And it is necessary, Queen Eleanor?"

She glanced at her ladies in waiting and then gave a sad smile. "The heir to the Scottish crown is a child. I must get to York and meet with the Norwegian representatives. Anything less than a king or queen would be deemed an insult to Norway and the guardians of Scotland. That troubled country bubbles with unrest. It is not the unrest of the people, you understand, but the nobles – there are at least fourteen who have a claim to the throne and the six guardians need stability. England is their only hope."

I could not help a wry smile. "England? They call us the auld enemy!"

She laughed and suddenly looked much younger. "I know! It is a cruel joke, is it not?"

Just then the door opened, and Sir Godfrey and Hamo entered. The queen's face became animated. Her illness seemed to dissipate as her smile made the fog of tiredness become the sunshine of joy. "I can see both his mother and you in him. Come Hamo, sit closer so that I may see you better."

He walked nervously forward, and she held out her hands to take his. He looked almost mesmerised. He had been brought up on my manor as a warrior, and this was the Queen of England. He was dumbstruck.

21

Queen Eleanor examined his face and then his hands. "His eyes and his smile are his mother's, but there is no mistaking the chest and arms of Gerald the archer. Sit next to me, for you are a giant and my neck aches."

To sit in the presence of royalty was unheard of, but Hamo obeyed. Sir Godfrey cocked an eye. Even he was surprised. "You know that my husband and I would not rule England but for your father, Hamo?"

He had heard the story, but I had made my part in it less than that of King Edward. "I know, Queen Eleanor, that he has been of some service."

She laughed again. "I can see that you will be as modest as your father. When others failed us your father was a rock, and it is why I have asked for him on this journey."

She turned her attention to me. "I am not a fool, Gerald, and I know that there are many in England who do not like me. I am Spanish and they are suspicious of me. The English do not like foreigners – which is ironic, as my husband is descended from Normans!" She shook her head. "I have given birth to sixteen children for England, and yet they dislike that my husband gives me the manors of debtors. Do I not perform good works for the poor?"

These were rhetorical questions, and no one reacted to them. She smiled and composed herself. "I do not think there will be an attempt on my life, but then I felt safe in Acre's walls and yet an assassin came close. I have my guards, Gerald, but it is you in whom I place my trust."

I bowed. "And I will do all that I can, Queen Eleanor. Forgive me, but I am a practical man. How will you and your ladies travel?"

"Just as I would have expected. My ladies are young and can ride. I fear that I cannot, and I will ride a horse litter. I know that will slow us up. I have two doctors, who will accompany us. They will probably slow us up even more than the horse litter! Whenever possible, we will stay in my manors." There was a sad smile on her face. "Some I have barely seen. I should like to see them again."

"And when do we leave?"

"Now that you are here there is nothing to prevent us from leaving as soon as possible. The day after tomorrow?" She put her hand to her head. "I am sorry Gerald, but I tire easily. This will be a foretaste of our journey."

"Of course." I bowed. "Come, Hamo. Queen Eleanor, I will speak with the captain of your guards."

I waited outside until Sir Godfrey emerged. "It is good that it is summer. I would hate to think of us making this journey when it was damp, cold and filled with autumnal fogs. Hamo, return to the men and tell them when we leave."

"Aye, father. She is a great lady."

I nodded. "None greater." He hurried off. "Who is the captain of the guard?"

"I do not think you know him. Rodrigo of Castile is a countryman of hers, but he is a sword for hire." I gave him a questioning look. "Do not worry Gerald, he is trustworthy. You value my opinion?" I nodded. "I would have him watch my back. He has with him ten men at arms. They are all English and are both good warriors and good riders. You can trust them – however Rodrigo is a Castilian, and they are a proud warrior race. What he may resent is your special position. He will not appreciate being ordered by an archer."

I smiled. "And you are telling me to be diplomatic?" He nodded. "And that goes against my nature. I will try. I can say no more than that. Lead me to him."

We disliked each other from the moment we met. He was a knight and saw that I was merely an archer. I had met his type before, for there had been many like him in the Welsh campaign. They were arrogant and whilst most were very brave, they believed that knights were the only ones who could win a battle. I took the initiative immediately.

"I am Captain Gerald Warbow, and I will be leading Queen Eleanor's party as we head north."

Shaking his head, he said, "I am the captain of the queen's guards and I will protect her."

I smiled. "I thought we were all there to protect her, but I am glad that you accept my authority and that I will lead."

"I did not say that."

"No, you said that you were there to protect Queen Eleanor, and I agreed." I sighed. "Captain, if there is danger then it will not be in the open, but in the forests through which we have to pass. Sherwood is a huge forest and therein lies the danger. My archers are at home in such forests. Are your mailed and plated men equally comfortable there?"

I knew that I had him there. He jabbed a finger at my chest. "I am Queen Eleanor's protector!"

When he had stormed off, Sir Godfrey laughed. "You have no future as a pursuivant, Gerald!"

"And I thank God for that. I know not how you do it, Sir Godfrey!"

We saw King Edward the day before we left. Parliament was not cooperating, and it showed in his face. He wanted money to pay for soldiers and his castles in Wales. They were both expensive. Parliament was filled with the self-serving nobles who did not go to wars but were happy to profit from them.

The king and his wife dined alone that night and we did not get to see him. The next morning, however, as we waited in the courtyard for the royal party, he did come to speak with us and, to Don Rodrigo's chagrin, the Castilian was ignored and King Edward spoke to me.

"Gerald, I am pleased that my wife asked for you. You cannot keep

24

her safe from her ailment, but I know that while you ride at her side then no harm will come to her from either man or beast."

"You will be with us, King Edward?"

"I will ride with you to Barking Abbey and stay the night." He smiled. "It will allow us to progress through London and receive the cheers of the city."

Inwardly I groaned, for the abbey was less than six miles from our starting point. I could not tell if he was joking or not. The populace of London was fickle, and King Edward preferred to stay either in Eltham, south of the city, or at Windsor to the west, rather than the Tower, in the heart of London.

"I will try to join you when I can. Her first manor is Hertford, and you shall stay there in her castle. Once you have passed further north, then my wife's residences are all manor houses and your men will have to work harder."

He seemed to notice the Castilian and, after nodding to him, put his arm around my shoulders and said, "Rodrigo is a good man, but my wife wished for *you*. You know that you will be paid?"

I had assumed so, but nothing had been said. I nodded.

"Good, then as soon as my wife is ready, we will begin."

That first day was a measure of the progress, or rather the lack of it, that we could expect. It took some time for Queen Eleanor to be ready and the horse litter, led by a groom on foot, was very slow. I understood why, but it galled me. We reached the abbey just before dark, having taken six hours for the relatively short journey. That was not all due to the litter, but we could expect the same crowds in every city through which we passed. The Castilian and his men rode next to the litter to prevent it from being jostled while we had bows at the ready watching for danger. That there was none, was a relief.

25

Chapter 2

The second day was easier, perhaps because there were smaller crowds, and we made almost twice the distance to reach Waltham Abbey. The king rode with us for a mile or two before he and his entourage headed back to London. Half of my responsibility left with him. I would now be able to give my full attention to the queen.

The abbeys were easier places for us to guard than her manors, although when we stayed in the royal castle of Hertford, when we visited that manor it was an easy duty. Rodrigo insisted upon his men guarding the queen in addition to my men. It was unnecessary and merely made all of us tired. I knew my men could cope with the extra duty, but I was not so sure about the royal guards.

The further north we travelled, the slower was our progress, for the queen was deteriorating day by day. It was the fault of her own kind nature and a determination to do her duty come what may. She insisted upon going through all the accounts of each manor, as well as speaking to those who were responsible for running them on her behalf. We stayed for three days in every manor.

As September passed, I worked out that we had been on the road for weeks and yet we had barely approached the true north. King

Edward tried to spend as much time with his wife as he could; often it was just for a night, or even a bare afternoon. He was not a fool and he knew how ill she was. Indeed, after we had visited Bingham we stayed with the king for a week at Nottingham. There we had an easier duty, for the castle was well defended and we had not had any trouble on the road.

King Edward came to me when we had escorted the queen to her quarters. "Gerald, you are more use to my wife on the road. Let the Spaniard guard her here, and you and your men can rest. I am appreciative of all that you have done thus far."

Although I was reluctant to abdicate my responsibility, I did as I was asked and my men and I took the opportunity of visiting both the market and alehouses of the city. For Hamo, this was exciting. He had been overawed by London and had wished to explore it. He had been unable to do so, but now he had the chance in Nottingham.

We went around the city in a large group; I wanted none of my men, nor my son, to become involved in fights. They were archers and their size meant that many who would wish to pick a fight with them. In the first tavern, I wondered if our decision to go drinking had been a wise one. There were two huge, hulking brutes of men in the corner and they were drinking heavily. I recognised them as former spearmen who had aspired to be men at arms. They each had a short sword and a ballock dagger. Their buskins were the type favoured by such men, but their clothes were tattered and torn; they had fallen on hard times. While I normally had sympathy for such warriors, the fact that they were spending what little money they had on ale made me take my men to the far side of the room.

Despite their presence, it was a good tavern, and the ale was tasty. We had three pitchers of ale and, inevitably, that made my son need to make water. The pot was outside the back door and he made his way there. I thought about accompanying him, but knew that he would hate it. Others had made water and I had not escorted them. Instead, I watched the door and when I saw the two brutes follow him, I tapped John, son of John, on the shoulder.

"Come with me!"

My men had been drinking but John was instantly alert, and he rose to follow me. When we neared the doorway, I heard the two men. The one who spoke had a slightly slurred voice. "So, little cockerel, you are wearing fine boots and I am betting that your purse is fuller than ours. How about helping out two old soldiers with a few coins? We did our duty for England, now you do your duty for us!"

I was proud of my son's reply. "Gentlemen, if you will wait until I have finished, we can go inside and speak. This is not the place for polite conversation."

As we emerged from the inn to the courtyard, I heard a sardonic laugh. "You misunderstand us! We will have your purse whether you will or not!"

Stepping out, John and I saw that the men had drawn swords. Hamo had managed to fasten his breeks but he was weaponless. I did not hesitate. I pulled back my arm and hit the nearest one so hard in his ribs that I heard them break. I pulled back and hit him again in the arm. The sword dropped. I smacked the side of his head with my left hand and he fell to the ground, stunned. The other had whirled to face us with his sword still in his hand.

"What the …?" He raised his sword and John ran at him as he swung it down. Archers have strong left arms and he easily held the sword. With his right hand, he punched the man so hard in the stomach that he fell to the ground and was gasping for air like a grounded fish.

"Hamo, take their weapons. John, bind them. We will let the town watch deal with these."

28

My other men had come to join us and I said, "Ask the tavern keeper to come here." The two men were just coming to and I said, "Stay where you are!"

The tavern owner had been told of my identity and when he came out, he fawned. "My lord, what is amiss?"

"It seems a man cannot relieve himself in your inn without being attacked. I have bound these two for you. See that they are kept for the town watch."

"Yes, my lord!"

"I am not your lord, for if I were then you would be punished severely for allowing such things to go on in your inn. Keep a better watch on your drinkers! Come men, let us find a better alehouse."

We pushed past his protestations and returned to the street. "I could have handled them, father," said Hamo.

I nodded. "I know, but taking on drunks might result in unnecessary injury. You are a fine archer, Hamo and you do not want to accidentally lose a couple of fingers, do you?" I saw him take that in. John and I had taken no risks hitting drunken men with our fists.

The next alehouse was smaller and quieter, but as we were drinking we were approached by two men. These too had fallen on hard times, but they were archers. They wore hats and I knew that they would have spare strings. I saw that they had retained their daggers and little else.

"Captain Warbow?"

I nodded.

"I am William of Ware and this is my brother, Edward. We served in the same army as you in Wales."

I waved over the tavern maid. "Two more beakers of ale for some old comrades. I pray you to sit." As my men moved to allow them to sit, I could smell them. They had that pungent aroma of men who had not bathed for some time. I knew that we smelled of horses, but their smell was that of human sweat and soiled breeks.

"Things have not gone well for you since that time."

"No, captain. We did not wish a garrison post and there were no wars. We hoped that King Edward would make war on the Scots, but he did not. We heard he planned a crusade …"

"But it did not happen." The girl brought the ale and I paid for it. "You have bows?"

They hung their heads. "We had to sell them for food."

"Could you not go home?"

"Our home is gone. Our father had a small farm. When we came back from the wars there was a new owner, put there by the lord. Our parents had died, and we had tarried too long in the west."

It was a common story. There were always people willing to farm for a lord who, sometimes, had no thought for his tenants. They both nursed their beer as men will when they know not whence the next one will be coming.

"And what do you wish of me?"

They nodded to the other archers. "We would join your company."

I shook my head. "We are guarding the queen."

They looked crestfallen. William said, "We thought that as old comrades …"

I put steel in my voice. "There is always work for archers. You could have gone to Gascony. There is war there. The fact is that you feel sorry for yourselves. Believe me, I know what it is to have nothing – but the one thing a man always has is his skill. I used my skill and took the chances I was given."

I saw Hamo and my men almost pleading with me, and I relented. "I will tell you what, and I pray that I do not regret this." I took out a silver shilling. "My home is at Yarpole, close to the Welsh border.

30

Make your way there and tell Peter of Beverley that I sent you. If you make it, when I return from this appointed task I will see if you are truly archers." My men smiled. "If you are archers then you can make a bow and any archer worth his salt can manufacture arrows. You can feed yourselves and walk to Yarpole."

Edward spoke for the first time. "But the punishment for poaching is a harsh one!"

I smiled. "Then do not get caught. I wasn't." I saw a platter of food being carried through. "What is the food like here?"

William frowned at the change in direction then he recovered. "I hear it is good, but we cannot afford it. We scavenge after the markets have ended."

"Then today you can try it, for I am hungry!" I waved the girl over and said, "Food for all!" I knew that the place was small enough that there would be no choice of dish. "And a last pitcher of ale!"

The food was a hunter's stew with rye bread. The two brothers wiped their platters clean and then, unashamedly, wiped ours. Then I rose. "We have work. I would advise you to husband your coins well. I may see in Yarpole, if not …"

I hid a smile as my men all slipped a coin into the hands of the two archers. I had known that they would, for there was a bond between archers I had not seen between knights.

As we headed back to the castle, Hamo said, "You did not give them much, father. Was that deliberate?"

"Aye, I gave them enough to buy an occasional meal. It is more than eighty miles between here and our home. I could walk the distance in three or four days. It would be hard, but I could do it. They now have enough coins for five days. Let us see if they are there when we have finished here."

He suddenly grinned. "And you know that mother will not let

31

them starve. If they do reach Yarpole, then they will be looked after, and we have weeks left for this task."

I sniffed. "Will she?"

He was right, and I had known that. I was not as hard a man as I had pretended to be.

We left Nottingham two days later. The disastrous news had reached the king that the Maid of Norway and future Queen of Scotland had died on her way to England. All of his plans were in disarray and his wife's journey had been in vain – but that was as nothing compared with his wife's condition. The doctors had been in close attendance and King Edward had tried to dissuade her from continuing, but she was a lady who understood the true meaning of duty.

King Edward dismissed his men, and he rode with us. He gave his orders to his nobles before we left: "Return to London. I am due another parliament. We shall hold it at Clipstone – ask my children to meet me there." His men knew better than to argue with King Edward and whilst they might not have liked the idea, they obeyed.

When I was alone with him, as we awaited our horses, I said, "The queen is that ill, my lord?"

"What?"

"When you summon children it normally means to say goodbye."

"You were always a clever fellow. She is ill, but she will not give up on this. I will ride with you for the rest of the journey, but I shall go in disguise as one of the queen's guards."

I could not help laughing. "My lord, I do not think that any would mistake you for a mere guard!"

He seemed offended. "We shall see – and besides, I have decided that we will wear plain cloaks, much as you wear, for the rest of the journey to York. We shall not be the King and Queen of England!"

He seemed to be in good humour, and I wondered if he was forcing it for the sake of his wife. I knew, better than any, of the love that they shared. He intended to make the journey as happy for her as he could. Even as we left the castle, King Edward rode close to Queen Eleanor and I heard them laughing. For the rest of the journey, they would be man and wife rather than royal consorts.

We had a bare fifteen-mile ride ahead of us and the day was quite pleasant. However, with King Edward accompanying us, we were more vigilant than ever. I rode with my men ahead of the rest. The litter was flanked by Rodrigo and his men. Hamo, to his chagrin, was with the servants and the baggage. He was not happy! The forest was quite close to the road and while it was not exactly thick by the roadside, we all knew that it could hide men. I heard not only King Edward laughing behind us but also the queen's guards. In contrast, we rode in single file and total silence.

We were all woodsmen and knew what to look for; we knew the scent and sign of bandits. We were barely a mile along the forest lined road when I noticed the birds suddenly take flight just two hundred paces to the north of us. It might have meant nothing, but we were ready for anything and I slipped my bow from its case. We would have to stop to string them, but we could all do that quickly.

My men saw what I had done, and they emulated me. When we neared the place I had seen the birds I slowed but did not stop. The forest was still and there was no movement. What I *did* detect was the faint odour of men. The wind was from the west and it was not a strong smell. I dug my heels in so that my horse hurried for ten paces and then I quickly swung my legs to the ground and strung my bow. Real archers can do this quickly and it is a matter of pride with most of them that they can string a bow and nock an arrow almost before a yeoman archer has started to pull the end of his bow down.

King Edward barely noticed that we had stopped. We had stopped before and walked our horses to keep pace with the queen's litter. I nocked an arrow and then walked with my horse between the western side of the forest and me. If this was an ambush, then my horse would protect me. Of course, if they were on both sides then I was in trouble.

I was beginning to think that my fears were groundless when I heard the thrum of an arrow and the sound of small twigs and leaves being broken. I turned and saw one of the servants with the baggage fall from his horse, clutching his arm.

"Ambush!" The cry was for the queen's guards and the servants, for my men and I were already running into the forest. The rear of the column was close to where I had sensed danger and I cursed myself for not investigating.

As we ran back to aid the rest of the column, my attention was on the forest ahead but from the corner of my eye, I saw that King Edward and the guards had placed their bodies before the litter. There were arrows in the guards' shields. King Edward had no shield, I saw a figure, eighty paces ahead in the trees, and he was drawing back a bow.

I did not hesitate, but stopped and pulled back. The bandit loosed his arrow and I heard a cry. I prayed it was not Hamo. My arrow flew a heartbeat too late and slammed into the upper arm and shoulder of the archer. I ran again, drawing an arrow as I did so. I had no time to select one. Time was more important than the type of arrow. My men were well trained, and they had spread out on either side of me. The result was that the bandits were suddenly faced with my archers loosing very accurate arrows at them and we came from their side. They would have to waste time turning to aim at us and our arrows were falling fast enough now to tell them that we were professionals!

"Run! We are undone!"

The cry from ahead had a Nottinghamshire accent. These were

local bandits. Unluckily for them, they had mistakenly attacked a royal column.

The king shouted to the Castilian: "Don Rodrigo, go and aid Gerald! Take your men to cut off these bandits!" I recognised anger in King Edward's voice. An arrow suddenly flew from the direction of the baggage train on the road and as I turned, I saw the bandit with the axe fall dead not ten feet from me. The two cries had distracted me.

I saw the fletch. It was Hamo's. My son had saved my life.

The thundering horses behind me clattered and crashed through the undergrowth. With another nocked arrow I sought more enemies but the only men I saw were dead ones. "Robin, secure a line here."

Robin, son of Richard, nodded. "Aye, captain!"

I hurried to the road where I saw that three men had been hit. Two were servants but one was a priest. Only one lay dead – an assistant to one of the doctors. I nodded to Hamo, who had an arrow nocked. "A good strike. Thank you!"

"I was lucky. He just stepped out from behind a tree."

"Lucky or not, I owe you." I nodded to the baggage. "They came for the baggage. The bandits must have thought it was worth the risk."

"Did they not know you were archers, father?"

"Perhaps not. We drew our bows on the right when we had passed the ambush."

Just then we heard hooves as Captain Rodrigo drove the eight prisoners towards us. Robin shouted, "There are twelve dead men here and four more who need a warrior's death!"

King Edward shouted, "Don Rodrigo, send four men to watch the queen. I would see these men who dare to prey on my road!"

"Yes, King Edward! Walter, take your men and the rest of you, watch these dogs!"

As the four guards reached the litter King Edward bent down to speak to his wife, and then rode to us. He was angry and he almost rode down the first prisoners. They were a variety of ages from a youth of perhaps thirteen to a greybeard.

The greybeard dropped to his knees. "King Edward, I beg you to spare us! We did not know it was you!"

He dismounted and backhanded the man. "And my people should have to endure attacks from murderers and thieves? It matters not that you attacked me, you attacked the king's road!"

Still on the ground, the man moaned. "We have to eat!"

"Had you just hunted game then you would have lived! You killed and wounded my people, and you risked the life of my queen. Don Rodrigo, hang them! When they are dead, collect their bodies and burn them. I want their very existence to disappear."

As the men were dragged by the men at arms and my archers to the nearest trees, King Edward turned and waved a hand around us. "Not a word of this will ever be spoken. This did not happen. If ever I hear this tale spoken, then the teller will suffer this fate." Everyone nodded. He turned to me and said quietly, "This is not for me, but if word got out then men would say it was an attack on the queen and a measure of her unpopularity. We cannot have that, Warbow, not now."

"No, my lord."

The king mounted his horse as the bodies were hauled up kicking and squirming as the would-be robbers tried to cling on to life. "Robin, have our men fetch the bodies and the weapons from the woods. Hamo, go with them and collect the bows and the arrows."

I remembered the two archers in Nottingham. We might not need the bows, but there were others who might.

By the time the fire had consumed the bodies and we had left it was late in the afternoon, and we reached Clipstone well after dark. The attack and the long journey had left Queen Eleanor poorly and the doctor shook his head as she was carried into the castle. There were sentries, but I arranged a rota for my men. I would take no more chances.

I had just walked the walls when King Edward found me.

"We will not be leaving here for a fortnight at least. I have summoned parliament and my family." His voice caught and he was silent as he tried to control it. "I fear, Gerald, that the woman I love is not long for this life."

Had Mary been there she would have known the right thing to say, but I was Gerald Warbow and words did not come easily to me. I did what I would have done with one of my men in the same situation. I put my arm around him. Such an act could have cost me my life, for this was the King of England, but I had known King Edward for most of his adult life and as I held him, his tears came. I said nothing, but held him until he nodded.

"Thank you, Gerald, but do not put your arms around your king ever again."

I nodded. "Yes, King Edward."

The moment had gone, and I had been reprimanded, but I did not regret it. Queen Eleanor would have wished it.

Her children arrived, as did the lords for the autumn parliament. My men and I were not needed for Don Rodrigo and his men stood guard on the queen, as well as King Edward's knights. We did not leave before the second week in November and the weather was atrocious.

The queen had said all that there was to say to her children, but she was determined to get to Lincoln. It was there the king and queen had been due to meet Margaret, the Maid of Norway, and Queen Eleanor was adamant that she would be there even though the Maid was dead. There was no sense to it but as Lincoln was a royal castle, she would be more comfortable there. We made barely eight miles a day and that was not just the fault of the weather. The queen needed constant attendance from her doctors.

We managed to make Harby, just seven miles from Lincoln, before her doctors insisted that we stop. We took her to the house of Richard de Weston and the priests were summoned. The doctors' faces told all that she was dying and when the priest gave her the last rites it was confirmed. The king came from the chamber for me. His drawn face made him look ten years older than he was. "The queen would have you present as a witness."

I went into the room where a wraith lay in the bed. I had seen little of her on the journey and this was a shadow of the woman I had spoken to in Eltham. The doctor stood in the far corner of the room. King Edward was a bitter man and I know that he had taken his anger out on the doctors.

The queen held out her hand. "I wanted you here at the end, Gerald Warbow. You slept across our door in Acre when we both nearly died. I am to make that last journey now, and I would like you here to hear the requests I make to my husband and for you to guard me one last time."

"It has ever been my honour to guard you, my lady!"

She nodded. "Husband, draw close, for my time is nigh."

He knelt and held his wife's hand. I could barely make out her words. The list was not a long one, but I heard my name. "And I would have Gerald knighted. He should have been in Acre. You know that better than any; remedy that now." A few moments later she stopped speaking and King Edward knelt to kiss her forehead. He was there for a long time. The doctor began to move forward but I shook my head and he moved back.

Eventually, the king stood and gestured for the doctor. He turned to me and said, "The queen is dead. She should have died hereafter.

God must need her." He shook his head. "She was right and, when we have taken the body to London, I shall right the wrong."

The body was escorted by my archers and Rodrigo's men to Lincoln, where the embalmers quickly removed the viscera and heart from the body. The viscera was interred in Lincoln cathedral. For three days King Edward did nothing except to eat and sleep by his wife's body. He gave orders that a cross was to be erected in Lincoln as a memorial. As we headed back to London, with an ever-increasing number of mourners, he ordered that crosses be erected in every place we rested on the journey back to Westminster. Grantham, Stamford, Geddington, Hardingstone near Northampton, Stony Stratford, Woburn, Dunstable, St Albans, Waltham, Westcheap and Charing were the stops we made, and each night there was an honour guard around the coffin.

Our work ended when we reached Westminster, although we stayed for the funeral held on the seventeenth of December. I was accorded the honour of attending the ceremony. It was moving, not because of the grief shown by the mourners but for grief shown by the king. He looked to be a shadow of the man I had followed for all these years. It showed me the depth of his love for his Spanish queen.

As he had promised, I was knighted and given an annuity the day after the funeral. There were few there to witness it: my archers, King Edward's closest friends and his children. When I was knighted, he took me to one side.

"It will take me some time to become King Edward once more but when I do, then I shall need you, Sir Gerald. The great cause we have to address is Scotland. Margaret, Maid of Norway, was of my blood and although I never met her, I feel obliged to ensure that north of the border is a stable and well-governed land and does not become a threat. I had hoped to go to Gascony or even return to the Holy Land. They are for the future, first we have Scotland. Enjoy your new lands and title. I shall not need you for a while, but keep your blade sharp and your men well-practised. I shall need my archer!"

We left for home that day. I was keen to reach Mary before Christmas. I had much to tell her.

We reached home on Christmas Eve as darkness fell. Of course, the news of the death of the queen had reached Yarpole, but not that of my knighthood. I was greeted with tears when Hamo and I entered my hall. Mary had been more than fond of the queen who had befriended her. I let her weep upon my shoulder and when her tears subsided, I said, "And you are now Lady Mary of Yarpole. King Edward has knighted me. I say this not as consolation, but because it was one of Queen Eleanor's last requests and is another reason we owe that great lady so much."

She hugged me. "It is no more than you deserve. Come, you shall wash, put on fine clothes and this Christmas will be one of celebration and remembrance."

As I turned to head upstairs, I said, "And did two archers come?"

She grinned. "Aye, William and Edward arrived the first week in December. They were weary and their feet were bloody, but they said you had sent them, and we made them welcome. They have been working to earn their keep and they are good workers." My wife had a kind heart.

"Good, then we have two more archers and I know that these two have spirit."

I did not see William and Edward that day, for Hamo and I were reunited with a family we had not seen for many months. Nor did I see them the next day, as it was Christmas Day and while

I normally spent some of the day with my men, I was selfish and wished to see just my family.

Margaret was the one most taken with the title and I knew why. Suddenly there would be young nobles who would now see her as a possible bride, for her father was now a noble. The king had told me that the title, Lord of Yarpole, was hereditary. Hamo would inherit the title as well as the land, but only when I died. Mary was more interested in the annuity, which amounted to two hundred florins a year, and the land which now included all the villages within five miles of Yarpole. Lady Maud and her son's loss was my gain, but I hoped it would not engender bad feeling. There had once been a lord of the manor, but his traitorous activities had lost it.

On St Stephen's Day I finally got to speak to my new men. In many ways, it was fortuitous that I had delayed, for it enabled Robin, John and my other archers to get to know them and, perhaps, to warn them about me. I could be short with my men. They seemed to understand it, but new men found it hard to take. They had made bows, but they were poor ones and the ones taken from the hanged bandits were better. Peter of Beverley had given them hose and tunics to identify them as my men and already they looked better. They had shaved, for archers do not like beards, they like to feel the bowstring on their cheek. Their hair had been cut, too, although I suspected that had been done to rid it of wildlife.

"We begin to practise today! You have all enjoyed two days of holiday and now we work." Surprisingly, perhaps, they were all happy to do so; my men enjoyed competing with one another and our practice always had winners and losers.

Robin asked, "And how do we address you, my lord? Is it to be Sir Gerald?"

I laughed. "I am content with *captain* if it slips from the tongue easier. The title just means that I can talk to lesser knights on an equal footing. No more *my lording* them!"

They cheered, for that suited them too.

I enjoyed the practice. Apart from the attack in Sherwood, I had not drawn my bow for months and it showed. I determined that we would practise every day until my body obeyed me and made my arrows fly as far as they had done when I was younger.

Hamo too had a reason to practise. He had seen my men in action and wished to not only be their equal, but their superior.

And so our life began to follow a pattern. We prepared for a war that was not even on the horizon and we worked our land. We taught the new men how to ride and I began to oversee the Sunday morning practice of my new villages. In theory, it gave me a force of more than a hundred and forty archers. Every man could use a bow, although few as well as my men. I wanted the Yarpole levy to be the best on the border.

Chapter 3

Yarpole, 1292

When Lady Maud died, my relationship with her sons, Sir Edmund and Sir Roger, worsened. The brothers had not been happy about the lands they had lost and when their mother died, Sir Edmund showed his displeasure. I was not invited to the funeral. Lady Maud had invited us, when she was well, to her castle at least once a year. That too stopped. It did not bother either Mary or me too much, but to Margaret it was almost the end of the world. We now felt as though we were cut off. We were not, of course, but we did not have the noble families to rub shoulders with.

I became irritated with my petulant daughter. When Mary had given birth to our second son, Richard, rather than Margaret becoming closer to my wife, my eldest daughter began to grow distant from her. The years since my knighthood had seen Hamo and I grow closer. He was now the age I had been when I had first gone to war, before I became an outlaw, and I was determined that his life should be easier than mine had been. We were constantly in each other's company and for us, in contrast to my daughter, it was a harmonious time. We rarely disagreed and I began to mould him, to become the captain who would lead my archers in battle.

We knew that we would be called upon sooner rather than later. King Edward had announced his intention to go on crusade and messengers had come to warn us that, as one of King Edward's knights, I would have to supply archers. If my men went, then so would I. I heard from a passing knight that King Edward had been in contact with the Mongols once more. For my part, I was glad that I had not been ordered to make that journey. I had managed it once, but I was not sure that I would survive a second such quest for I was getting no younger. A man had only so much luck!

It was a glorious summer and life was good. Margaret apart, my family was happy. She was fifteen and those with children told me that the age might be to blame. I did not understand that, as Hamo was the same at eighteen as he had been at fourteen! Joan was still largely a child and my youngest son was happy and mischievous.

When Sir John Malton and his men rode into my manor I wondered if I had been summoned to fight sooner than I thought.

The young squire I had first met in Gascony had, like me, aged and now had grey hairs in his hair and beard. He had been with me on the mission to the Mongols and while we were never as close after that time, I still viewed him as a friend and one I could trust in battle. He was a baron and he owned lands not only in Yorkshire but also in Wales and, as he dismounted and spoke to me it became clear where he had been for he had come from the south-west and his men were all mailed and well-armed.

"Gerald ...." He smiled. "I'm sorry, *Sir* Gerald, it is good to see you. Congratulations on your elevation."

"Thank you, Sir John. It is good to see an old friend."

He put his arm around me. "None of that *Sir John* nonsense. We are friends. I have not forgotten that I would not have survived the journey to the Mongol court without you."

We entered the hall and Mary, who was attending to Richard, beamed when she saw him. "Sir John! You should have warned us you were coming!"

"Any chambers you have, or even a stable, will do, Lady Mary."

She laughed. "It is still Mary and we have rooms. Sarah! Have rooms made ready for Sir John."

"Yes, my lady!"

Margaret and Joan had joined Hamo. "This is my eldest, Hamo, and my daughters Margaret and Joan." Just then, young Richard hurtled into the room at his normal break-neck speed. "And this my youngest, Richard."

Sir John laughed. "A fine family. I see you named your eldest son after our old friend. He is the image of you, Gerald and I can see the archer in him."

"Sit. Peter, wine!"

Peter had anticipated my command and brought in a tray. Mary stood and said, "Let us leave the two men to speak. Hamo, go and show Sir John's men to their chambers. Margaret, come with me and we will help Sarah. Joan, go outside and play with your brother."

Margaret looked as though she would object, but one look at her mother's face warned her of the foolishness of such an action. We were left alone.

We spoke first of our families. I confided in him about the problems with Margaret and my pride in my son. He told me of his pride in his son, John whom he hoped to knight soon. That done, I asked him questions that were pertinent to his journey. "So, John, I am guessing that you have been in your lands in Wales."

"I have. There was trouble between Hereford and Gloucester. King

45

Edward asked me to accompany him to settle it peacefully. After we had done so, I found time to visit my Welsh lands." Many lords who were close to the king had been given Welsh estates. They were not particularly valuable and certainly not worth living in, but as they paid little or no tax it was a way to reward knights and give them additional income. The Marcher lords had to defend the lands, not King Edward.

"The King did not need me?" I was not upset to have been left out, but I wondered at the reason.

Sir John laughed. "He wanted diplomacy and not a warrior. He uses his archer as a decisive tool in war. He just needed some grey-haired nobles to impress upon the new lords that King Edward was not happy at the dissension on the border. And now he has gone to Berwick to settle the matter of the crown of Scotland. As I am a baron of the north, I have been asked to accompany him."

"And who shall the new king be?" He did not look happy and I added, "Come, old friend, if you cannot trust me to be silent then you have truly forgotten me!"

He nodded. "Balliol of Barnard Castle and de Brus of Annandale are the forerunners and as Balliol is almost an Englishman, then I think that King Edward will favour him."

I had not missed the intrigues of King Edward's politics, but it was good to hear what had been going on. I learned that the King of France was conspiring to gain more of Gascony. King Edward's brother, Edmund – called Crouchback – lived in France and was married to a French woman. Perhaps King Edward would be able to outwit the French with diplomacy. It seemed to me, as my wife came to tell us that food was ready, that there was little prospect of war in the foreseeable future.

As we sat down to eat, I found myself disappointed. When I was at war, I always missed my home and my family, but peace did not sit easily with me as I was a man of war and I did war well. I knew that Hamo would be the same. His action in Sherwood had told me that he was a natural warrior. When others had frozen, he had not, and his prompt action saved lives, not least mine.

War was not a subject for the table and so Mary asked about Sir John's family. His son, also called John, was his squire and he, along with Hamo, served us.

"I have another two sons, both younger than John, and two daughters."

"And do you live in a fine castle, Sir John?" Margaret had dressed in her finest clothes and she was keen to impress both the squire and the knight. It was inevitable, I suppose, for we had few visitors of such standing.

"No, Mistress Margaret. Malton is quiet, although I do have a moat around my hall. York is close enough so that if the Scots were ever bold enough to risk English ire, my family could take refuge there – but as they would have to cross the Tees at Stockton, which has a fine castle, then I do not fear for my family."

He turned to Mary. "You should come and visit, for it is a most beautiful part of the world. When I was first given the manor, I confess that I was slightly disappointed, for it is so far north of where I grew up, but I do not regret it. There are many fine manors there and the barons and knights who are my neighbours are all fine fellows and we enjoy a lively social life."

My wife smiled, but it was a sad smile. "That is what we miss here, Sir John. When the old Baron Mortimer, God rest his soul, was alive then we enjoyed good company and met other lords. Since he died …"

Margaret nodded. "And I am left here without a single person to speak to!"

My wife shook her head. "Am I invisible?"

"You are my mother! I mean those of my own age!"

Hamo had just carved himself another slice of the venison and he adopted an outraged look. "Then I am either ancient or, like our mother, invisible!" He had little time for Margaret's tantrums.

Defeated, she bowed her head. Sir John was an astute man; I had always liked that about him. He understood women far better than I did and he chose the right thing to say.

"Gerald, I wonder if you and your family might be able to help us out. My daughters are young, Mistress Margaret, and my wife needs help. You would be helping me out if you might agree to come to Malton. My wife would deem it an honour to have you as a lady in waiting."

I saw the relief on my wife's face, and I was pleased that I had raised the issue with him at our first meeting. "I was Queen Eleanor's lady and I learned much. This might be good for you although I would be loath to have you leave us, even if it might only be for a short time."

Margaret tried to feign indifference, but she failed badly. "I suppose I could come for a short time. You say many other lords live close by?"

"Aye, and they have young sons and daughters too."

"If you could do without me, mother?" The sweet smile did not fool her mother or me.

"I shall try."

It was decided that Hamo and I would accompany Sir John to Malton. I would take my archers with me, if only to give the new ones the opportunity to ride abroad with my company. We now had more archers, and I could take just ten in addition to Hamo, knowing that I left my home well protected.

That night, as my wife lay in my arms she said, "Should I feel guilty that I am happy that Margaret is leaving us?"

I laughed. "I had no brothers or sisters and my mother died young, but I can see how Margaret is a trial."

My wife sighed. "Had she endured my upbringing then I might have understood it, but she has had nothing in her life of which she can complain."

I kissed her head. "And yet you would not wish your childhood on her, would you?"

"No, but I worry that we have done wrong by her."

"Look at Hamo. He has turned out well."

"But he is a man, and you spent a long time with him. I look to myself and wonder if I could have been a better mother."

"Now stop that! Perhaps this is the best thing for our daughter. She thinks that the green grass of Yorkshire will be better. It will not. Do not worry, Sir John is a good man. I know that we fell out a little in the Holy Land, but that is past. I know his heart and he will care for our daughter as though she is his own."

Both of my daughters could ride. I took no credit for that. My wife had lived amongst the Mongols and they were the finest horsemen I had ever met. We also had good horses, and I had no worries about Margaret as a rider, but we would be travelling through some parts of the land which were devoid of people. Unless we detoured further south than I intended, the spine of England would need to be crossed.

I had Sir John's son, John and Hamo flank Margaret as we rode. She would be safe. She was happy, for she liked John. Sir John deferred to my experience and I set the vanguard, which was made up of my archers. His men at arms and servants would bring up the rear with our baggage. I knew that the journey back would be quicker, but I did not mind the long journey north, for I had the opportunity to catch up with Sir John. Yarpole was a backwater since Prince Llewelyn had been defeated.

It was as we passed through Derbyshire that he told me of the capture of Rhys ap Maredudd. A Welsh rebel, he had been a thorn in King Edward's side for some time. He was more of an irritant than a danger, but he had been eventually captured in the Tywi Valley and was in Edward's hands. He would be hanged, drawn and quartered. That I had not been summoned told me that the new lords of the newly-captured Wales felt confident enough to handle the Welsh. That, and the king's increasing involvement in Scottish affairs, let me know that the eyes of the crown would no longer be on Wales. The next wars in which my men and I fought would either be in Scotland or Gascony – and whilst that meant we would be further from my family and my people; they would be safe in the backwater that was Yarpole. That was good.

When we reached York, we met up with King Edward at the castle. I know it was not planned, for Sir John would have spoken of it, but sometimes fate has a way of arranging events to change your life. One such event had allowed me to meet my wife, while another had made me an outlaw. When I saw the king, I knew that the death of his wife still weighed heavily upon him, for when he spied me, he pointedly came to speak with me – and yet I was the lowliest knight in the room.

"You are well, Gerald?"

"Yes, my lord."

"Good! This is propitious. I would have you come with me to Newcastle and then to Berwick. It will do the Scots no harm to see that I take my archers."

"My lord, I am to take my daughter to Malton with Sir John."

"And I am to take a ship from Hartlepool so you can join me there." He leaned in. "While the port belongs to the Palatinate of Durham, the de Brus family own the lands that surround it. The younger de Brus is lord of the manor there." He smiled. As Sir John had told me that the two contenders for the crown were the de Brus and Balliol families, I could see King Edward playing a game with them.

King Edward was no longer the grieving husband and had become, once more, the driven king who would brook no opposition to his plans. I was resigned to a longer journey. "I shall be there, my lord."

He nodded. "It is just a pity that we shall miss the punishment I intend to mete out to Rhys ap Maredudd." He shrugged. "It cannot be helped, and when you return through York you shall see his head adorning the city gates."

The next day, as we headed for Malton, I reflected that King Edward was not a man to cross. He was ruthless and I hoped that the Scots did not underestimate him.

Lady Anne, Sir John's wife, was a real lady. It did not surprise me that Sir John had chosen to marry her; she was soft and gentle. I could, however, see why Sir John had wished Margaret to come; it had not just been out of kindness, he really needed someone. His wife did not look well. The last childbirth, he had told me on the way north, had taken much out of her.

I accompanied Margaret to her room, and we were alone.

"Daughter, I know that you have been unhappy at home and your mother and I are happy that you have a chance, here in the north, to enjoy new company." She nodded. "But you are here to help Lady Anne and not to add to her woes." I put steel in my voice and the smile left her face. "You are the daughter of a lady who understands hard work and duty. Put those first and yourself second." She nodded. "If you do well, then you will be rewarded."

She spoke as she threw her arms around me. "I will, father, and I swear that I shall not let you down. I felt I was drowning in Yarpole. Hamo had a future and I saw nothing ahead of me save becoming a spinster."

I laughed and stroked her hair. "You are still a child!"

"Inside I am not, but I will help Lady Anne all that I can, for I can see that she is unwell."

We could not even stay for one night, as King Edward would not brook tardiness. We bade farewell to Margaret and she wept. I hoped that this experience would do her good.

Sir John told us that the shortest route lay across the Tees and the ferry to Stockton. Once we crossed the river we were in the Palatinate. I knew from my conversations with King Edward that the Palatinate had even more freedom than the Welsh Marches, but the prince bishop managed them better. They were ever a buffer against the Scots. Bishop Bek was a strong ruler of the land and that showed when we landed on the north bank of the Tees and were questioned. I did not mind and as my name was known we were allowed on and we rode the last fourteen miles to the port, reaching there just before they closed their gates.

King Edward was already there along with his pursuivant, Sir Godfrey, who secured stabling for our horses. While King Edward enjoyed the hall in Hartlepool, we slept aboard the ship. For Hamo, this was all exciting. He was, once more, guarding the king. He was aboard a ship for the first time, and he was about to sail the seas. Admittedly it would be a relatively short trip, but it all added to the excitement. For the men I had with me this was nothing new.

I still could not see why King Edward needed us. He was going to be a broker, an arbiter of the crown. I knew there had to be a motive, but I could not see it.

52

We were awoken early as King Edward boarded and we left on the morning tide. The journey was a quick one. I believe that was the first time that King Edward had used Hartlepool, but it would not be the last. He was in deep conference with Sir John Vescy and Otto de Grandson on the way north. We passed Newcastle and then the islands where the seals and seabirds outnumbered men by many times. It was not long after that we sighted the mouth of the Tweed and the fortified town of Berwick.

I was disappointed in this southernmost Scottish stronghold, for there were no stone walls, just wooden ones, and the castle was not the fortress it would become one day. As we sailed to our berth, I looked at its defences from the viewpoint of a warrior. A large company of archers could inflict so many casualties that the walls would soon fall. It was then that I saw why King Edward had asked for my men. The only men at arms he had with him were the nobles he had brought.. We were, in effect, his bodyguard and he was letting the Scots see where his strength lay. We followed King Edward into the castle, but not the hall where the conclave would be held.

"Sir Gerald, wait without!" He tapped his right ear as he entered. I was to keep my ears open.

We were in the heartland of Scotland and some of the conversations could not be overheard, for they were in Gaelic. I quickly deduced that those who spoke thus were not important, for all the ones who spoke a language I could understand were the ones who sought the crown. I identified the various camps of lords who were there to support their own claimants. The two largest were those of de Brus and Balliol. It was the Balliol faction who appeared the less belligerent of the two. The de Brus nobles glared and glowered at me and my archers. I thought it strange, for the de Brus lands in England were more valuable than those in Annandale. Guisborough and Hartness both had religious houses upon them and, as such, were a good source of income. All I learned was that no matter who King Edward supported, the losing sides would not give in. There would be war in Scotland and a civil war suited King Edward. My archers were there to show that we not only had a threat of heavy horses, but also of archers. Their schiltrons might be able to defend against mailed horsemen, but not against the longbow.

We had a fortnight of debate and at the end of it, we were no closer to a decision about the future ruler of Scotland. It was frustrating, especially for my men and me. All that seemed to have been decided was that Florence of Holland, the third major candidate, had been paid by King Edward to withdraw his claim, and it was just between de Brus and Balliol.

It was as King Edward was departing that I discovered the real reason we had been brought. Sir Godfrey took me to a small hall on the outskirts of the town, just inside the wooden wall. My men were already on the ship and finding comfortable berths. I was expected to sail back to Hartlepool and then Malton.

"Where are we going, Sir Godfrey?"

He shook his head. "You should know by now that King Edward is close-mouthed. You will find out when we get there. To be honest, all that I know is that we are meeting a Scottish nobleman." I did not move and he shook his head again. "Sir Gerald, this must be important, It is the reason you are here. Had we not met you in York then he would have sent a ride from there to fetch you." I nodded. The spider that was King Edward spun complex webs.

When I saw the squire of John de Warenne, the Earl of Surrey, standing guard outside the house, then I knew who we would be meeting. John Balliol was the son in law of the earl and that told me that John Balliol had been chosen to be the next King of Scotland. It was just that the Scots had yet to decide that for themselves! When I entered, my suspicions were confirmed. John Balliol, John de Warenne and King Edward were seated around a table and there was no one else.

King Edward stood and smiled as though this was a casual meeting. "You have not yet met Baron Balliol. This, Baron Balliol, is Sir Gerald Warbow, the finest archer in my army and the leader of a company of longbowmen who are without peer."

The baron stood and gave a slight bow. He struck me as a nervous man and in all my dealings with him, I had no reason to change my opinion. "It is good to meet you, Sir Gerald, and I thank you for your help in this matter."

I looked directly at King Edward, who did not show any surprise. "I have yet to tell Sir Gerald of his task, baron. I shall do so now. Sir Gerald, we believe that the baron will be in danger until he reaches his castle at Barnard. You showed me, in Sherwood, that you have great skill in such matters, and I would have you and your archers accompany the baron and his men back to Barnard Castle."

I could not refuse, but I was not happy, and I quickly thought of excuses. "King Edward, we left our horses at Hartlepool!"

He laughed. "A minor consideration. Sir Godfrey will be accompanying you and he will procure you some." He frowned. "I thought you would have been delighted to be of service to me. Has the knighthood given you an inflated view of yourself?"

I felt myself colouring at the suggestion. "No, King Edward, I am merely surprised that this was not mentioned earlier."

He said, calmly, "I am doing so now. The baron will be leaving on the morrow." He waved an airy arm at the house. "There are servants' quarters here and you will occupy them. The baron has just a squire, four men at arms and a pair of servants, Warbow. It is your men who will keep him safe!" With that, I was dismissed, and I headed back, with Sir Godfrey, to the ship.

Sir Godfrey knew I was angry and once outside he said, "Gerald, take this as a compliment. King Edward needs Baron Balliol alive. You guarantee that."

"I do not like to be used."

He shrugged. "One way or another, we are all used. I will get good horses and you shall keep them when this is done. It is not far from Barnard Castle to Hartlepool."

I gave a sardonic laugh. "Then that makes everything better!"

Chapter 4

My men were not as angry as I was. In fact, they seemed pleased to have the opportunity for action. As John, son of John, said, "If we escort this baron back safely then I do not doubt he will reward us, and if we have to draw a bow in anger and save his life then we will be rewarded even more. None of us fears any Scotsman, captain, and certainly not one who employs others to do his killing for him!"

I was, it seemed, in the minority, for even Hamo was more than happy to be on what he thought of as an adventure rather than hanging around while old men spoke. Sir Godfrey was as good as his word and the horses were not the small ones used by the Scots, but showed English breeding and were valuable beasts. When we returned to the house, I did not speak with Baron Balliol but his sergeant at arms, Gregory of Boldron. I was a knight and outranked him, but I did not wish to make an enemy of him, and so I requested rather than ordered. I remembered how I had antagonised Rodrigo.

"Sergeant, I do not know the road twixt here and Barnard Castle, but I am guessing that much of it is in woods."

He nodded. "You are right, Sir Gerald. There are not many settlements and it is a wild and empty land. If we took the coastal route, through Newcastle and Durham, then there would be fewer woods and there would be more villages, castles and towns.."

"Then why not take that way?"

He smiled and I saw that he had teeth missing. This man was a fighter. "Enemies, Sir Gerald. The de Brus family have friends in Newcastle and lands in Durham. I will be blunt. We need you because the de Brus family wish to eliminate Baron Balliol, for they know that King Edward favours him." He shook his head. "I do not like this deception. You should have been told from the outset that the threat came from a particular family. I wanted Baron Balliol to bring more men, but he said he did not wish to start a war. We have a war – it is just a secret one."

"Thank you for your honesty. Then if we are to go through forests and woods, I would have your men ride as close to the baron as you can while we form an outer defence. I have enough woodsmen to scout aggressively."

"I am comforted that you are with us, Sir Gerald. I know of your skill. I was at Evesham and saw the effect of your arrows. Another reason for choosing that route is that we travel through lands which support my lord, and we will have accommodation we can rely upon but you are right, there are many places where we might be ambushed."

The eleven archers I would have with me now seemed an inadequate number for the task in hand. When I had spoken with him, I joined the baron and Sir Godfrey. I had forgotten Sir Godfrey. He could handle himself, and the extra blade could be crucial.

The baron spoke. I could not see him as a king, for his voice was querulous. "Sir Gerald, all is well? I could see that you were not enamoured of the task the king gave to you."

"It is not the task, my lord, but the sudden nature of it. I have spoken with Gregory and he seems a good man. So long as all obey my commands, then it will be well."

He cocked an eye. "Your commands?"

"King Edward charged me with this task because I did so before when King Edward was the target and the king obeyed my commands. I will be blunt, Baron Balliol, I am a warrior and a fighter. I think Gregory is, too. You are a gentleman and, I think, unused to war." He nodded. "Then let a warrior command on the road." He smiled his acceptance. "I would like to do the journey in three days rather than four. If there are enemies then our speed will be our ally." His face told me that he did not relish such a journey.

Gwillim and Dick of Luston were our best two scouts and hunters. It amounted to the same thing. Once we had worked out the route then they rode, one to the east and one to the west, a half mile ahead of us. They rode in the woods whenever possible. John, son of John, and Robin son of Robert rode four hundred paces ahead of us on the road. Half of the men rode with strung bows. We had taken spares with us: these were the ones we had taken from the bandits. Our best bows were in their leather cases. Hamo led the sumpter with the spare arrows and other war gear. He was happier to do so this time because he knew that if there was an attack then he could simply let go of the reins and fight alongside the rest of us.

The first day was a good one and we made thirty-two miles, staying in Rothbury castle on the Coquet. Even though it was without incident I was glad when we reached the castle and the gates slammed shut behind us. I had not spoken to the baron on the journey but when we dismounted, he came over to me. "Thank you, Sir Gerald. That was well done. Your men and you were vigilant the whole time. I feel safe in your hands."

"Thank you, my lord, but the most dangerous part is yet to come. Once we reach the wilder parts of the journey then ambush is more likely."

We crossed the Tyne at the end of the next, shorter ride of just twenty-five miles. Bromleye Hall belonged to the Balliol family but it was not as secure as Rothbury, as it was not a castle, and we had to keep men on watch all night. That was not a problem, but I knew that they would be more tired the next day and that was always a danger.

The weather did not help us, for even though it was summer with long days there was an early morning mist. Gregory had already warned us that this part would tax our horses and our riding skills. I was pleased I had not brought new men. They could ride, but not as well as these, my best men. My two outriders had worked out just how far to ride from the road. They had spied men in the forests twice, once on the first day and once on the second. Both were innocent encounters, but my men learned from them. We passed Stanhope and rested our horses at the River Wear where Baron Balliol was known, and we were fetched food. My two outriders had not stopped and, indeed, they had not even crossed at the bridge. I had not seen them, but I knew that they would have swum the narrow river. John and Robin ate sparingly and then carried the still-warm bread as they crossed the bridge. We were not far from Barnard Castle, although it would be a hard ride there. The baron was smiling, and it showed that he was happy. I still did not take to the man, although I could not say why. He was not what I would call regal.

"Time for us to go, Baron Balliol." Sir Godfrey was the one who kept close to the baron and spoke to him for me while I did my job. I was scanning the faces in the village and the road ahead. I knew that the two scouts would have crossed the river where they would not be seen by watchers. I spied a farm and a copse just five hundred paces upstream. It was the only cover I could see until the woods a mile away.

"Must we? I think that I need a new saddle." The baron tended to whine.

I mounted, and so did my men. Gregory said, "Come on, my lord. Not far now, and I will have the saddler make you a new one when we reach the castle."

The baron mounted and I waved my men to follow John and Robin, who were now more than four hundred paces from us. I whistled and they stopped and turned. Such are the margins between life and death. I led my men over the bridge and glanced behind me to see the baron had mounted and, flanked by his men at arms, was crossing the bridge. I spurred my horse to close with John and Robin. This encouraged the baron and his men to ride faster. The result was that by the time John and Robin had turned, we were less than two hundred paces from them.

The Scots on the ponies charged from behind the two men. They had been hiding at the farm. In an instant, I knew that Gwillim and Dick had crossed further upstream and missed them. It was a clever trap, for they had cut us off from the bridge.

"Archers, dismount! Gregory, put the baron behind our horses!"

As I dismounted, I saw Sir Godfrey take the reins of the baron's horse and drag him towards us. I took my bow from its case as the four archers with the strung bows sent arrows at the thirty odd men who rode at us. Although speed was important, stringing a war bow was not something to be rushed, and I had to trust my archers who had strung bows to discourage the Scots. John and Robin threw themselves from their saddles as they re-joined us, and as I drew my first arrow I wondered where Gwillim and Dick were. We needed their bows.

The Scots were just fifty paces from us when I released my first arrow. I saw four riderless ponies and knew that my archers had already enjoyed success. My arrow slammed into the mailed chest of the Scottish attacker with such force that he was thrown over the back of his saddle; I had another arrow nocked before he had hit the ground. The second Scotsman I slew was barely twenty paces from me, and this time the arrow struck his face, for he wore an open sallet.

We were exposed and the riders had wisely spread out. I loosed another arrow at a horseman who raised his sword to strike at Robin. In many ways, it was a lucky strike, for it hit him in the shoulder and, as he fell, sideways, his pony tumbled and crashed into two others. We had accounted for a third of their riders but now they were so close that our bows would not help us. I dropped mine and, drawing my sword, ran towards the nearest Scottish warrior riding a pony. Had they been riding horses this might have been more difficult, but we were all tall men, and I swung my sword two-handed as the spear came at my chest. Although the spear hit my shoulder, I had a leather brigandine beneath my tunic and whilst it hurt, the Scot had no chance to strike a second time as my sword hacked through his arm and into his side.

Some of my archers were still loosing their arrows, and Gregory and Sir Godfrey were using the extra height afforded by their horses to great advantage. It was the return of Gwillim and Dick that turned the tide. They appeared behind the Scots and, dismounting, sent their arrows into their backs. Their leader, or perhaps the most senior warrior left alive, decided that they had failed, and I heard a shout of, "Fall back!" The twelve survivors turned and ran. Twelve did not reach the bridge, however, for two more were thrown from their saddles by arrows.

I had picked up my bow and nocked an arrow when I heard the shout for aid. The surviving attackers were too far from me and I had no clear target. I looked around and saw that my archers were whole, but one of the baron's men lay bleeding on the ground. The baron had a sword drawn but I could not see blood upon it.

"See if any live. We will question them before they are hanged!" I was angry, but mostly with myself. I had thought my plan was perfect and I now saw the flaws in it.

"Here is one, captain!" Hamo shouted me over and I saw one on the ground. The arrow had come through his back and from the blood, the man did not have long to live. I ran to him, dropping my bow as I did so.

"Who sent you?"

A trickle of blood came from the corner of his mouth. "No one, we were out for a ride and thought to rob you!" He was young and had a smile on his face.

"You have courage, my young friend. Suppose we just leave you here. The night is coming, and the wound will kill you, but it will take time. I can see that blood seeps rather than pours. You look fit. You might last until dawn, for you are young. Would you like a slow death with rats and foxes taking bites from you?"

The smile left his face. "Do you have a priest with you?" I nodded. "Then let him hear my confession."

I shouted: "Father Godfrey, come and hear this dying man's confession!"

Sir Godfrey was quick thinking, and he came behind the youth so that he could not be seen. "I am here, my son. Confess."

He put his ear close to the youth's mouth. When he had finished, he made the sign of the cross and said, "You can meet God with a clear conscience, my son. Now tell Sir Gerald who sent you."

"It was the Lord of Annandale, the older one. He paid us in silver. Now I beg of you, give me a swift death." His death was close, for as he spoke, he coughed up blood. I took out my dagger, but it was not needed. His eyes glazed over, and he died.

Sir Godfrey stood. "King Edward's precautions were necessary."

I nodded. "Aye, but we were nearly undone. Let us hope that there is not another ambush further down the road." I stood up. "Fetch the ponies and let us ride." My men had found the silver and taken any weapons worth having. The villages would take what remained and perhaps bury the bodies.

Gwillim and Dick rode over. "Sorry, captain. The ford was a mile upstream and we were so eager to avoid being seen that we overlooked the farm."

"We lost one man. That he was not of our company is immaterial. See that you do not make another such mistake. Men die, and I would avoid any further deaths."

We left with the Scottish ponies. If nothing else, they might make an equine barrier if we were attacked again. I kept John and Robin closer to us as we completed the journey. I saw more places we could have been ambushed but, thankfully, they had chosen the river. Our swift journey had helped us. When I saw the mighty bastion that guarded the upper Tees, Barnard Castle, I breathed a sigh of relief. Had Baron Balliol died in the attack, then King Edward would have blamed me. I would not expect praise for having succeeded. As far as he was concerned, Gerald Warbow had merely done what he was asked – but failure would have been heaped on my doorstep.

We stayed but one night and despite the baron asking us to remain we headed east the next morning, to ride to Hartlepool where we would pick up our horses. We made quicker time without the baron and I spoke with Sir Godfrey as we rode.

"Is it not a gamble to be so blatant in his backing of Balliol?"

"Perhaps, but he is English more than he is Scottish. It was his mother, who recently died, who was the one encouraging him to put himself forward as king – for she was also closely related to the royal family and ambitious for her son. He will be a reluctant king."

"And de Brus seems more belligerent. It was a bold move, to attempt to kill his rival."

Sir Godfrey shook his head. "There is no evidence of conspiracy or collusion. The man we spoke to was dying, and it is just our word against that of de Brus. Trust me, there will be no connection for any to follow. The one who led them away will report what happened. You had best watch your back. You have no castle in which you can take shelter."

"If he comes for me then he is doubly a fool. Firstly for I am unimportant and secondly because any he sent to harm me would be dead before they could get close. My men and I do not know the land hereabouts, but we know Yarpole and Luston!" He smiled his agreement with my affirmation. "I shall return to Malton to see how my daughter fares, but what next for you?"

"There will be a ship waiting for me at Hartlepool and I shall join King Edward. We have three months to find out just what the Scots will do."

"And what will that be?"

"Why, to accept King Edward's authority. Robert de Brus, the Lord of Annandale fought alongside King Henry at Lewes. He will obey King Edward."

"Yet, he sent killers to end the life of Baron Balliol."

"He was a rival. As much as they hate England, they know just how strong we are, for he has fought alongside us. If they were in a position to challenge King Edward, then they would have done so. No, the danger is his son, also called Robert de Brus. He is a young man and, I have heard, he is ambitious. If he were Lord Annandale, then he might challenge the king's decision to appoint Balliol."

It was as we were approaching Hartlepool, close to the manor of Elwick, when we met the horsemen from the north. The roads met and then dipped down to cross a small stream. It was customary when you met someone at a crossroads to stop and speak. It was considered bad manners to ride ahead of someone, for you did not know their rank. We reined in at the top of the brow just beyond the crossroads. It could have been that they were heading south to use the ferry at Stockton, but I did not think that was the case. As they approached, I recognised the de Brus livery. I had seen it in Berwick many times. The red saltire on the gold background was distinctive. They were riding, like Sir Godfrey, without helmets as this was not a dangerous part of the world. I saw that they were young and guessed that it was not the claimant to the Scottish throne who rode at their head.

They reined in and Sir Godfrey said, "Good day, Sir Robert."

The young man frowned and then smiled as he recognised Sir Godfrey. "Ah, Sir Godfrey. I did not recognise you without your pursuivant livery. I thought you would have gone back to London with King Edward."

"No, my lord, I had a task appointed to me by the king." I saw the question form on the young Scottish knight's face, but I knew he would not ask. It made me wonder if he had been party to the ambush and attempted assassination. "This is Sir Gerald Warbow. He was King Edward's captain of archers in the recent Welsh war."

Sir Robert turned to me and it was clear that he had heard of me. "The archer knight! You are unique, Sir Gerald, or so rare as to count the same. King Edward must have thought much of you to confer a knighthood on what amounts to a commoner."

If he thought to insult me, then he did not. I knew I was the stuff of the earth to the noble but I also knew that I was a warrior and that counted more than noble blood.

"I have been lucky, my lord."

"You ride to Hartlepool?"

I nodded. "Sir Godfrey takes a ship south and I have left horses there when we sailed to Berwick."

"Then let us ride my lands together." He was letting me know that these were his lands and we would have to obey him. It was a small thing, but it showed me that the young noble was a thinker.

As we passed through the village, along the side of the green, the young Scot showed that he was well known, for the villagers doffed their caps as he waved at them. The road twisted, turned, fell and then rose again until we had a sudden vista of the port and it could be seen as the stronghold it was. With a good wall, and dominated by St Hilda's church and abbey, it was an important place. We reined in again.

"One day there shall be a castle here!"

Sir Godfrey's face showed not a trace of the disbelief I knew he felt. The Bishop of Durham and the king would never condone or allow Sir Robert to build a castle. This was not anarchy, when any lord could throw up a castle and challenge the king. I saw then the young man's ambition. He was not afraid to challenge King Edward and when his father was gone, England would have a thorn lodged in its side.

He turned to us. "You must come to my hall and dine with me."

I shook my head. "I fear, my lord, that I have been absent from my home for too long a time and the Welsh border is many leagues from here."

He smiled. "Aye, it is strange, Sir Gerald, that King Edward should have brought you all the way from your home for something which does not really concern you."

Sir Godfrey answered: "Did you not know, Sir Robert, that Sir Gerald here saved King Edward's life when in the Holy Land on crusade? They are close."

"You were a crusader?" I nodded. "One day, I shall take the cross." He gazed wistfully east and then shook his head. "I doubt I shall see you again, Sir Gerald, for your world is Wales and I am a Scot, but it has been interesting to meet with you. And you, Sir Godfrey, will you dine?"

"It would be an honour, Sir Robert."

I hid my smile. The Scot was letting in King Edward's man and the astute Sir Godfrey would discover all that there was to know.

We parted before the gates of the town, for the Scot's hall lay outside them. "Farewell Sir Godfrey."

He clasped my arm, as warriors do. "We shall meet again, Sir Gerald." Quietly he added, "Keep your eyes and ears open, my friend. The fire in Wales is not yet out."

I held his gaze. "And stay safe, Sir Godfrey."

We passed through the gate into the town and headed for the port and the stables arranged for us. Once we had ascertained that our horses were well, we found someone to take the ponies we had captured off our hands. They were of little use to us. We also sold half of the horses. As was my wont, the profits were shared between all my men. The weapons we had taken would be sold at a better market, and so we headed south.

This time we were forced to spend the night at Stockton, as the meeting with de Brus had delayed us and the ferry did not cross at night. The lord of Stockton was absent, but his steward knew me, perhaps from King Edward when he had passed north, and we were accommodated.

As we left, the next day, I was pleased that the bastion that was Stockton would bar the advances of any Scottish incursion. English rivers were our best defence and I wished that we had more such rivers on the Welsh border. The Severn apart, the rivers ran in the wrong directions.

We had not been away for long, but Margaret had already begun to change. The scowls she had adopted at Yarpole were replaced by smiles. She seemed part of Sir John's family already. That hurt a little, and I knew that if I told Mary she would be upset too, but we had brought Margaret into the world and it was our task to make sure that she was happy. We were parents, and our happiness was immaterial. We stayed a week at the insistence of Sir John, and we hunted and rode. He had something he wished to say to me.

"Gerald, one of my tenants and his wife died last year when they suffered the winter flux, and we have been raising his son, Jack. He is just eight summers old, and he will grow to be as big as was his father. I think he would make a fine archer."

I nodded, but there was something about Sir John's words that did not ring true. "And you wish me to train him?"

He looked relieved. "If you would, then I should be grateful."

"And there is no other reason, Sir John?" Whilst the northern knight was happy to ignore my title, I had always called him Sir John. I held his gaze and his eyes dropped first.

"There has been trouble with my youngest, Edward. They do not get on. It is another reason I was so pleased that Margaret came north. Edward can be a handful. He has moods, sometimes he is the sweetest child you could imagine and at other times, he is like a fiery demon. Jack is a strong boy and if he stays, then I fear he might hurt Edward."

"And that might be the best thing for your son."

"He is my son." I did not agree with Sir John, for I believed you gave your own child discipline, but fathers were all different and I nodded. "You will not be put to expense, Gerald. I sold his family tenancy and there is a small chest of coin for the boy and the expense of training him."

I had already decided to take the boy, and the money would be for the child. It was Sir John with whom I was disappointed. I thought our falling out in the Holy Land was an aberration, but I now saw that we were different. I hoped that Margaret would be influenced more by Lady Anne than my old comrade in arms.

"I shall take him, but only if he wishes to be trained as an archer. You cannot force an archer as you would rhubarb. A man is either destined to be an archer or he is not."

When we met Jack, I saw that God and his parents had given him the frame of an archer. Although he was still a child, I saw that he would grow to be strong in arm and legs. He looked nervous as Sir John waved him over. "Jack, this is Sir Gerald Warbow, the celebrated archer."

He looked at me and not Sir John. He smiled. "It is an honour, Sir Gerald. I have heard your name."

"Indeed?"

He nodded eagerly. "Sir John's men at arms speak of your prowess with the bow and your daughter, Lady Margaret has told me tales of your skill."

I smiled – and part of it was a surprised pride that my daughter spoke well of me. "And would you like to learn how to use one?"

"I would, Sir Gerald, but Sir John does not have many archers."

"I meant that you should join my company, so that we could train you. It would mean moving from here and living with us at Yarpole."

"I would dearly love the opportunity, my lord." His answer came almost before I had finished speaking.

"Hamo, take Jack and find his gear. He shall stay with our men until it is time to leave."

"Aye, father. Come, Jack of Malton, you are now part of the illustrious company of archers whom all enemies fear and all friends respect!"

As they left, Sir John said, "Thank you, Gerald. You have solved a problem."

I hoped I had not created one by leaving my daughter with him. The night before we left, I walked with Margaret through the village. She had her arm in mine and I felt closer to her than I had since she was a toddler.

"Margaret, if you are not happy here then you can return to Yarpole with me."

"I am happy here, for I can learn things I cannot at Yarpole. This will not be forever, and I shall write to you."

I laughed. "I doubt that there will be many messengers crossing this land just to deliver a missive from you!" I saw that she had not thought that through, and she frowned. "Let us say that you will write to us by Christmas and again at Easter of next year. Whenever you are ready to return, I shall come for you."

"You are a good man, father, and I am sorry for the trouble I have caused."

I squeezed her hand. "Your mother and I chose to bring you into the world and any trouble you may have brought is our own doing. All will be well."

She stopped. "It is good that you are taking little Jack with you." I looked down at her. "Edward hurts him. I know not why, but he seems to take pleasure in inflicting pain. I have had to stop him on more than one occasion. Jack is a lonely child, and he has lost his parents. Edward is a bad child."

"Thank you for that and we will care for him. Are you sure you wish to stay here?"

She laughed. "Oh, I can handle Master Edward!" My daughter had changed already.

The journey back was a pleasant one, for the archers had all heard

71

the story of Jack. Hamo and his sister had been close for the last day or so and she had told her brother what she had told me. The result was that Jack laughed more and seemed a happier child than the one I had seen diffidently approaching Sir John as though he expected to be punished.

Mary, of course, was keen to know about Margaret and it was only when I had put her mind at rest that she asked about Jack. After she had heard it, she nodded. "This is God's work. Jack shall live in the house with us. He can have Hamo's old room and he shall be treated as one of the family. To lose your parents is bad enough, but to be bullied and hurt is inexcusable. I think less of Sir John now." She knew what it was like to be helpless and to be used, not as a person, but a thing.

And so our family changed a little. There was more harmony now, for Joan took to Jack and Jack seemed to take to all of us. I forgot Scotland and put my efforts into the manor and the training of my men.

Chapter 5

Yarpole, June 1294

We did not hear the news of King Edward's decision until a month after the event, To the people on the Welsh border, Scotland seemed a distant world. It was early December when we heard that the Scottish auditors who decided the matter had chosen Baron Balliol. It was no surprise, for forty of the auditors had been chosen by de Brus and forty by Balliol. The other twenty-four had been chosen by King Edward. All knew that King Edward had picked Balliol.

As a result, Robert de Brus gave up not only his claim to the throne, but also the title of Lord of Annandale. His son, the knight I had met outside Hartlepool, now took the title and the claim. I, for one, knew that the Scottish problem had not been solved. That had been two years since and much had happened to my world in that time.

Margaret had not only prospered in Malton, but she had also changed enough that she had wished to return. In all, she spent a year in the north and when we brought her back, I brought back a woman. The reconciliation with her mother was heartfelt and Mary decided that we should open our hall to the other lords, ladies and gentry who lived in the neighbourhood. Sir Edmund still shunned us, but my association with King Edward meant that others were happy to enjoy our hospitality.

I was a rich man and Mary knew how to spend my money wisely. Six months after Margaret's return, she met a young gentleman from Ludlow, Richard Launceston. His father was a rich merchant and while Richard was not a noble, he was training to be a man at arms. The two got on well and a month after they had met, I was asked for her hand. I knew my daughter better by that time, and I happily gave it. The news of the wedding was joyous one although there would be few of noble blood there as Sir Roger did not approve. I had not asked his permission. That Margaret was moving to Ludlow was not an issue, for it was close enough for us to visit. Margaret and my wife were constantly together, spending my money on a wedding that would be the talk of the county!

It was not Sir Godfrey who brought me King Edward's gift for Margaret, but Henry de Lacy, Earl of Lincoln. I knew him because he had been prominent in the last war and when King Edward attained the throne, he made him Protector of the Realm. He was not a fool and I liked him, for he did not waste men's lives in battle. That such a high-ranking lord should bring a golden locket for Margaret was explained when he spoke with me.

"Sir Gerald, I had been sent back to my castle at Denbigh and Chester already and King Edward asked me to fetch the gift when he heard of your daughter's marriage. The King needs you and your men. The French have claimed all of Gascony, and he is raising an army to sail there to recover it."

I nodded. "Of course my lord. And when is the muster?"

"The first day of September at Portsmouth."

Before he continued his journey, he gave me more information about what we might expect in France. We had enjoyed almost four years of peace and I now had more archers. I think I was ready to go to war once more. I had time to prepare for a campaign that I knew would last the better part of a year. Operating in France meant I needed arrows, spare bows – not to mention horses – cloaks, swords and the like. The king had paid me when I had escorted Baron Balliol but the expense of maintaining a company of archers had been borne by me. The lands I now owned were enough to pay for them, but it had meant that Mary had not been able to spend as much as other ladies of such lands. She was content, for I was still King Edward's man.

Hamo was delighted when I told him the news. He was now a grown man and I had expected him to have wed one of the many young maids who saw him as attractive. He had committed himself to becoming an archer as good as his father, and I took that as a compliment. He saw the opportunity as some heroic quest to regain land stolen by the French. I knew it was not as simple as that. With Scotland under his sway and Wales subdued, King Edward was building an empire. We learned that many of the lords in the west of England had been asked to join the king and one of them was my future son in law, Richard Launceston. He was going as an independent man at arms. At least I would be able to keep an eye on him, but as archers usually fought separately from men at arms, I could do nothing to save him on the battlefield.

Jack was not the only one of my men who would be new to campaigning. William and Edward had not been on campaign and we had another eight archers who, whilst they had fought in battles and wars, had not been part of my company. Hamo was now my lieutenant and he used John and Robin to help him organise the men. Arrows, bows and bowstrings were all needed. We had enough horses as well as spares. Ralph the fletcher and his sons would make the arrows. Ralph's sons would be with the company and, like Jack, would be with the two servants we took who would lead the horses. When we fought, Jack and the two boys would be the ones sent to the rear to fetch arrows. All had to be explained and the boys given clear instructions. When boys went to war it was not the game they imagined. We would not bother with tents as Gascony had a milder climate than Wales. We would make hovels.

Margaret's wedding day would have to be postponed. They were due to be wed on Michaelmas, at the end of September. By then we would be in France! Whilst upset, she was calmer than she might have been before her visit to the north. She and her mother decided that the wedding would take place just as soon as we returned from France.

We planned on leaving Yarpole in the last week of August. The Earl of Lincoln's men had already passed through Ludlow on his way to Portsmouth and Richard had joined them. The earl was charged with watching over the northern Welsh border. I knew that it mattered not if we arrived a day before the muster or a week before, we would not be moving any time soon.

However, fate intervened and I, who had rarely suffered a wound and never endured a day of sickness, fell ill. It began just three days before we were due to leave and I was attacked by a fever, which made me dizzy and unable to keep down food. I was ordered to bed by Mary and I had little choice in the matter, for my eyes refused to stay open.

I entered a dream world, and I knew not if I was awake or asleep and time meant nothing to me. Faces came and went. I saw my children and my wife as well as, bizarrely, Jack. I did not know how long it lasted, but one morning I opened my eyes and saw Jack asleep in a chair next to the bed. I tried to raise my head but I could not and so I attempted to speak. No words came forth. It was as I tried to speak again that a croak came out of my mouth and Jack sat bolt upright in bed and seeing my eyes open shouted, "Mistress! He is awake! My lord, we thought you dead!"

I still could not speak. My wife came into the chamber and her face broke into a huge smile when our eyes met. "He lives! Praise God! Jack, ask Peter to fetch the doctor and ask Sarah to warm up the broth!" She sat on the edge of the bed and cradled my head in her arms. She took a beaker and poured some liquid into my mouth. It was honeyed ale. I guessed it had been warm once but now was cold. I cared not, for my throat burned as though a hot brand had been thrust down it. Mary poured it down in small amounts until I nodded, and then she laid it down.

"How long have I been ill?"

"It is seven days since you were laid low."

I laid back and closed my eyes; that was a lifetime. I suddenly remembered my plans and my eyes opened and I tried to sit up. "The muster!"

"Peace! Hamo left the day after it became clear that you would not be able to lead the men. The doctor was so concerned that Father Michael came and gave you the last rites. Hamo did not want to leave you, but he knew that our men had to be at the muster, and he wanted to be on time, arriving as they would, without their captain. He left Jack so that you could join him when you were well enough."

I struggled to rise. "I am well enough now. If I ride quickly, then ..."

She pushed me back and she smiled. "If a mere woman can restrain you then I think that is evidence enough that you are not yet fit. You would be late in any case, and King Edward would prefer, I think, a tardy archer to an archer who could not draw his belt tight, let alone a bow!"

I knew she was right. "What did the doctor say it was?"

She shook her head. "He had never seen the like. None were allowed close to you save the doctor, Jack, and me. He thought it was

77

a new plague and he wore a mask. It was only after three days that he relented, for Jack and I showed no signs of the contagion." She smiled. "Jack was most concerned about you. When Hamo suggested that he stay here as your servant he looked as proud as any newly knighted squire. When you are ready, then he will ride with you to Portsmouth."

"But the king will have left."

"And you know that it will take time for his army to be close to the French. Your health is more important."

A servant appeared in the door but looked nervous about approaching. "Here Anne, give the bowl and spoon to me. You can catch nothing from Sir Gerald!" Her voice sounded irritated. The young woman handed the bowl to my wife and scurried away.

I felt like a babe again as my wife fed me the bowl of soup. It had been made from fowl and was as delicious as anything I had ever tasted. I had just finished it when Doctor Erasmus, who now lived in Yarpole, entered. He waved away my wife and Jack and closed the door. He began to examine me. He prodded and poked. He put his head close to my chest. He opened my mouth and my eyes. It was a strange experience and took some time.

Doctor Erasmus was an interesting man; he had arrived two years earlier on his way to Chester. He had lived in the Eastern Empire but the attacks by the Turks had made him fear for his life and he had fled. He believed that Chester was as far away from the east as civilisation extended and he had been on his way there when his horse had become lame in Yarpole. He was forced to stay for two days and liked it so much that he remained. This was the first time I had experienced his company as a doctor. It was a strange one.

"Well, Sir Gerald, you appear to be over it."

"What was it, doctor?"

He smiled. "I do not know. We doctors are more comfortable with what we know, and this has puzzled me. I had seen similar diseases, but they were in the east. Talking to Lady Mary I know that you, too, had spent time there; however, unless the disease lurked in your body for these years then I think it is unlikely you were infected then. No, I think it must have been when you were on the ship with the king which took you to Berwick." I widened my eyes. "No magic, Sir Gerald, I questioned your wife and son at length to see if I could find a cause. I thought, at first, that it might be like the plague, which sweeps through small towns, but your wife, the boy and I had no ill effects from tending to you. We must put it down to God reminding you that you are mortal." He stood. "As far as I can tell, you are over this, whatever it was. Perhaps I shall call it Sir Gerald's Ailment!"

"And when can I join my son and my archers in Gascony?"

He laughed. "If you are able to rise in a week I shall be surprised. You are as weak as a new-born babe, Sir Gerald. First, we feed you up to regain your strength. I will visit each day and when I deem it right then I shall allow you to rise. Another week will see you able to walk outside for short periods and a week after that you might begin to draw a bow."

I said nothing, but he did not know me. I was the master of my body and not the other way around. I nodded my compliance.

The doctor shook his head, for he saw the defiance in my eyes. "No matter what you *believe* you can do Sir Gerald; your body will determine what you *can* do." He leaned in. "And I, for one, would not wish to cross Lady Mary!"

He was right in one way; my recovery was not as quick as I wished it to be, but it was quicker than he expected, for I was a determined man. Jack helped me, for when Mary was absent from the bedchamber seeing to our family and the manor, I used him as a crutch so that I was able to stand and try a few steps. When I collapsed, he slowed my fall. I ate meat at every meal and drank the strong red wine I liked – unwatered. I know that the doctor disapproved of my diet, but I knew my body better than he did and four days after I awoke, I was able to walk around the room and, with Jack's help, I ventured downstairs. My daughters and son had visited me in the bedchamber but when they saw me descend, both Margaret and Joan burst into tears.

Mary shook her head and gave me a wry smile. "I should have known, husband, of your inner strength."

A few days after the day when Margaret should have been wed, Michaelmas, I could ride my lands and attempt to draw a bow. I had received good news, too, for a rider heading for Sir Edmund's castle told us that the army had not yet sailed for Gascony and that bad weather had kept it from departing. That evening as we ate, I said, "Tomorrow, Jack and I will leave with two of the archers my son left. Walter and John are both good men. We will ride for Portsmouth."

My wife frowned. "You have done well, my husband, but I feel it is still too soon."

"Look upon this illness as a gift from God, for I have been able to stay at home for a month longer than you expected."

She laughed. "And as a week of that saw me wondering if you would live or die, it is a mistake to remind me!"

The conversation was ended by a banging upon the door. It was late and as nights were drawing in, we expected no visitors. Peter answered the door and even as I began to rise to go to the hallway the door burst open and Peter stood there with a rider wearing the livery of Earl Henry.

"My lord, sorry for the intrusion but I have been sent to summon you. The Welsh have risen. Caernarfon and its castle has been taken. Earl Henry requests that you join him at Chester with as many archers as you can."

This was treachery of the highest order and I gathered as much information as I could, but the rider was keen to ride to warn the other local landowners. I learned that all the new castles along the Conwy valley were in danger. After he had gone, I spoke with my wife and Peter. "I fear that the Welsh have planned this well. With the king in France, it is the perfect opportunity for mischief. I have just twelve men left to defend my home."

Peter said, "We can raise the levy, lord. We can muster more than a hundred men."

"But who will lead them?"

He nodded towards his maimed limb and said, "I may not be the best warrior any longer, but I still remember how to command men. If you will raise the levy, lord, then I shall lead."

I looked at Mary, who smiled. "You have made our home strong. We bar the gates and defend the walls but there are many strongholds that lie closer to the danger than this one. If they reach here, then King Edward has lost Wales."

I was satisfied and I began my preparations. The twelve archers who remained were the older, married ones. Having said that, they were more than happy to follow me. This was their land and they were defending it. Raising the levy took longer than I had hoped and I had forgotten that I now had more lands to manage. It took seven days, by which time we discovered that Castell y Bere, Hawarden, Ruthin, and Denbigh castles had all fallen and Criccieth Castle, as well as Harlech, was besieged. It was Madog ap Llywelyn, a distant relative of the last Prince of Wales who led the attacks in the north but Morlais Castle, further south and west, had been captured by Morgan ap Maredudd of Gwynllwg in Glamorgan in the south, and Cynan ap Maredudd besieged the castle at Builth for a period of six weeks. Half the town of Caerphilly was burnt, although the castle itself held out and, further south, Kenfig Castle was sacked. The three-pronged attack had been well planned and all the attacks had been simultaneous. The good news was that King Edward had not been able to embark for France, due to the weather.

As Peter said to me, "It shows that God is on the side of the English, lord. Now, with an army ready to fight, King Edward can hurry north."

I hoped he was right, and, at the start of the second week of October, I led my small company of archers to Chester and the muster to retake the Earl of Lincoln's castle at Denbigh. I avoided the Mortimer castle – but that was mainly because there was a shorter route to Chester. I had an archer leading the sumpter with the arrows and supplies. I did not intend our men to starve.

It took a couple of days to reach Chester, but that was mainly because we had refugees fleeing east to safety and we could not make our normal good time. The old Roman amphitheatre by the river was a huge camp, but I noticed fewer men at arms than I would have liked. There were archers present; the Cheshire archers were renowned, but the better archers were, like my men, all with King Edward. As a knight and captain of archers, I was summoned to Chester Castle and a conference with the earl. He must have spoken to the other lords, for there was just his clerk, captain of the guard and a priest with him when I entered the chamber he was using.

"How bad is it, my lord?"

"A disaster, Warbow. All the land we took in the last Welsh war we have lost, and we have few enough men to retake it."

I asked the question that was prominent in my mind. "How many archers do we have?"

"Mounted? Just the ones you bring. The rest is the levy. There are four hundred archers."

My heart sank. "The Welsh will have many more and they are at least the equal of our best."

His face told me that he had worked that out for himself. "And we have fewer than one hundred men at arms. The greatest numbers we have to fight the Welsh are made up of the fyrd." He forced a smile. "King Edward is heading north with the army intended for Gascony, but I fear it will take him too long to reach us. He has ordered me to strike. He wishes at least one castle retaken. Sir Reginald Grey is heading to Flint and Rhuddlan. They have not yet fallen and if we can hold them, then Chester is protected. I will lead the bulk of the men we have. We march for Hawarden and then Denbigh in two days. I hope that I can count on you to command the archers?"

"Of course, my lord."

"The king is sending ships to aid us. Harlech and Caernarfon, not to mention Criccieth and Conwy, can all be blockaded or supplied by sea."

"I have spare arrows, my lord. I am happy to share them amongst the army, but we will need recompense."

"Of course, and as Chester is paying for this army then you know you will have prompt payment."

We would be recovering the earl's own recently-built castle, and he would not penny-pinch.

The news was bad, but there was hope. If King Edward could bring the army before Harlech, Conwy and Criccieth fell, then the others might be recovered. I went to speak with my men. I had already decided that each of them would be a vintenar and command twenty men. They knew how to obey my commands and what was needed in battle. Then we went to the camps of the archers. I was fortunate, in that many men remembered me not only from the Welsh war but the battle of Evesham. I did not have to impress anyone. The archers tended to camp together and although there were spearmen close by, as well as other members of the fyrd, I raised my voice so that every archer could hear me.

"I am Sir Gerald Warbow, and I will be your captain in this campaign against the Welsh. Some of you know me, for I was Lord Edward's archer." I saw some smiles and nods and felt that I was amongst friends. "My men, the archers of my company, will lead you. You will be divided into twelve groups and you will obey the orders of my vintenars as though I had given you the command. You will know them by my livery. We have brought arrows with us. I know you are all fine archers and like your own arrows, but trust me that the ones we will share with you are the best that you will ever use."

I waved my archers forward and counted off the men that they would command. That night as we sat around our own campfire, I spoke to my archers to give them instructions. "We have less than two days to get to know the men you lead."

They were all experienced archers, having campaigned with me before. One of them, Will of Leek said, "Captain, we know how to draw a bow, but we have never given commands. Can we do it?"

I laughed. "Will, you have sons and I have heard you shout at them when they have made errors. Being a vintenar is much the same and you have all heard my commands often enough. You are the stiffening of the ranks. You are the bodkins amongst the hunting arrows. We need the archers to loose as one and to keep up a good rate. It will not be the same as it would if all were my men, but we need our arrows to thin their ranks. We fight the Welsh, and all know that they are as dangerous as any enemy." I paused. "We will lose men."

Geoffrey of Banbury had recently become a father again and his wife had not enjoyed an easy time. Of all my archers, he was the most unhappy to be with me and not his family. He asked, "We can win though, captain?"

"The earl is a good leader, but we do not have enough good archers, nor do we have enough men at arms. We are attempting to capture a castle and that is not easy. I would be happy if we just occupied his attention until the king and the Earl of Warwick arrive with Hamo and the rest of our archers. We do this, Geoffrey, so that the Welsh cannot reach Yarpole and our homes." I saw realisation set in and he nodded. I knew I had not explained our situation well enough. This whole three-pronged attack had caught us off guard and even I was making mistakes. How would the rest of those who led it react?

It was not far to Hawarden and we were such a large host that the Welsh, who had overextended themselves, tried to set fire to the castle and then fled to Denbigh. Many thought it a victory and the levy became excited thinking that this would be an easy campaign. Neither the earl nor I were of that opinion. The size of the army had frightened the Welsh. When their real leaders saw the lack of quality, then they would fight us. The earl left a sizeable garrison to repair and guard the castle, which was very close to Chester, and we continued our journey to Denbigh. My archers and the knights and men at arms were mounted but the army was largely afoot. I felt a little lonely as I led the archers. Normally Hamo would be next to me but my men were spread amongst the levy from Cheshire. Now, there was just Jack. This was his first campaign and I saw how nervous he was. Without turning when I spoke, I tried to calm him by explaining what we were doing. It was a help to me, as it organised my thoughts, and I went through the elements of the army to explain to him how we would operate. The men ahead of me were the levy spearmen and they were unknown. The men at arms were the earl's and I had not fought with them. I knew just twelve of the archers. This was a strange experience for me. Like me, my men led their horses, for the others walked. It would save the horses but would tire us.

As we trudged towards the Conwy Valley, I felt my recent illness. I was unused to walking and usually rode everywhere. I gritted my teeth. Perhaps this would make me stronger – but as I stepped onto a stone that felt like a huge rock, I could not see that happening. My feet ached and I struggled for breath, but I was Captain Warbow, and I could show no weaknesses.

We only had twenty-five miles to travel and, mounted, we could have been there in half a day. However, we trudged. What concerned me, apart from my aching feet and heaving chest was that my scouts were not at the fore. They were hurrying north from Portsmouth. The archers were in the middle of the column. We were before the ordinary farmers and behind the men at arms, spearmen, and the earl. The scouts were his Cheshire men who knew the land through which we travelled.

We had the Clwyd 'mountains' to climb. I had ridden this road in the war against Llewelyn and had disputed the fact these pieces of high ground, which dominated the plain, were referred to as mountains. I had even travelled them as a youth – but that had been many years since and I was getting old. Now as I walked up it, I understood why they had been so named. When last I had ridden them, I thought them little more than pimples! We stopped at the top. I smiled wryly as I drank from my water skin and let my horse graze. The last time we had been here I wondered why we stopped after a climb that had taken little out of me. Now I scanned the road ahead. I saw the road headed due west and that the sun had passed its zenith. We would descend through trees and Denbigh Castle would only be in sight when we were three miles away and in the cultivated part of the valley.

I was also unused to being away from the leaders. I understood it, but I would normally be with King Edward or the Earl of Warwick. Here, I was like every other ordinary warrior. I listened for the commands, which rippled down the column. The result was that once we started our descent gaps appeared, for the men at arms and knights were all mounted and the men on foot had taken the opportunity to sit down. We had gone barely half a mile when the first arrows slammed into our whole column from the trees on the northern side of the road. We were lucky that they did not concentrate their missiles on one part. It was not the arrow storm that I liked to use, but it was bad enough.

I now saw that the victory at Hawarden had been a hollow one. The garrison at Denbigh had known we were coming.

Even as I drew my bow and shouted, "Ambush! Ware right! Jack take the sumpter to the baggage!" I saw men falling to the Welsh arrows.

"Aye, lord!"

Praying that Jack's first battle would not be his last, I took my bow from its case. I saw four spearmen hit by arrows and as I began to string my bow, two of the archers close to me had no chance to loose their missiles, for the arrows struck their chests. My men and I strung our bows first for we were the strongest and most practised. I drew a war arrow and nocked it. This would not be the first attack I had envisaged us making. We had no time to nock, draw and release as one. We had to hurt the enemy.

I caught sight of a face in the trees. The range was less than a hundred and twenty paces from me and I loosed. I did not see if I had hit, but as the face did not reappear I assumed I had. As I drew another arrow, I slapped the rump of my horse to send her into the trees behind me. Our horses were well trained, and they would not run off; they were used to the sound of war.

I heard my vintenars shouting commands and encouragement. They might have had doubts about their ability, but they had risen to the challenge. It was one positive to take from the disaster that was unfolding before me.

I sent another arrow at a bold Welsh archer, who had stepped beyond the trees to loose an arrow at a man at arms. The man at arms was rallying the spearmen, who were in danger of breaking. When he drew back, the Welshman made a tempting target and my arrow drove deep into his chest and he fell to the ground. The Welsh were now pouring from the trees to attack the disordered men at arms and spearmen. They also made the mistake of racing towards us – and as soon as they did then the arrows which had been thinning our ranks ceased to be as deadly, and I shouted, "Archers, nock!" It was a risk, as it allowed the Welsh to come closer, but I knew the effect of a large number of arrows. "Draw!" The Welsh were now less than fifty paces from us. "Release!" The arrows slammed into the Welsh and so many were hit that the line was halted. "Loose!"

I already had a bodkin arrow nocked and I sent it at a mailed man, whose shield had arrows in it, who was encouraging the rest of the attackers to fall upon us. His shield was held above his head, but my bodkin hit his mail hauberk and drove through to his back. I could tell that, for the fletch was all that stopped the arrow from disappearing into his body. The attack failed and men fell back to the safety of the trees. Of course, as soon as they did then arrows fell upon us again – but this time there were fewer of them, as many of the Welsh archers had been slain in the attack. As I sent a war arrow into the back of a fleeing Welshman I glanced west and saw that the Welsh had broken through our lines.

This would be a defeat.

I had never tasted defeat before and I did not like it. However, having been on the other end of the situation myself I knew what I needed to do. I shouted, "Yarpole archers, prepare to withdraw east. We will need to discourage the Welsh when the earl and his men fall back." No one answered me and I shouted, "Yarpole, answer me!"

I did not hear twelve voices, but I heard enough cries of, "Aye, my lord", to know that most of them had survived.

I turned and saw that the baggage and most of the fyrd behind us had fled. Jack was there, holding the reins of his horse and the sumpter with the arrows. He had, in his hand, a short sword. I wondered where he had acquired it.

The ground was littered with the bodies of those who had been guarding the baggage train and we were in danger of being cut off. The horn from the west was the earl's signal to retreat, but it was too late as the spearmen of the fyrd had had enough and were trying to flee through us. I whistled and my horse trotted next to me. I hung my bow from my cantle, and I mounted. It was not to help me to escape, but to afford me a better view.

I saw the scale of the disaster. The earl and the mounted men were racing down the road and having to fight their way through Welshmen trying to kill them and our own men on foot who were trying to escape.

The earl's surcoat was covered in blood and I saw that he now had a sword rather than his lance. The sword was also bloody. The earl had fought! As he neared me he shouted, "Warbow, take your men and fall back in good order." He whipped his horse's head around and rode back to charge the Welsh with his familia.

"Aye, lord!" Turning, I shouted, "Yarpole, March fifty paces turn and release! Jack, stay by me."

I saw that four of my men were dead. One-third of my archers would not be returning to their families. I drew my sword. I could not use a bow from the back of a horse. The men we had driven back saw that we were moving and began to emerge from the trees once more. I spurred my horse towards them. Being at the front of the archers meant that their attention was behind me and when

I brought my sword down on the unprotected head of a Welsh archer, he had no idea that death was descending. I rode through them knowing that I had height, speed, and a powerful arm. I did not kill every Welshman I struck, but I stopped enough of them so that my archers had time to withdraw. When an arrow hit my cantle, I knew that I had used up all my luck, and I turned my horse to follow my men down the road.

I spied Will of Leek and Geoffrey of Banbury. They had mounted their horses and were reorganising men. I reined in. "I want you two to take it in turns to stop your men, one company at a time and discourage the enemy. When you fall back the other can cover you. I will go and tell the rest of the vintenars."

They nodded and dismounted, to make themselves a smaller target. "Aye, captain."

I hurried down the road and passed my instructions to the others. We looked to be the only ones with any kind of order. Everyone else was fleeing. I saw some of the spearmen discarding equipment to hasten their flight. I could not see the four horses that belonged to my vintenars. They had been taken. If they were not returned, then I would seek out the thieves.

By the time I reached Will of Leek, I saw that he had gathered four of the men whose vintenar had been killed, but two of his own men lay dead some twenty paces away. We were not yet the rear-guard. The Earl of Lincoln and the mounted men at arms were fighting their way to us. "Jack, stay with Will and keep them supplied with arrows." Shouting, "Keep them occupied!" I drew my sword and rode to attack the rear of the men fighting the earl.

My men's arrows had cleared the road before the earl, but the men who were slowing down the retreat were too close to our men and the archers could not risk hitting a horse or man at arms. I hurtled towards them and made no attempt to slow. My horse would naturally stop, but his weight might well crush a Welshman. I leaned from my saddle and slashed at the unprotected back of a Welsh archer who was attempting to send a bodkin into the earl's back. My arm jarred against his spine. The forehooves of my horse struck the back of another and he fell screaming. Those two deaths were like the unjamming of a dam and the ones on either slide were slain by the earl's familia.

Earl Henry was bloodied but unwounded. "Thank you, Warbow."

"My men hold the road. The rest have fled."

He nodded. "Fall back to the archers but keep good order."

So began a long fighting retreat to Northop, where the Welsh finally gave up. My archers discouraged the Welsh and, thankfully, they did not have enough bodkins and their war arrows failed to penetrate the mail of the earl and his oathsworn. It had cost us twelve brave archers to do so although thankfully, no more vintenars. When we finally reached Chester it was midnight, and we were no longer a fighting force. If Sir Reginald had suffered a similar fate, then King Edward had lost Wales.

Chapter 6

I thanked the levy before they were sent home. They had done well, but they were broken men. They had seen their friends and family slaughtered and maimed by the Welsh. They had witnessed the spearmen who were professional, fleeing. Earl Henry let them go because he knew that by December, King Edward would be in the north and we could retake North Wales. We needed men with hope to fight the Welsh and not the ones who had broken. We also had good news; Sir Reginald Grey had fortified and reinforced both Flint and Rhuddlan. They were held for the crown.

After the battle my men and I found three of the horses which had been taken. Their riders had foolishly returned to Chester and made the mistake of not seeking their owner. The three of them were spearmen and, as such, were paid for their service. That they had taken the horses from my men meant that they had fled before the horn had sounded the retreat. It was Will of Leek who found the horses in the same stable, and after a few questions discovered that their owners drank in the inn attached to it. He sent for me and I brought the rest of the archers. There was anger amongst us all, for this was deliberate theft. I had men watching all the exits and entered with Will and

Geoffrey. The three men were easily identified, for they had short swords and each had a coif about his neck. However, to be certain I approached them and asked, "Are those your horses in the stables?"

One of them appraised me and when he spoke, I took him for the leader. He looked at my spurs. I had not worn them when I went to battle but wearing them in Chester often afforded me more courtesy. "Yes, my lord, they are for sale if you wish to buy them."

I smiled and he smiled back. "Why should I buy back my own property from horse thieves?"

Their hands went to their swords, but the man's two companions found an archer's bodkin blade pressed at their throats whilst I rested my hand on the pommel of my sword. "Please, draw your sword. There is nothing I would like better than to kill you here and now."

I could see him debating it, but one of the others said, "Fool! That is Sir Gerald Warbow!"

The man put his hands up palms outward. "I am sorry, my lord. We found the horses. We would have returned them!"

I laughed. "They had my mark on them and the battle was almost a fortnight since. Take their swords and bring them with me. We will let the constable of Chester mete out justice." They stood. "First, pay for the stabling of the horses."

I know that to many it would seem petty, but I wanted the men punished and they were. There had been desertions and the three of them were the only ones we could prove had deserted. They were whipped and put in the gaol at Chester at the constable's pleasure. Basically, that meant they would be given their freedom only when Earl Henry decided.

After the punishment had been meted out, Earl Henry told me of the progress of King Edward. "He is approaching Wrexham even as we speak, and you and your archers are to join him on the road to Denbigh. I will raise another army. Do not worry, Sir Gerald, we will find those untouched by the disaster. The rebels, it appears, have progressed no further than Denbigh. They are attempting to reduce Flint, but Sir Reginald is made of stern stuff."

In truth, I was glad to be free of Chester. My men apart, there was an air of defeat that hung in the city. We left early the next morning for the twelve-mile ride to Wrexham.

We arrived simultaneously with the vanguard of the army. I felt a huge sense of relief that I would see my son and my archers. My makeshift company had shown that they had lost nothing of their skill, but I knew the ones with Hamo were at the peak of their prowess. This time, I would be commanding the best of archers and not Sunday morning bowmen! The archers were not at the fore, and that reflected the fact that many of them were on foot and whoever commanded them in my absence wished to keep them together.

The king saw me as he entered the town. He was riding next to the Earl of Warwick who acknowledged me as the king waved me over. "Warbow, tell me all and spare no one's feelings. How were we so soundly beaten?"

"We had an army which did not have enough steel in it, King Edward. The scouts were inadequate, and we lacked leaders amongst the men."

He nodded. "And it has hurt us, for men who have been so soundly beaten are ever likely to run."

"The earl is raising another army from those who did not fight."

The king waved a hand at the darkening skies. "And we are fighting at the end of autumn which in this land is like full winter in London. This will not be easy."

The earl and I nodded our agreement. The king did not like wasted words. "Warbow, you will command the archers."

"How many do I have?"

"Do I look like a bookkeeper?"

The earl said, quietly, "Two hundred mounted archers and six hundred on foot."

"We need more mounted horsemen."

The king snorted. "Ask for the moon while you are at it. We have what we have. Your mounted archers will be the scouts. Captain Geoffrey of Cheadle has led them hitherto. We rest here for two days and then advance on Denbigh. I would have you scout out the road. This is, after all, your land."

"Yes, King Edward."

I was quite happy to be given the task, for there would be no lord to tell me what I did was wrong. I waited until the archers rode in. My men were with the other mounted archers, but I ignored them as I spoke to the captain. He dismounted and came over to me. We knew each other from Evesham and the Welsh wars. He had been a young archer at Evesham, and I knew that I could rely on him, for he had experience.

"Captain Geoffrey, the king has appointed me to take command of the archers, but you will still be captain, for I need someone I can rely upon to command the foot archers."

"It will be my honour. We heard the earl was ambushed and his army routed. Surely that was an exaggeration, Sir Gerald?"

"No, it was a disaster, but this time will be different, for my archers will scout the road. We need more archers to be mounted. Have the town scoured for any animals or ponies you can find." He cocked an eye. "Legally, if you can but get as many as you can. We will camp on the northwest of the town. The king and the nobles will take the best places within the walls. We can endure a little cold and damp."

95

He smiled as the rain began to fall. "I fear, Sir Gerald, that we will have to endure many such nights before the castles are recovered."

I mounted my horse and shouted, "Mounted archers, follow me!" Led by Hamo and my men the archers cheered, making some of the newly-arrived lords turn around. I had not been introduced by the king, but many would remember me from the last war we had fought in Wales.

Getting through the crowded town was tortuous. I hoped that Captain Geoffrey had done as I would have done and ensured the men carried enough supplies to be fed. The archers who had been in Chester with me had a sumpter laden with food. It would feed my contingent of archers, but I could not perform the miracle of the loaves and fishes!

We kept going until Will of Leek found water, woods, and grazing. I could not tell if we were on some noble's land or not, but I circled my hand to indicate that we had found our camp. My horsed archers had followed me closely and they went into their well-practised routine. Others emulated it and we soon had a cheery fire going and hovels erected whilst food was cooked. It was not until the food was bubbling and we had used our cloaks to make shelters from the drizzle that I was able to talk to Hamo, John, son of John, and Robin, son of Robert. My news could wait; I wanted to know how the men had fared.

Young Jack took my horse. He had grown a little in the time he had been on campaign with me, but it was something different I noticed about him. I saw more of a swagger in his movements, which were now far more confident. He led his horse and mine easily. He had been close to danger and battle. He had survived and he had learned from it. I found myself smiling. The battle had been a disaster, but I felt more hopeful now that my men were with me and Jack was a symbol of that hope. He was the sapling who would grow to be an oak.

Hamo spoke, and I knew that the time away from me had been

his coming of age, too. He was now assured and confident. Robin and John happily nodded their agreement as he talked. I discovered that the wait in Portsmouth had not done the king any favours. There had been desertions and fights but at least the army was on the right side of the Channel when the Welsh attacked.

I told them of the battle and our losses. The four men from Yarpole who had died were all known to them. "I will keep the others as vintenars, and they shall lead the dismounted archers. The rest of my men will become vintenars for the ones who are mounted."

"Some companies have vintenars already."

I smiled. "Hamo, I command and the men I know, and trust are my men. Do not worry if I ruffle feathers. Think of the archers as a puppy that needs to learn who is master. The Earl of Lincoln's army was saved by the discipline I instilled, and we are going to need that discipline if we are to winkle the Welsh from their nooks and crannies. King Edward has built good castles and they should not have fallen. Now that they have, we will have the devil's own job to shift them. This will be bloody work we face."

They nodded.

A voice shouted, "Food is ready!"

We each had our wooden bowl and spoon in hand already. The men moved aside to let me to the pot and the stew was ladled into it. It was what we called a hunter's stew. You had to hunt to find out what was the main ingredient, but it was tasty and filling. I had a stale loaf I had brought from Chester and when we sat, I shared that with the others seated the closest to me.

"Have you seen Richard of Launceston?"

Hamo nodded and wiped his mouth with the back of his hand. "When we were in Portsmouth, we saw him each night, but he rides with Sir Edmund and Sir Roger's men."

97

"Are there any problems?"

Hamo laughed. "Sir Edmund regards us as the droppings from horses and would not deign to speak to us. I think that the fortune of Master Richard's father ensures that Master Richard is treated well. I like him, and think that my sister has made a good choice."

"Then let us hope he survives this war, for I believe it will be harder this time than the last. Tomorrow, we scout out Denbigh. Robin, you and John fought here the last time. Take half of our men and ride beyond Denbigh towards Ruthin. I want you to secure as many horses as you can take and discover if they patrol the land between the two castles that they hold. Stay there to stop it from being reinforced until we arrive with the rest of the army. Hamo and I will take the rest and we will ensure that the land around Denbigh has no nasty surprises for the king. We want the castle cut off completely."

If Hamo was disappointed to be riding as my deputy he did not say anything. It was a deliberate act on my part. I wanted him to learn how to lead men he did not know. It was far easier for him to order around men like John and Robin than it would be total strangers, who might resent a young man giving orders. I had endured conflict when I was given command. It had made me more ruthless and, I believe, stronger.

We left before dawn. Of the men around me only Hamo was well known to me, although some archers nodded at me and smiled a welcome. I might have led them the last time. After discovering which of the archers had fought here with me, I took them and Hamo to be the advance guard. We were only five horse lengths from the others, but I was familiar with this land and knew what to look for. When we rode in the open areas, we kept to the road, but when I spied trees, undergrowth, or settlements then I sent ten archers to our right and left to ensure there was no ambush. The twenty-mile ride, which would be an easy one in summer, was a longer and wetter one at this time of year. With days lasting barely six or seven hours and dark clouds making visibility even worse, it was an unpleasant duty. The advantage we had was that the wet meant any Welsh archers who might choose to ambush us would have a much shorter range, making it easier for us to see them. Most of the archers I led had swords, and the ones who had fought here before knew how to use them.

We had just left a wooded section of the road and my outriders were closing back in with us when we saw the ten Welshmen on ponies ahead of us. They saw us as we saw them, and they turned to flee. I spurred my horse, as did Hamo and the others. The outriders had an advantage that they were riding over open fields and they had little to obstruct them, as the crops had all been harvested. It meant that the Welshmen had to stay on the road. We began to catch them. Our horses had longer legs. Perhaps the Welshmen thought we were armoured and would be slower – but we were not.

When we were just thirty paces from them, I bellowed, "Halt and surrender or you will die!" One of them turned and shouted something which, from his gesture, I took to be a curse. He had signed the death warrant for them all. We could not allow them back to Denbigh as they would warn the garrison. That the defenders of Denbigh would know we were coming was clear, but the longer we delayed that knowledge, the fewer supplies they could gather.

I drew my sword. Hamo had a long sword like me but most of the archers only had a short sword. Hamo put his horse next to mine as we closed with the Welsh. I allowed Hamo to ride to my left. He would have the easier strike. I was the experienced horseman. The Welshman at the back was labouring and he was not helping himself by constantly turning in his saddle.

"Yours, Hamo!"

The Welshman drew his short sword and tried to turn to hack at my horse's head. Hamo's sword almost decapitated him and he fell from the saddle. The fall slowed Hamo, who had to swerve to his left. The next two Welshmen were side by side and I reached the right hand one before Hamo reached the other. The slash by the Welshman with the short sword was a blind one and my sword took off his right arm. He was not a skilled rider and he fell to the ground to be trampled by the horses which followed us. Hamo easily disposed of the other as a Welsh pony had veered into it. The outriders had now managed to get ahead the remaining riders and the two archer arms closed shut. All of the Welshmen died. For my archers it was a strange victory as it had been achieved with a sword and not a bow.

"Take their ponies and their weapons! Jack, stay with the ponies." We needed the ponies, and I did not want the Welsh to have access to their weapons. I detailed four men and Jack to take the ponies and weapons back to Wrexham.

The capture of the animals delayed us, and I knew that it would be dark before we could return to Wrexham. The hard chase had been longer than I planned. We rode steadily to Denbigh. I knew the castle well and we watched from the woods. It was clear that they had no idea of the proximity of our army, for their gates were open and the walls were unmanned. It was clear that John and Robin, along with their men, had managed to remain hidden. If they had been seen, then the walls would be manned and the gates shut. That they would be spotted was inevitable, but the Welsh might assume that they had come from Flint Castle. Satisfied that there was no Welsh army close by we turned and headed back.

It was far later than we had envisaged when we reined in our weary horses. Leaving Hamo to see to the horses and men, I went to speak with King Edward. He, the Earl of Warwick, and his senior nobles were in the largest hall in the town. It belonged to a merchant who was keen to gain the favour of King Edward. I was aware that I stank of horse as I entered; I saw some of the lords wrinkle their noses.

The Earl of Warwick beamed and stood to pour some wine. I knew that he liked and respected me. "Here Sir Gerald, you look weary, have a goblet of wine."

I shook my head and waved over a servant. "Beer is what I need!"

The servant scurried off and King Edward said, "Well?"

"I do not think that they know we are close, my lord. The gates were open, but they did have patrols out. We eliminated one and they will learn soon enough that we are here."

"As we leave tomorrow, then there is no problem."

The servant brought the ale and I unceremoniously downed it in one. It slaked my thirst. I handed it to the servant and nodded. I wanted a second. "I have half of my mounted archers on the far side of Denbigh. They will delay any attempt to reinforce and prevent a sortie from that side."

The king nodded and nudged Sir Walter Bigod. "You see, I told you he would think of everything. Well done, Sir Gerald. I am sending sixteen thousands of my men to join Sir Reginald Grey and they will march along the coast road. The Earl of Lincoln will bring the men from Chester to join him. The six thousand I retain should be more than enough to retake Denbigh. Conwy still holds out and we will reunite there. I have ships sailing north to resupply the castles even as we speak." The servant arrived with the beer. "Drink that, Warbow and then get some rest. You will be in the saddle before dawn. I would have Caernarfon back in my hands by the New Year!"

As I left, I knew that the king was being overly optimistic. It was not just those with aspirations to rule Wales who had risen, it was the people who did not like English law and English lords. All of Wales and its people would fight.

I did not so much fall asleep as collapse. My illness still sought to trip me up and I hated it. I liked to be in control of my body and not the other way around.

Jack shook me awake. "Sir Gerald, your son said to wake you. The men are preparing their horses."

I nodded. My illness had changed my body and I hoped it would be a temporary thing, for I did not like to be the last awake. It was not my way. As we were close to a town there was fresh bread, and we had ale. As campaign breakfasts went, it was better than most and having a full stomach made the ride easier.

Our job was to ensure that the road was clear for the main army. Over half the army was on foot. Jack was not the only one leading a sumpter. Hamo had taken two servants and Jack rode with them and Ralph the fletcher's boys. They were used to the road now.

I had asked Jack about the sword which now hung from his belt and he told me how he had come by it. A Welshman had raced from the woods to try to take the sumpter but in his haste, he had tripped in the ditch which lay before him. Jack had been quick-thinking enough to ride his horse at the man who lay on the ground. His horse had killed the man and Jack had armed himself. I knew then that, despite his upbringing, he was a natural warrior and not a farmer. I was glad that we had brought him from Malton.

By the time it was dawn we were at the place where we had met the Welshmen on ponies. Sending Hamo and twenty men to ride to Denbigh, we awaited the king. There had been little opportunity to stop people leaving Wrexham and I knew that by now those in Denbigh would know of the presence of King Edward's army. I had to admire the cleverness and military skill of King Edward. Those who would have fled to Denbigh would have reported an army of over twenty thousand. When the defenders of Denbigh saw our banners, they would assume we had that number with us not knowing that Sir Reginald Grey and more than twenty thousand men were on their way to the coast road to cut them off.

The king and the earl of Warwick reined in next to me. I waved my archers forward. "We have seen no Welshman and a company of archers now watches Denbigh."

"Good. Then let us move. I would have my food tonight in the hall of Denbigh Castle!"

We headed towards the castle, now watched by my son; Hamo stepped from the woods when I approached. "Dismount," he said, and pointed as our horses were led away. "They have the gates barred and the walls manned." He waved forward one of the men I had sent with John and Robin. "Harold here brought word that the valley road is blocked to the coast by our archer, but they saw no sign of any reinforcements coming."

"Good, then the king will be happy. Take our men and have them form lines beyond bow range. When Captain Geoffrey arrives, I would have him do the same. Keep our men together in the centre so that we can attack the gatehouse."

"You think that King Edward will use us first?"

I laughed. "We are far cheaper than his men at arms and he would have the Welsh waste their arrows on us rather than him and his nobles."

Hamo nodded. "There is cover." He led the men off.

I had sent an archer with orders for John, son of John, and Robin, son of Robert. They were to keep the northern wall under attack. There would be a limited number of archers inside the castle and I did not want them all on this wall. Jack, Ralph's sons and the two servants arrived. "You five will be kept busy today. Your task is to keep the Yarpole archers supplied with arrows." I knew that Geoffrey had his own supply of arrows but fewer men to resupply them.

The king and his commanders soon joined us, and he viewed the castle from the trees. He waved me over. "I will give them the opportunity to surrender. I suspect that they will spurn the offer but I have to appear to be fair. I want fifteen flights of arrows sent into the castle when they refuse."

"Many of the arrows will be wasted, King Edward."

"Do not worry, the Welsh will recompense you for the loss. I see now that I was too kind when we took this valley. There will be a stronger hand upon the reins from now on. Join your men. I will wait until all my nobles are here and we will blind them with our shining armour and glittering banners."

I took my bow and a war bag of arrows and headed down to my men. I saw Captain Geoffrey dismount and hand his horse to one of his servants. "Captain Geoffrey, have the foot archers flank our other archers. The men will need fifteen arrows, at the very least," I told him.

"Aye Sir Gerald!"

Once I joined my men, I strung my bow. My recent illness showed, for it took me longer than it normally did. I knew that my full health and strength would return, but it would be a slow process. "Hamo, tell the vintenars that when I give the command, we will send fifteen arrows in swift succession into the castle." He raised his eyebrows. "The king orders it. Make sure that every vintenar and Captain Geoffrey knows what we have to do. They fight under my command." I had a banner, but I had not brought it. Jack was better used in fetching arrows than flaunting my flag.

I looked down the lines and saw the lines being straightened by vintenars. We had some archers with us who had never fought in a battle. They had marched to Portsmouth and then to Wales, but their bows had been in their cases until this moment.

King Edward, the Earl of Warwick and Sir Godfrey – in his pursuivant livery, bareheaded and with open palms – rode forward. We parted to let them through. Hamo returned and nodded. The message had been passed. Sir Godfrey demanded that someone come to speak with the king. When one spoke, we knew that Madog ap Llewelyn was not in the castle.

"I am Gruffyd ap Rhys and I command here for Prince Madog ap Llewelyn."

King Edward's voice was, as ever, commanding and imperious. "You have taken the castle of the Earl of Lincoln and done great mischief in this land. Surrender the castle now, lay down your arms and return to your home. If you do so, then you will keep your lives – all save you, Gruffyd ap Rhys, who will be tried for treason."

The Welshman laughed and shouted, presumably to the defenders. "You hear the words of this Englishman? He thinks this is England!" The man turned and pointed at King Edward and said, "This is Wales, ruled by Prince Madog, a Welshman, and we hold what is ours!"

"That is your answer?"

"It is."

The king whipped his horse's head around and as he passed me, he said, "Now it is your turn, Warbow. Let death rain down upon them and they will see who truly reigns here."

I raised my bow and advanced to within arrow range. As the king had been speaking, I had noticed that the men on the wall were a mixture of archers and men at arms. I had not seen nocked arrows. It did not take us long to close the distance, and as we were in straight lines it took a moment for me to shout, "Nock!" I had chosen a bodkin arrow, for I saw metal on the walls. "Draw!" The creak was not as sharp as I would have liked when the bows were drawn back, but it would have to do. "Release!"

We had caught them unawares. They would have expected the normal preliminaries of battle and that would have allowed them to replace the men at arms on the walls with archers. I used war arrows once I had sent my first bodkin. I nocked, drew and released as fast as I could, but I was not as fast as I had been and Hamo had sent his fifteen arrows an arrow before me.

The concentration of drawing and releasing so quickly had emptied my head of everything else and I had heard nothing. The thrum of bowstrings and the *whoosh* of arrows had filled my ears and head. Now I heard the cries from within the walls. Many arrows had missed flesh and hit buildings, the walls, the stone roads within the castle – but so many arrows must have had a devastating effect.

Behind me, I heard the Earl of Warwick shout, "Advance!"

It was not over, and I shouted to my archers, "Nock but do not draw! Await my command." I heard my vintenars praising where necessary and chiding those who had been tardy. They were earning their extra pay. "Open ranks!" Archers never stood too close together and by turning our bodies to the side the men at arms with shields and axes were able to pass through us.

Hamo said, "I see bows!" He drew back a little but did not release.

I drew back and shouted, "Draw!" I spied a few archers, obviously sent from the other walls and I shouted, "Release!" Our arrows made the archers duck. I was unsure if we had hit any, but the axemen were able to make the walls and to begin hammering on the gate.

The voice from above was not Gruffyd ap Rhys, it was a priest, who shouted, "Cease! We surrender! Lord Gruffyd is dead!"

The hammering stopped, but we did not relax our vigilance. When the gates swung open, I unstrung my bow. The archers' work was done.

Some of our archers began to walk towards the castle. I shouted, "Archers, hold!"

I knew that the king would wish to be the first into the castle. As he rode past me, he nodded. "You did well, Warbow. Join your other men on the far side of the castle. I will send food and instructions to you."

Some of the men grumbled as we headed around the castle to join the rest of our archers. I heard Captain Geoffrey admonishing some of them. They had expected to sack the town. That would not happen, for this was one of King Edward's castles and he wanted no harm to come to it. I turned to Hamo and said, "When we reach the other side and the camp there, send some men into the castle to recover any undamaged arrows and the heads of any arrows which we can reuse. I do not think this war is over yet."

"Where do you think we will be heading next?"

"Conwy first. The last intelligence we had was that it held out. The town has a good wall, and it can be supplied from the sea."

Jack was close by us, leading two sumpters, He was followed by Ralph and Roger, sons of Ralph the fletcher. Jack already appeared to have the potential to lead and he said, "That was easy enough, Sir Gerald. Will we be home by New Year?"

I laughed at his youthful innocence. "You are of the same opinion as the king. We may, but it depends upon the Welsh. It is winter and this land is a harsh one, even in summer. We will have an army of thirty thousand to feed. I fear that we will have tight belts for a while."

John and Robin had made a sturdy camp with embedded stakes all around it. While our horses were tended to, they told Hamo and me of their side of the battle.

"We chased away the handful of men they sent against us and captured twenty ponies." Robin pointed to the walls. "They did not have a large enough garrison to attack us and so we waited. When we heard the attack begin, we started to pick off archers from the walls."

Hamo asked, "Where was the army which ambushed you, father?"

My son was astute and the same thought had crossed my mind. "That is a good question, Hamo. Perhaps the king's decision to send the bulk of the army to the coast road has made them withdraw. It does not change what we have to do. Have you enough food?"

John, son of John, grinned. "The Earl of Lincoln will find fewer deer when he returns to his castle. We will eat well."

The king sent food and Sir Godfrey. "The king wishes you and your mounted men to accompany him on the morrow, Sir Gerald. He will ride with chosen mounted men for Conwy. The Earl of Warwick will keep the bulk of the army and they secure this valley and find all those who are rebels. Captain Geoffrey will command the archers in your absence."

I nodded. We had been lucky. We had lost a mere ten archers in the attack and that was far fewer than I had expected. The king's plan of attack had taken them by surprise.

Chapter 7

Conwy, 1295

A far smaller force than I had expected left the next day, for Conwy. We had been able to mount more foot archers and I led two hundred mounted archers. King Edward took just four hundred men at arms. Six hundred men with a few servants was a risky move, but King Edward was nothing if not confident. Conwy had been a crucial part of the defences King Edward had built, and when I had last been there it had been a low wall less than six feet high. Master James of St George had taken just six building seasons to finish both Conwy and Harlech. The fact that both new castles had held out was a testament to the skills of King Edward's castle builder. The whitewashed walls made the castle look like a sailing ship in the harbour and it must have been a sight which told the Welsh who, despite the recent setbacks, was master in this part of the world.

We crossed the river and entered the castle. When they had subdued the surrounding countryside then the army would join us, but King Edward wanted to be behind walls for the start of the new year so that he could plan his campaign to retake Caernarfon and the other fallen fortresses.

Our lack of supplies soon began to have an effect. King Edward was forced to keep a large part of the army on the other side of the Conwy where they could forage. He summoned me on the first day of January.

"Warbow, we are blind here in this castle and I need to know what lies to the west of us. Take your mounted bowmen from Yarpole and scout out the land. I need to know where the Welsh are to be found."

"And the rest of the army, King Edward?"

"They will cross the river when they can. I intend to strike at the Welsh wherever I can find them."

We had rested and I knew that with such a small force of archers we would be well capable of supplying ourselves and living off the land. I left the eight vintenars with the other archer companies and took the rest. Jack and Ralph the fletcher's sons led the sumpters loaded with our arrows, and we left Conwy to head along the narrow coastal road which nestled beneath Snowdon's brooding peak.

This was Madoc's heartland. Here were the most fanatical of all the Welsh, in a place of steep slopes and narrow paths. It was perfect country for an ambush. Gwillim knew this part of Wales well and he, along with Dick of Luston, were our scouts. They both had noses for ambush and for finding the Welsh. Penmaenmawr and Llanfairfechan were both places where the Welsh could have held us up, but we passed them without seeing any threat to our army. Bangor, on the other hand, being close to the island of Anglesey and a port, did have a sizeable garrison. We spied it from a small wood which lay just half a mile from the small town walls; the leafless trees would not have hidden a larger force but they hid my men and we saw that there were men at arms as well as the usual archers. We counted a thousand men. I suppose we could have returned to King Edward with that news, but I liked to be thorough and we continued south and west, keeping away from the coast. The slopes and terraces along which we travelled afforded us a view to the sea and yet gave us plenty of escape routes.

We camped above the Llyn Padarn. This was sheep country, but in the heart of winter and with wolves still roaming the desolate mountainside, all of the flocks were safely protected lower down in the valley. I confidently had the men light a fire for hot food and warmth. I set sentries and we enjoyed a hot hunter's stew. My men laid traps to catch rabbits and some looked wistfully down at the lake. Fresh fish would have been a treat, but I did not wish to push our luck further.

We were close enough to Caernarfon so that by leaving early, before the sun had risen, we were able to be in a position to spy out the castle and see if it was defended. I had never seen the castle, but I had spoken with Sir Godfrey and knew that this was supposed to be the great fortress which would control Wales. As the sun came up, we could see that the castle was not defended, and the reason was clear. It had been half-finished when the Welsh attacked, and the walls would not have stopped any from entering at will. All the wooden buildings had been burned and the scaffolding for the walls set afire, resulting in the collapse of huge sections. King Edward would have to build again, and that would cost money.

We did not need to go any further and I continued to lead my men further down the coast towards Nefyn, where King Edward and his army had defeated the Welsh the last time we had subdued them. We reached the tiny hamlet of Cennin just before dark. Gwillim knew the place and we chose it for, despite the danger of being spotted, it afforded a view both towards Nefyn and south to Criccieth and Harlech. Once the inhabitants realised that they were safe and that we intended no harm, they went indoors.

While my men prepared food, I went with Hamo and Jack to spy out the land. Nefyn was defended. I saw, in the distance, a banner flying from its walls. It was too far away to identify the noble. I saw, too, that Criccieth was defended. We knew it had fallen but the Welsh had not wrecked it, they were defending it.

"Well, Hamo, we can return to the king with the news he wishes to hear. The Welsh are within striking distance. Once our army crosses the Conwy, he can reclaim this part of Wales."

"And we can go home?"

"Perhaps, but I would not count on it."

The bulk of the army was still heading to the Conwy, but my news heartened the king and he decided on an immediate foray down the coast. He would not be gainsaid by any. "Warbow has brought us good news for I had feared that Caernarfon would be defended and that we would need to besiege it. The Welsh mischief will be their undoing. Warbow, I need you and every mounted archer." I nodded. I would be leading two hundred men. "We take the four hundred men at arms I brought with me and a good baggage train to keep us supplied. With the Earl of Warwick and Grey on the other side of the Conwy then the castle will be safe until they have cleansed the land. We will leave at the end of the first week of January!"

For Wales, the weather was clement as we set off. There was neither snow nor sleet and, by Welsh standards, the wind was almost gentle. King Edward had my archers as his vanguard and scouts. The baggage train at the rear was protected by twenty young knights while the king rode with his potent force of mounted men at arms. Jack and Ralph's sons stayed with us. They would act as horse holders if we were needed.

I had not seen any Welsh force on our scouting expedition which could face us. The king's bold move might prove to be a successful one. I knew that he was disappointed not to have begun the year with more of Wales under his control; his ships still supplied Harlech but all else was under the control of Prince Madog.

We did not move as fast as when I had scouted, and it took a day or two to reach Bangor. There, the Welsh decided to face us. They had equity in numbers, but not in quality. Their archers apart, the men who faced us were either well mounted and armoured nobles or peasants armed with a variety of home-made weapons. Designating ten archers to guard the baggage train, the king dismounted the archers and his men at arms took lances from the baggage train and stood behind us. The Welsh formed up much as we did.

I might have been tempted to stay behind the walls of Bangor but whoever led the Welsh must have been confident he could defeat us. They had four hundred mounted men, but half were light horsemen who would be swept aside if King Edward led a charge of heavy horses. They had many spearmen and appeared to have adopted the long spears favoured by the Scots.

"Warbow, advance and annoy the Welsh. We will be close enough to protect you." With my men sprinkled amongst the other archers, I knew that the men would do as I commanded. The field of battle was small enough that my voice would be heard across it.

"Archers, advance!"

"Men at arms, prepare to follow."

We set off, each with an arrow nocked. I heard when we had moved a few steps, the sound of the horses as they followed. I knew that the Welsh might choose to release before we were in position. They had a delicate problem. With the mailed men advancing behind us they would be uncertain as to our intentions. If they nocked a war arrow and the horsemen charged, then their arrows would avail them nought. On the other hand, if they had bodkins and they used them against archers, the missiles would be wasted. They waited with arrows in the belts. We each had a war arrow. There were too few mailed men ahead of us to waste bodkins upon. I halted and raised my bow. My vintenars shouted "Halt!" almost as one.

I heard the horses for a moment before they stopped and I shouted, "Draw!" The Welsh now saw their target and they reached into their warbags for war arrows. Even as they nocked an arrow and began to draw, I shouted, "Release!" Our arrows flew and plunged down on the Welsh archers. I drew and released – again and again. Arrows landed amongst my archers and I heard men cry out as they were struck. This was not a time for the faint hearted, and I kept releasing my arrows at an ever-diminishing enemy. Arrows showered me. One struck so close to my buskin that it scored a line down the side.

"Open ranks!" King Edward's voice gave the command that I normally issued. We all turned sideways. As we did, I saw a Cheshire archer fall as an arrow slammed into his skull.

The huge horses brushed us aside, and when they had done so I shouted, "Prepare to follow! Nock an arrow!" Jack ran up with a bag of arrows. He gave some to me and some to Hamo before running to John and Robin. It was a brave act, although the Welsh archers were now scrabbling in their bags for bodkins. We had won the duel, and the Welsh archers sent a few desultory arrows at the charging horsemen before fleeing. They broke through the spearmen and, their integrity shattered, were swept aside by King Edward and his mailed men.

I had been in enough battles to judge the moment. "Archers, let us get amongst them!" I loosed the arrow I had nocked at the back of a spearman and then slung the bow over my back. It made running easier. This would be a test of my fitness. As I had expected, Hamo soon overtook me but then he ran just before me. My son was protecting me. When had our roles changed? I cursed the illness which had made me a weaker man.

The whole Welsh army was fleeing. Those who could were heading for the town, but most simply took to their heels to seek an escape somewhere a horse could not follow. While King Edward and his men at arms might struggle to climb the rocks and hedges, my archers would not. I suppose that had they chosen, the Welsh archers and spearmen could have turned and made a stand when they realised that it was just archers who followed. My men still had their bows and when the terrain slowed the Welsh up, then arrows were sent at a range of forty paces into unprotected backs. It meant that we prevented them from rallying. As the Welsh began to ascend into the rocks they slowed, and I stopped and unslung my bow. My chest was heaving and enough of them were in my range. I nocked an arrow and targeted an archer who was attempting to get behind a large rock. He was forty paces from me, and I almost pinned his body to the stone. My breathing became a little easier and I took the life of a spearman next.

Most of the archers I had brought from Yarpole did the same. Running into a warren of rocks was a recipe for disaster. By the time I had emptied my bag, there were no Welshmen close to me and I shouted, "Re-form! Archers, re-form!"

Jack joined me with more arrows. "I shall not need them now Jack, but put them in my warbag, draw your short sword and let us see what we can find."

Hamo joined me. "We have lost some archers!" He pointed to the rocks above us, where I saw the bodies lying at awkward angles, bloody marks showing where they had been caught.

I nodded. "Fewer than we might have, although more than I wished." I turned and saw the royal standard flying over the gates of Bangor. The king had won. "Have the men find as many arrows as they can and bows. Shatter the spears and make a bonfire of them and any bows we do not want." We had to deny the enemy weapons. We had plenty, but they would find it hard to replace the metal heads on the spears. I did not need to tell the men to collect treasure, that came as second nature. None of the dead was wealthy, but coins collected from the bodies soon mounted up and with swords and daggers, which could be sold on, my men would all make a profit. Friends carried the dead back to Bangor.

It was dark by the time we had finished, and we saw, in the rocks, the fires we had lit burning in the night. While my men made food, I went to the king who was settling into the town.

"You did well, Warbow. What did it cost us?"

"We have thirty dead archers and another twenty who are wounded."

"A quarter. A higher cost than I would have liked."

I shrugged. "It is war and we slew a far greater number. Bangor is now yours, King Edward. Do we return to Conwy?"

He laughed. "No, Warbow. We push on. Let us see if we can retake Criccieth or Castell y Bere, eh? I saw nothing today to make me fear another battle."

We left the next day. The town was burned, but as much of it was made of stone the Welsh could rebuild. Had we enjoyed the luxury of more men, we could have garrisoned it. I sent the wounded back to Conwy. That way we had fewer mouths to feed.

Over the next days, the Welsh proved to be like fog or a will o' the wisp. We saw them in the distance, but by the time we closed with them they had disappeared. The king had not bothered to view Caernarfon and so we were able to make time down the peninsula. As my men and I had discovered, this was an empty and desolate coastline. There was no opposition and our scouts reported nothing ahead of us. That was, until we were nearing Nefyn. The road passed through some rocky scrubland. There were a few trees, but it was mainly gorse and wild bushes. My scouts came hurrying back to us.

It was Gwillim who led them. "My lord, the Welsh are ahead. There is a battle line and we saw horsemen!"

King Edward beamed triumphantly. "We have them! Warbow, take your archers and ride to hold them. Sir Edmund, keep your men with the baggage train and the rest come with us."

I spurred my horse and saw the Welsh a mile ahead on the flatter ground. They had bowmen arrayed and their horsemen guarded the flanks. Even as I rode towards them, I noticed that they had no spearmen. There looked to be just four hundred men all told, and I guessed that they were counting on the fact that this time, they would be drawn and ready. We had taken horses at Bangor and we had spare mounts. It might mean losing a few horses, but we could use them as an equine barrier to allow us time to string our bows and draw. Being without armour meant that we were faster, and I halted my men just two hundred paces from the Welsh.

"Dismount and use your horses for protection."

As we stopped, King Edward and his men at arms galloped past. They had no lances – they were on the baggage train – but all had swords and axes. They thundered beyond us. Even before we had strung our bows the Welsh had raced to their hidden ponies, mounted, and were now galloping off.

Gwillim shook his head. "Now what is *that* about, Sir Gerald?"

I did not know. "A trick, perhaps? Are they leading the king into a trap? Mount and let us go to the aid of King Edward!"

The Welsh men at arms had turned and raced away before the ponies of the Welsh archers. I should have known there was a trick of some kind when there were so few archers and no spearmen. That was not the Welsh way. I doubted that we would catch them, and I was looking for places where they could spring their trap. The best place would have been where we first spotted them. There was an old hill fort southeast of Nefyn and I wondered if that was where they waited for us. When Sir Edmund and the men designated to guard the baggage train arrived just behind us, I saw where the trap had been. The foolish knight had abandoned the baggage train for a chance of glory.

"Archers. Halt and follow me!"

Not all obeyed. All my Yarpole men did, but many of the others were caught up, like Sir Edmund, in the chase. Hamo and I led the men. Jack, and Ralph's sons, along with their sumpters, had been behind the main body of archers and Jack stopped and turned when he heard my command. He rode with us.

Hamo stared north. "What is it, father?"

I shook my head. "The Welsh have outwitted us, Hamo. They have taken our supplies and spare weapons!"

As we neared the place at which we had left the wagons, we saw the slaughtered drivers – but there was no sign of the wagons. As we had not seen the perpetrators, I deduced that they had headed east to the woods and the peak that was Cefn-caer-Ferch.

I dismounted to string my bow and my men emulated me. "Robin, take the three boys and five men. See if there are any left alive and make a fortified camp. The rest, follow me." I saw that I led fewer than sixty men. The others had all been caught up in the chase. "Gwillim, use your nose."

"The wagons will be hard to hide, father."

"Hamo, if they planned this well, they will have organised some way to get the wagons to safety."

The route we followed was clear. We saw not only horse droppings, rare in this part of the world, but also items that had fallen from the wagons and the damaged trees through which they had passed. We did not really need Gwillim to discern the route, for any of us could have done so, but his nose was remarkable and he proved that I had made the right decision when he left from his horse and shouted, "Ware, ambush!"

I dismounted as quickly as I could, unslung my bow and grabbed the first arrow that came to hand. I heard the arrow before I saw it, and it slammed into the tree just behind me. Had I not been warned then I would have been hit.

I knew the direction whence the arrow had been released and I peered into the trees. The track along which the wagons had fled was empty and that meant our attackers were hiding. The Welsh had used the old trick of smearing mud on their faces and hands. It made them hard to see, but you can't put mud on an eye, and it was the eye I spotted. I drew and released in one motion. It was a hurried strike but a lucky one. I hit the Welshman's bow and shattered it. Small shards of wood must have hit his face, for he screamed.

I nocked another arrow and sought another enemy. I could hear the noise of archery duels as my men looked for targets. It was the sound of arrows cracking through leaves and twigs. It was the thrum of a string as the arrow was released.

The Welshman I next hit was falling back. An arrow, presumably from Hamo, had hit the man next to him and he was moving away when I snapped off an arrow at him. I hit his right shoulder and the arrow drove into his chest. Like a wounded stag, he managed a few steps before falling to the ground, presumably to bleed out.

"Mount and after them!" It was a risk, but one worth taking if we were to recover the wagons. I hung the sword from my cantle and drew my sword. Once I made the track, I found that, as I had given the order, I was ahead of the rest and I spied a wagon which looked to be within two hundred paces. We were not travelling over a road, but it was – largely – a flat surface. The piece of high ground over which I rode, twisted, turned, rose and fell. There was a rise ahead and I closed to within fifty feet of it. As it disappeared over the edge, I urged my weary horse on, knowing that the draught horses would be in an even worse condition. As I reached the top, I heard a cry and a crash; I saw that the driver had lost control of the wagon and it had slewed around, crashing into a tree and throwing the two men to the ground. The exhausted horses just stood, and I galloped up to capture the two men. I was too late. One had been impaled on a broken branch and the other lay crushed beneath the wagon.

Hamo and my men arrived. "Gwillim, take four men and see if you can catch them."

He nodded, glumly and pointed to the darkening sky. "Night will soon be here, captain."

"Do your best."

He chose his men, and they rode off. "The rest of you, right this wagon." I saw that while the wagon had neither food nor tents, it was filled with arrows, spears and lances. It was a disaster for the king, but we had salvaged something.

We did not reach our improvised camp until it was dark and the king, along with the rest of the army, was at Nefyn. An angry King Edward was making the locals pay for the loss of his baggage train. We were isolated and few in numbers. I had a small fort made using the wagon and stakes cut from the wood. We always had food, for my men were opportunist hunters and gatherers.

We set sentries and dealt with the few minor wounds my men had suffered. We sat in a large circle and I shouted to Gwillim, who was on the other side of the circle: "Your people have shown just how cunning they are, Gwillim."

"They are not fools, my lord. We showed them at Bangor that the archers you lead are the equal of the Welsh and all know that none can stand up to your horsemen."

"You are right."

Hamo said, "Then they will not risk battle again?"

Shaking my head I said, "They do not need to. We have enjoyed a benign winter up to now, but it will worsen. We have long lines back to England and our only hope is to be supplied from the sea. We have a large army, but it needs to be fed!"

A messenger arrived as we were preparing to leave to join the king. He was returning. Although we had not lost many men the loss of supplies and wagons meant that we had to return to Conwy and await seaborne supplies. When he re-joined us, the king had me ride next to him.

"You salvaged arrows then?"

"Yes, King Edward. We were lucky. They had a good route planned but we caught the last wagon before it could escape."

"We will have to make the rations we have last. Have your men divided into two groups. I want your archers at the rear. Sir Edmund has proved that he cannot be trusted to follow a simple order. We will take all that we can find on the way back."

We found very little. The Welsh had removed everything edible into the mountains. In revenge, King Edward burned every building we could find.

We were still half a day from Conwy when first the wild wind and then the savage winter rain began. It was not unexpected, for this was winter, but we had been deceived by the clement weather thus far. We had not even needed furs to sleep outdoors. Now, however, the wind scythed in – bringing not just rain, but also sleet and the hint of snow. By the time we made Conwy even the most hardened of veterans was frozen to the bone. As the gates slammed shut we prepared to sit out the storm.

After a week it was still unabated, and King Edward ordered rationing to begin. Then began a time of real hardship. My men and I were too used to foraging and hunting. We rarely went hungry. I knew that the king was worried, but in typical King Edward style when we were down to the last barrel of wine, he insisted that all share in it. We both knew that if help did not come soon, either men would die or we might have to surrender the castle. The bulk of the army was still across the Conwy. but enough had entered the castle to mean that there were too many men for the short supplies we had.

The storm only eased by the second week of isolation, but it was still too stormy for either men to cross the river or for ships to bring us supplies. We were being besieged by nature itself. I daresay the Welsh took heart and thought it was punishment for the arrogant English oppressors. It was February before the first supplies were landed. After a week of filling our stomachs, I was summoned by King Edward. Whilst we had food for the men our horses were becoming weaker thanks to the lack of grazing.

"Warbow, I intend to send horses out to graze but I am loath to lose them to Welsh raiders. Take your men for a sweep around the land to the south and west. Your men are well led and intelligent. Be as the spokes on a wheel and get as far as you can. I need to know if there are Welsh close by and I would have as much as I can returning from the baggage train." Many of the lords liked comfort when we rode to war and they had fine goblets and furs, which were carried in the baggage train. Unlike his antecedent, King John, King Edward did not take the crown jewels with him, but he had precious objects which he wished returned. One was a beautiful psalter given to him by Queen Eleanor. He would read from it each night before bed, and I knew that its loss hurt him. I was not hopeful, but I was ever King Edward's man and I would do my best.

"Yes, my lord."

I was pleased, for the incarceration in the castle had resulted in some fights and disagreements. My men needed action and I for one was pleased to be riding abroad. I divided my men into four columns. Hamo, John and Robin each led one while I had the fourth. I gave my best men to the other three; I had commanded for longer.

There were really just two roads that we could use. One went along the coast and the other down the Conwy. The route along the Conwy had tracks and poor roads which led off the main one and most of them ended close to the base of Snowdon. The Welsh did not need roads, but I knew that the wagons they had taken must have used roads and that we might find evidence of the Welsh. Messengers had brought news that the Earl of Warwick's army was in good condition, having been supplied from Chester and Shrewsbury. He was ready to ride forth in March and another part of my task was to see what lay to the west of the River Conwy.

I sent John, son of John, along the coast road and I gave Gwillim to Robin. His task was to scout out the places where the roads were little more than tracks. Hamo and I headed south towards Pen-y-Pass. It was an ambitious ride. Hamo's men and mine were chosen because they had the best horses. When we reached the pass Hamo would turn around and come back to Conwy, but my men and I would ride along the old Roman road towards Bangor and the coast.

If there was a military presence close to Conwy, then it was well hidden. We patrolled aggressively and Hamo and I sent men to search halls, barns and outbuildings but, as we headed along the Roman road, we saw nothing save the best warriors the Welsh had, Snowdon, Glyder Fawr and Carnedd Llewelyn. Those peaks dominated the landscape, and they determined our route. The only place we found signs of an enemy were at the bridge of Llanrwst. We found more horse droppings than one might expect and the hoofprints in the soft and muddy ground suggested larger horses than the Welsh normally used. The people were sullen and unhelpful, but we saw no mailed men nor even archers.

Hamo and I parted where the road headed for the Pen-y-Pass and then Llanberis. I would re-join the coast road close to Llandygai. John would await me there, after having investigated Bangor. Hamo would ride to the head of the pass and scan the land to the west. His return would be the way we had come, hoping to catch any Welsh warriors unawares.

"Take care, son, and do not assume that the Welsh will be tucked up in bed. They will be planning mischief." He nodded. "And if you find spare sheep on the fells, then take them. If nothing else, we can starve the Welsh into submission!"

Hamo laughed. "I have our lucky charm with us!" He ruffled Jack's head. "We will be safe enough. You have the harder ride, and you are getting no younger, father. This weather might bring on your illness again."

"Begone, I will be well."

I took Ralph's sons with me, as I felt responsible for them. Ralph the fletcher was with John, son of John. Although I was riding with men I did not know as well as my own, I had chosen one who was a Welshman. It was he who had translated when we had asked questions. Mordaf ap Tomas was a typical Welsh archer. Shorter than the men I led, he had a chest which was as broad as a firkin barrel. When we left Hamo, he joined me at the fore. I had been brought up to the east of these mountains, but I had rarely travelled through them.

"Mordaf, is there a danger of ambush?"

He shook his head. "Trees and bushes do not grow well here,

captain. The Welsh can perch in the peaks if they choose but the scree close to the road makes a treacherous footing and if they were there then we would be alerted."

"Then where *are* the Welsh?"

He grinned. "The Welsh? Why, captain, they are all around us – but if you mean where King Edward's enemies are, then they will be further south close to Llanfair Caereinion and Powys. It is winter and they will eat better there. There will be warriors here." He waved a hand at the brooding crags above our heads. "They will be doing as we do, and they will watch us. When we have passed then they will report to their prince. We are too few in number to worry them."

I was pleased I had him with me, and I was already preparing my report as we headed down the road towards the coast. We approached the village of Glanogwen as the afternoon light began to fade. The ride had taken longer than I had expected. I spied a hall, which Mordaf identified as being the home of a local lord, Maredudd ap Maredudd. There were people there, for I could smell woodsmoke. I knew that we would have to ride most of the way back in the dark no matter what we did and so I decided to seek the Lord of Glanogwen. I sent Mordaf with twenty men around the back of the hall and dismounted the rest of the men. Ralph and Roger watched the horses.

As I banged on the door, I heard noise from the back and then the sound of steel on steel. I barged the door and it cracked open. Drawing my sword, I led my men into the well-lit hallway.

I could hear screams and shouts. A man stepped from a chamber to my right and I saw that he held a sword. He was not one of my men, and I lunged at him. He tried the same move, but the difference was that my left hand was gloved in a leather gauntlet and while I was able to fend off his sword, mine slid into his middle – for his hand was sliced to the bone when he tried the same move.

"Search the chamber!" Two of my men went to the room and I led the rest through the large hall. When we reached the kitchen, I saw bodies on the floor. One was one of the archers Mordaf had led. Once we were outside, I saw that there had been a battle. Mordaf had a nasty looking cut on his cheek, but the rest of my men were whole. Three men lay dead and a woman was weeping over the corpse of one of them. She spat at Mordaf and spoke in Welsh.

I cocked my head to one side, and he shrugged. "The man is Lord Maredudd, and this is his wife. She has cursed me!"

"Secure the women but do not harm them. If they fought, then there is something they are hiding."

It was dark by the time we had searched the building. We were rewarded. We found one of our wagons. We also found Queen Eleanor's psalter, as well as other precious items which had been taken. I was tempted to take Lord Maredudd's family as hostages but decided not to. We took the wagon and supplies from the house; we had enough to please the king.

Scouts from John's company of archers met us coming in the opposite direction. "Captain, the Centenar was worried about you!"

I laughed. "Thank you, Will. It is like having a company of mothers to watch over me."

When we met up with John he had much to report. "We saw few men, and Bangor looks to be deserted, but when we neared the port, we saw a boat with warriors heading across to Anglesey."

I nodded. "That makes sense – and we saw none either, but Mordaf thinks that they are gathering closer to Powys. We will report to the king and let him try to make sense of this."

We were the last to enter the castle and it was so late that I did not bother the king. We devoured the food that had been left for us and I listened to Hamo and Robin, who confirmed what I already knew; the Welsh were in Anglesey and Powys. King Edward could graze his horses with impunity.

Despite my body complaining I rose before dawn and joined the king at his breakfast. His scowling face told me that was not pleased with my late arrival. I waved forward Ralph. son of Ralph the fletcher, who presented the king with the psalter and the other precious items we had retrieved. The scowl became a beaming smile, and he held the psalter close to his face and kissed it.

"All is forgiven, Warbow! What did you learn? Sit and eat while you talk."

It was not easy to do both and so I nibbled rather than ate. I gave him the facts first and then the opinion. Sir Godfrey was with him and I now saw that Sir Godfrey acted as a sort of adviser. He said when I had finished: "It is what we thought, King Edward – the breadbasket that is Anglesey is the key to controlling Wales. We need a castle on the other side of the straits."

The king was, as ever. decisive. "Aye, and I shall take the army thither. Warbow, take your archers and join the Earl of Warwick. While I take Anglesey, I would have the earl clear out the rat holes of Powys."

Chapter 8

The earl was at Y Trallwng, which was close to the English border. Sir Godfrey told me, just before I left the castle, that he had been sent there to prevent mischief from the Welsh. The last thing we needed was for Shropshire and the Marches to be raided. He did not have a large army and my archers would bolster it considerably.

We had sixty miles to cover, but it was still late February and Wales was empty. The fields were too cold to be ploughed and the livestock too valuable to be let loose on the hills. There were too many of us to be threatened by locals, but they showed their displeasure by barring their doors. We used their water troughs, and that was the only hospitality that we were shown.

Y Trallwng was a small town. In England, it might have been called a large village. The earl had taken over the largest house, but I could see that we would have to camp. Leaving Hamo to organise the camp, I went with Jack to see the earl. Jack was a handy messenger. I had a letter for the earl and while his squire served me some local ale, he read it.

"So, Sir Gerald, we are to control a land size of Yorkshire while King Edward takes an island the size of the Isle of Wight! We have a handful of men and he has the whole army!"

I was honoured by the openness of the earl's words. He was, of course, being realistic. Anglesey was flat and his fleet could follow him all the way around the coast to keep him supplied and act as his eyes and ears. I smiled. "Take it as a compliment, my lord. How many men do we have?"

"Five hundred men at arms, a thousand spearmen. With your archers, we have four hundred and I have raised the levy which gives us five hundred men although their quality is in doubt."

I thought he was being unfair. My levy came from the same stock and I would happily have led them into battle. If the levy was well led, then they were stout men. The problem came when they were faced by mailed horsemen with no support. As I had shown at Denbigh, they could be managed and used effectively if someone had a strong hand.

"And have we any idea where the Welsh are to be found, my lord?"

He smiled and folded the letter up. "Now that you and your mounted archers are here, we should be able to find them. There are few places where Madog could gather an army big enough to threaten us. It is twenty miles to the mountains and high ground. If we were to draw a line twenty miles from here, then that should be where the Welsh are gathered. They are, as you know, largely a foot army."

"They used horses, my lord, to take the king's baggage."

"Just so, but generally they are on foot." I nodded. "And that means that a distance of twenty miles is as far as they could reach us to attack the border."

"We will need a day to recover. Have you any remounts?"

"A few, why?"

"I would send a couple of scouts out tomorrow. I have men who are able to sniff out our enemies."

"I will have four sent to you."

129

I chose my best four men and sent them to ride just ten miles to the northwest and southwest to look for signs. I then divided my horse archers into the four groups we had used in the north. When all was arranged, I sought out Captain Geoffrey. He and the other archers were unhappy at the lack of action. "We have had desertions, Sir Gerald!"

I frowned. "Then when we have time, we will find them and punish them. We do not want others to copy them."

"I do not blame them. Sitting in winter camps, eating thin stew and enduring the cold and wet is not an archer's work."

I knew what he meant. The men had signed on to go to Gascony, where there would be wine, warmth and loot. Wales had none of those things. "Hopefully, we can give them work and we can bring the Welsh to battle."

"That might occupy them, my lord, but it will not give them what they think they have lost."

"Captain, we are the king's archers, and we serve him. No matter how much sympathy you have with the men you need to lead them. Do I make myself clear?"

"Yes, Sir Gerald."

It was good that I had returned, Had Hamo and my archers been led by Captain Geoffrey then I knew their character would have been changed.

Gwillim and Mordaf led the two groups of scouts. When they returned, Mordaf spoke first. "We think we have found a band of rebels, captain. To the west are many rivers. The River Banwy is the largest and it is in flood. I saw signs that men had forded it before it came into flood. They headed north."

Gwillim nodded. "And we were well to the north and found the hoofprints of ponies and men on foot. They also looked to be heading south."

I took a wax tablet out and marked Y Trallwng. I gave the stylus to Mordaf and said, "Mark the river and the direction of the tracks." He frowned and did so. Handing the stylus to Gwillim I said, "Mark your tracks."

When they had done so I saw that there was a village close by – Llanfair Caereinion – and if you extended the two lines they intersected there.

"Tomorrow, you two and twenty chosen archers will come with me and we will scout out this village."

Mordaf said, "It may just be a large warband, captain."

"True, but we have to start somewhere and as this is just ten miles away, we will start there."

I had Hamo with me as well as the two Welsh scouts and the others I chose were all good at concealment. We forded the river close to Cyfronydd, which consisted of a pair of houses set back from the road that led to the ford. The river was lively, but we were all experienced riders and we made it. I sent two of the archers north to see if there was a better crossing. If the earl had to cross the river, we did not want to risk losing men. Once across the river, we walked our horses, crossing two small streams which were just knee-deep. That was for a couple of reasons: we were harder to see and we saved our horses. We spied a house just half a mile to the north of us and that encouraged us to stay by the river, where overhanging trees hid us. We were just a mile and a half from the ford when we stopped. Gwillim's nose detected something and he held up his hand. I gave my reins to Hamo and then joined Gwillim, who had given his reins to Dick of Luston.

Gwillim dropped to all fours and began to crawl along the tree line. The ground rose a little to our right and we were hidden from whatever was there. Thin spindly trees, along with elder, blackthorn and hawthorn, afforded some cover and Gwillim and I crawled through them. Once at the top of the bank, overgrown grasses and weeds made us hard to see. We both peered through them and there we saw the Welsh camp.

They had tents, although there were few of them, and they had horses, for we could hear them. From what we could tell they were mainly foot soldiers. Spears were stacked together close by where the men were camping. I recognised the banner of Madog ap Llewellyn. He had adopted the Welsh dragon. They had sentries but they did not appear to be too vigilant; I heard laughter from them. I saw men heading towards the other side of the camp carrying pails and when they returned, I deduced there had to be a stream there, where they could get water.

Gwillim pointed to the south and I saw the smoke and roofs of the village. It was more than a mile away. As I looked back to the camp, I saw that it was set in a natural bowl. All the streams we had seen fed into the river.

I was about to return to our horses when I heard shouts. More horsemen and archers were arriving. There were just twenty of them, but it explained why Madog had not yet attacked. He was waiting for more men. The arrivals were warmly greeted and their horses, all three, led to the place we had seen the pail men fetch water. The three horses were ridden by men wearing mail.

I had seen enough. I had estimates of their number and we had their position.

We said nothing until we reached the ford. We dismounted and awaited the two archers we had sent. Hamo asked, "What did you find?"

"We found what we hoped. A Welsh camp. I saw the flag of Madog. Gwillim, how many men did you see?"

132

"There looked to me to be almost fifteen hundred. I was counting the fires."

I nodded. "And more arriving all the time. That gives us a little time."

The two archers did not keep us waiting long and Harry, the older of the two, pointed north and said, "There is a better ford not far to the north, for there is a spit of land between the two riverbanks; it makes the water slower and safer."

"Good."

We arrived back at Y Trallwng just before dark and I joined the earl and his senior leaders. I used my wax tablet to give them an idea of what we faced.

"You say they had sentries?"

"Aye, but they were not too vigilant, my lord."

He shook his head. "No matter how poor they are, we would be spotted before we could get into position and with the bridge at Llanfair, whatever the name of the place is, we cannot let them escape. I am thinking of a night-time attack. It would allow us to surround their camp and then charge with our horsemen."

The knights all nodded but I shook my head. "My lord, an attack at night means that my archers will not be as effective, and you will need my arrows to deter the Welsh archers."

The earl saw the wisdom in my words. "Then we surround them in the dark and when it is light, we attack. Does that suit?"

"Aye, my lord."

"We will need tomorrow to prepare, for I want the hooves of the horses muffling. Warbow, send some men to watch them from a safe distance. I need to know if they are likely to move and I also want to know if they have the bridge defended."

He spent an hour going through the plan and I had to admire his speed of thought. He had as sharp a mind as any man I had ever met. Every contingency was considered. He intended to use his heavy horses to charge the Welsh and to break them up. My archers, along with the spearmen and the levy, were merely there to hold them and prevent an escape.

When I returned to our camp, I assigned the camp watching duties to Hamo and I took the riskier task of scouting out the bridge and the village. Mordaf was a mine of information. He had a cousin who had lived in the village and he had given Mordaf the valuable nugget of knowledge that there had been a Roman fort there. The stones had all been robbed out and used to make the houses, but the ramparts and ditches remained.

"And where is this old fort, Mordaf?"

"Just outside of the village on the south eastern side."

I had seen many Roman forts in my time, and I knew that they liked the high ground, especially if there was a river. It would be the perfect place to spy out the bridge. Many Welsh were superstitious and the thought of living close to an old Roman fort and that along with, I assumed, an accompanying Roman graveyard, would deter many. We headed to the fort across country and avoided the roads. We would be clearly identified as English if we were seen. Welshmen who rode horses like ours and wore helmets and mail were rare and if there any would be men at arms.

Our bow cases and hoods marked us as archers. The overcast day helped, and there were just four of us.

Mordaf had never been to the village, but his cousin had told him enough to help my Welshman guide us. The fort rose above the ground around it. Some trees had colonised the approach and that only helped us. We dismounted and led our horses for the last three hundred paces. We left them amongst some of the trees with one of my archers and the three of us headed across the overgrown ditch, up the rampart and into the fort. Although the stones had been taken their foundations still gave the layout and we followed the main road in the fort to the north gate. Crawling to the top of what would have been the supporting earth bank for the gates, we lay down.

The village was less than half a mile from us. I was relieved to see that there were no defences on the bridge, although I did see two mailed horsemen who were speaking to a pair of villagers. The Welsh camp was hidden, and I now saw the cunning of Madog. Had we ridden up the road and crossed the bridge, we would still not have seen the camp. We managed to get back to our horses and thence back to Y Trallwng without being seen. I reported to the earl and we were both relieved when Hamo returned to say that the Welsh were still encamped but another one hundred men had joined them.

We left the village after dark. With Mordaf to guide them, the earl sent twenty men at arms and ten archers to the Roman fort with orders to seize the village and hold the bridge. We had many men on foot, and they would hold us up as we marched to our position. The earl was keen for us to be in position and so we did not move at the pace of the foot. I left Gwillim and Dick with them to guide them and we hurried, through the dark, to the place I had selected for the archers; it lay just north of the camp. Hamo designated a mixture of our archers and foot archers to go to the place we had first spotted the camp. The rest of the archers and spearmen were placed in a large horseshoe around the camp. We had to leave the road to the village open, but that would be closed once our attack began.

The horsemen waited a mile north of the camp. There was a large gap between the archers led by Captain Geoffrey and Hamo. The gap would be closed once the men at arms had charged. We all had to remain silent. Amazingly, we did. I think the horses were too far from the camp and were downwind of the Welsh while the night sentries appeared even less vigilant than those on duty in the daytime. I knew this because I managed to get within twenty feet of a pair of them. They spoke in Welsh and I could not understand a word, but I guessed that they were in good spirits, for they laughed a lot. Had I wished to, I could have slit their throats, and none would have been any the wiser.

I made my way back to my men, who had tethered our horses more than a mile away. Our archers were too valuable to be used as horse holders and even young Jack and Ralph's sons were vital to us. I designated some of the younger levies. My archers each carried a spare bundle of arrows. Jack, Ralph's boys and the other servants began to fetch other bundles from the horses. As dawn approached, we were almost ready.

The earl and I had fought alongside each other before. Trust and confidence were the bonds that shackled us and gave the risky plan the hope of success. I knew that when he sounded his horns to attack then we had just a short time – the time it took to cover five hundred paces – to loose as many arrows as possible. The last thing we wanted was to hurt our own horses. My men commanded the best archers, and Captain Geoffrey and I had spread those most experienced of bowmen amongst the foot archers, who had not had much to do thus far. For that reason, not one of my men was close to me. The forty archers who were closest to me were foot archers, and the need for silence meant that I could not encourage them with humour as I would normally have done. Instead, I had to use encouraging smiles and, as I walked silently amongst them to check they were ready, pats on the back. I knew from my men the high regard in which I was held. I was an archer who had been knighted by the king. I was the physical proof that a man could rise from the bottom and become a man of means.

I saw the sky begin to lighten and I returned to my place. I strung my bow and I lightly nocked a war arrow. I had already chosen one. All of my arrows were good ones, but I had picked the one which looked, to my eye, to be perfect. I watched the sky and listened for the horn. It was too dangerous for horses to attack in the darkness. Although surprise could be guaranteed, there was just too much danger that a horse might trip over a hidden obstacle. This way, the archers had a greater range.

I had to judge the moment well and when I could see forty paces from me, I raised my bow and began to walk closer to the Welsh. The centenars and vintenars all raised their bows and the horseshoe of archers walked forward. Behind us, the spearmen and the levy rose to their feet to copy us.

The move was a risk but a necessary one, and the Welsh spotted the shadows moving closer to them. There were shouts of alarm which was my signal to begin my attack.

"Nock!"

I heard the horn sound and I shouted, "Draw!" I could now see the camp clearly and it resembled a disturbed nest of ants as the Welsh awoke and rushed to get their arms. There was an echoing creak as bows were drawn back.

In the distance, I could hear hooves as the horses began their move. "Loose!" The crack of the bowstrings as they sent their missiles high into the air was rippling all around the Welsh, telling them that they were surrounded, and I gave the next command: "Loose at will!"

I drew and released until I had counted to ten and then I shouted, "Hold!" Out of the corner of my eye, I caught the flash of colour and heard the drum of hooves as the Earl of Warwick led our horsemen into the Welsh camp. The brightening sky showed many corpses lying before us, but they were now organising their spearmen with archers behind.

"Move closer!"

Captain Geoffrey and Hamo would have closed the gap already and now we needed to tighten the noose. Either we would have to send more arrows at them, or we would draw swords to end the battle. Whichever it was, we had to be closer to the Welsh.

As we moved just thirty paces closer I heard the crack as horses and mailed men struck the wooden spears. The sound of spears shattering was louder than any sound yet. I saw some of the levy close to me flinch.

"Fear not! That is the crack of doom for the Welsh! Soon we shall pick over Welsh corpses! Stay vigilant!"

The archers who were closest to the village were the furthest from the horsemen and I saw arrows falling into the rear of the Welsh ranks. The Welsh, however, were fighting back and I saw men at arms fall from their horses. When the Earl of Warwick ordered his men to fall back, I roared, "Archers! Loose!" I knew that this would be a more ragged shower, but it mattered not, for we would now keep releasing until we were too weary to do so. The light was now good enough to target individual men. The levy archers and the ones who fought on foot would just keep their arrows heading for the mass of men before us but my men, the best men, the centenars and vintenars, would choose those who were leaders or represented a danger to us.

It became a duel between Welsh and English archers. Had we not had initial surprise, it might have been more even than it was – but the first ten flights of arrows had killed some of their archers and now, as arrows fell amongst the men I led, we began to kill their archer leaders.

I quickly emptied my first war bag and as I reached down to pick up a second, I saw Jack running towards me with another. He was grinning. I knew, having spoken to him, that he could not wait until he was a warrior too. I grinned back at him. "Do not run in a straight line, Jack, and keep to as much cover as you can find. Tell Ralph and Roger to do the same." As if to emphasise the point, as Jack ran away, an arrow struck a Kentish archer from the Weald. Had Jack not ducked behind him, he would have been killed.

My illness had slowed me some months ago, but I had worked hard, and I was now sending three arrows to the two of those around me. I saw a mailed man encouraging his spearmen to hold firm. I picked out a bodkin. We had a different fletch on them, to make identification easier. He was moving and so when my arrow hit him it was not a killing strike, but it hit his shoulder and knocked him to the ground. It weakened the resolve of the spearmen. Had we had more mounted horsemen then the earl could have launched a second charge, but we had not, and the archers would have to finish off the Welsh. Men were falling around me, although none were killed. I seemed to bear a charmed life. The Welsh, when they broke, did so almost to a man. It was as though a dam had broken. They seemed to be firm and then they dissolved as they fled. One of the prisoners we later took told us that this occurred at the instant that Madog ap Llewelyn fled.

The Earl of Warwick was mounted and had a good view of the battlefield. He sounded the horn for the charge, and I shouted, "After them!" Slinging my bow, I drew my sword. There was little point in telling the men around me to take prisoners. This was the levy and they had endured arrows. They would kill any man they found.

I ran and tried to keep ahead of them. I knew that the earl would need prisoners to discover the whereabouts of the rest of the Welsh rebels.

Isolated knots of men tried to make a stand. They were brave men, but they were outnumbered. My sword made short work of the spearmen whose long weapons were better suited to fending off horses rather than agile swordsmen who could knock aside the wooden headed weapons. The Welsh could not cross the narrow, guarded bridge into the village and so they threw themselves into the river. That was a mistake, for it was swollen by the recent rains and more men drowned than we killed in the battle. By the time we reached the river, the Welsh camp was filled with their dead and dying. Men were searching the bodies for treasure and weapons. I managed to take one prisoner, a Welshman who was wounded. Leaving Jack, Ralph and Roger to watch him, I went to the tent I had seen the Welsh leader using. It was when I entered it that I noticed how little was within. Hamo joined me.

"Any treasure, father?"

I shook my head. "No and that is strange. It is as though we found the Welsh not long after they arrived. Where is their baggage train and supplies?"

Hamo nodded. "Aye, for we found no arrows ready to be used. I think they fled because they had no more arrows to send."

It was noon by the time the earl and his mounted men returned from the chase. Madog ap Llewelyn had escaped. The earl dismounted. "Your men did well, Warbow, and won the day for us." I nodded and told him what Hamo and I had discussed. "Aye, well tomorrow you and your mounted men can search for the baggage train. My guess would be that it would be found to the northwest."

"I agree."

"What is this place called, Warbow?"

"One of the wounded men we questioned called it, Meismedoc or perhaps Maes Moydog. He was hard to understand. Why do you ask?"

He laughed. "King Edward likes to keep a record of such things. He will want to know the name of the battle that saw the Welsh defeated."

In all, just seven men had died, and as six of those were men at arms it was an unusual result. We found seven hundred bodies on the battlefield but many more would have been swept to their deaths. The river was in full spate and as cold as ice. After burning the bodies we camped in the village. The Welsh there did all that they could to accommodate us; they obviously did not relish us taking our anger out on them. The earl took the prisoner, but I was not sure he would have any information that might help us.

I divided my mounted archers into four and used the same formations as the last time we had searched for the Welsh. I led my men towards Abertridwr, which lay close to two rivers: Nant Tridwr and the Vyrnwy. It was not far away, but on the road from the mountain vastness of Snowdon. I had deduced that the Welsh kept their supplies hidden there, for we had searched all the towns, villages, and halls.

It was spring, and in the Welsh mountains and valleys that meant the weather could change overnight. We set off through a fog. We could have followed the river but, instead, we chose the twisting narrow road. This was not a Roman-built road and its surface was uneven. That, added to the fact that we knew there had to be survivors from the battle close by, made for a cautious ride through the fog.

None of us had been along this road but we knew that the confluence of the rivers lay twelve miles or so away, for we had questioned the prisoners. They were happy to give us information about the land but not about their comrades. The fog, thinning a little above us, allowed me to see the sun and that told me it was noon, but the valley bottom was still wreathed in a grey, clammy, fog. One of my archer's horses had picked up a stone and we halted while he picked it out with a knife. I saw that the road descended and twisted just ahead of us. The visibility was now thirty paces and that was a distinct improvement on what it had been.

The fog had sapped all the joy of the victory from my archers and we sat in silence on our horses. Then, I heard voices and sounds from ahead. Although none had spoken, I held up my hand to ensure that the men remained silent.

The voices spoke Welsh and there were horses. That meant an enemy. It had to be either the remnants of the battle or reinforcements. Fog was an archer's enemy and so I drew my sword and raised it. My men raised theirs too, but remained silent, I kicked my horse in the flanks and rode down the road.

As our hooves clattered on the stone-covered road the voices ahead stopped and then a Welsh voice shouted the alarm. That confirmed we had found an enemy. The fog was burning off quickly now and I saw the Welsh wagons, guarded by warriors, labouring up the slope.

We had the advantage, for our weapons were drawn. The Welsh drew their own, but it was futile. We fell amongst them and when four had been slain, the rest surrendered. We had found the supply train. Not only was there food and weapons, but there were also some coins.

Madog ap Llewelyn might have escaped, but he had neither men nor coins. No matter what happened further north, the rebellion here was ended. I knew in that moment that we had won.

Chapter 9

King Edward had taken Anglesey without suffering any losses. It was not a place that could be easily defended, and his campaign had been short and swift. His ships had ensured that his army was well supplied, and the Welsh were defeated each time they attempted to fight. He had vented his anger on Llanfaes, which had killed his Sherriff earlier in the year – it was completely levelled. Combined with the defeat of the Welsh as Maes Moydog, we now had all our castles restored to us. Harlech's garrison of thirty-seven men had fought off the Welsh and it was now being reinforced. The king was pleased with the Earl of Warwick, who was quick to point out that my archers had played a pivotal role. The king sent for me.

"Once again, Warbow, you have proved your worth. As a reward, I release you and your men from my service."

"Thank you, King Edward."

He wagged a finger at me. "But keep your men honed, Warbow, for I shall need you again when I go to France. However, your men have been away from home long enough and I have been absent from London more than half a year. Once I have begun work on my new castle in Anglesey and taken the funds from the Welsh to repair Caernarfon, I shall return to London."

"Could I beg a favour, my lord? One of your men at arms, Richard Launceston, was due to marry my daughter. He has been with the army for almost eight months. If he is not needed, then I would take him back so that we can make plans for the nuptials."

He gave a strange smile and said, "I have not seen this side of you before. Earl, make it so."

With that, I was dismissed. We did not need a long goodbye and we packed our horses and headed back towards Y Trallwng and thence Yarpole. Until we had found the supply train there had been little opportunity for treasure, but the horses I claimed and the coins I sequestered added to that taken in battle and all my men were a little richer.

I was not unhappy with the time away from Yarpole, for I knew it had made better warriors of my archers. They had all experienced leadership and Hamo, in particular, had shown himself to be calm and dependable. Leadership cannot be taught; men are either leaders or they are not. I was a leader and I knew that when the time came for me to hang up my bow forever, my son could carry on.

We were still travelling through a land ravaged by war and so we were vigilant, but we had fought across this land and the scouts who rode ahead knew where the dangers lay. Jack too had enjoyed the responsibility of watching over Ralph and Roger. He was better for it.

I was able to talk to my son and Richard, my future son in law, as we rode across land which now seemed warmer and burgeoning with new life. Hamo was looking to the future, for he had enjoyed leading men in war and was not yet ready for peace. "So, father, we go to France?"

"Perhaps. Sir Godfrey told me that while we were in Wales the French had raided the south coast. First, the king will need to make the south secure."

Richard, too, had grown since we had been in Wales. He had not been with us close to Y Trallwng for he had been with the Earl of Lincoln on Anglesey. Although he had enjoyed an easier campaign it had changed him and made him, in my view, an even better prospect as a husband and father.

"Sir Gerald, will I be required again?"

"Your lands are worth more than £40 a year?" He nodded. "Then it is likely to be so, but I would not worry. If you wish to stay in England, I have men who can provide your service."

"I would not be seen as a coward!" He coloured.

I smiled and said, "No one would consider you thus. It is not as though a campaign in Gascony would serve any except the king. That is his fief and the profits from it would provide for him and the crown. If my men and I were called upon to go then we would, but that is because we know how to profit from war."

He looked shocked. "Sir Gerald, I thought you were the king's man!"

"I am, but that does not mean I do not see that King Edward does all he can for his family, the future rulers of England. I do the same for Hamo, Margaret and my other children."

He shook his head. "I thought war would be noble."

Hamo put his hand upon Richard's shoulder. "Dick, I have seen only a little of war, but I have spent my life amongst warriors and I know that what my father says is true. The only real war worth fighting is to defend your home. My father and the men of Yarpole have done that. Like my father, I will happily serve King Edward as an archer, for I know I have a skill and I am no farmer. You, it seems to me, are a brave man, for you went to war with little experience. You can fight – but I suspect that you have no love for it."

He suddenly started, as though Hamo had read his mind. "If you spoke those words to Margaret she might not wish to marry me!"

I laughed. "My daughter knows her own mind. She has fallen in love with you, Richard, and she would rather you were safe at home with her. The sooner you are wed, the happier she will be. King Edward has delayed your marriage long enough. As soon as we are home, we shall have the banns read and you will be wed."

My news ensured that I had the most wonderful of welcomes from my wife and daughter. The fact that all my men returned safely and with a little profit made me popular with all the other wives, too. I basked in the glory knowing that we had been lucky. When we had been stuck in Conwy and down to the last barrel of wine and salted meat I had wondered if King Edward's luck and mine had run out!

The wedding went well, for we were celebrating not only the marriage but life itself. We had fought and won and there were no deaths to mourn. The only sadness was when Margaret went to Ludlow to live with her new husband. The rift between the girl and her mother had ended when we went to war and the time since had made them closer than ever. That too meant that Joan would be closer to her mother, who sought to fill the void of Margaret with her younger sibling. I was not as sad as Mary, but the reason was simple: I was a warrior who was used to being parted from those I loved. I knew that, as autumn approached it was highly likely that Hamo and I would be summoned to King Edward's side once more. I made the most of my time in Yarpole.

Hamo and I began our work to train Jack in earnest. It was not so much a matter of his learning how to draw a bow, although we practised that each day, it was making his body stronger and more suited to archery. He lifted, carried, chopped, and generally worked his body so hard that, at times, he could barely lift a spoon to eat his evening meal. He was not alone. Some of the men who had followed me and now farmed small holdings in my manor also had sons whom they wished to follow an archer's life, and they worked alongside Jack.

Ralph and Roger were with Jack each day and the three grew in many different ways. I saw friendships formed which could only help them when the time came to go to war. I enlivened the tedium of hard work by holding weekly competitions for the aspiring archers and the rest of my men. The targets we used were small ones for the archers and larger for the younger ones. I provided prizes and although the prizes themselves were not valuable, the fact that they won them meant that they were precious.

In the first week of September, we had a visitor. It was Sir Godfrey and he had with him four royal men at arms. My heart sank, for I had not heard of any summons to serve the king. When he dismounted, his serious face did not bode well. He put his arm around me and said, "Where can we speak privately?"

"The courtyard. The men are taking their midday break and it is empty."

When we reached the courtyard where we had the pel and the targets I saw that Jack was still there. "Jack, go and have some food. Tell the men not to return until I send a message to them."

"Aye, Sir Gerald." He left, but curiosity was all over his face.

Sir Godfrey shook his head. "King Edward has been betrayed and much of the good that you and I have done, and the king planned us undone!" I said nothing, but waited. That there were traitors was not a secret but that they could hurt King Edward was. "Sir Thomas Turbeville was a most trusted knight of King Edward's household. He was taken prisoner in the wars with France and when he escaped, the king rejoiced. This was soon after the king returned from Wales. The king lauded him with honours. Three days since, a letter was intercepted. sent from Sir Thomas. It was written to the Lord Provost of Paris. In it, he details the king's plans for Germany, how many ships he is sending to Gascony and that the south coast is undefined. I remember this part. He said, *And know that we think that we have enough to do against those of Scotland; and if those of Scotland rise against the King of England, the Welsh will rise also. And this I have well contrived, and Morgan has fully covenanted with me to that effect.*" He shook his head. "A most vile and dangerous man. Now the king fears discontent in Wales and Scotland." He leaned in. "He escaped, for he had friends who told him we had the letter, and he has fled. The king has sent men, such as me, who know him, to find and return him to London and his execution, after he has divulged the names of others who are traitors. I believe he has come to Wales and that he seeks sanctuary with Morgan ap Maredudd of Gwynllwg in Glamorgan. The king has sent men north and there is another column of men led by the Earl of Warwick heading directly for Glamorgan, but I believe that he will try to get to Glamorgan from the north. I need you and your men to hunt him."

"Of course, but you realise the enormity of the task. Wales has many rat holes into which a small group of men could disappear."

"We have to try, Gerald, for England and King Edward. If he succeeds in raising the Welsh and the Scots, then we would be hard-pressed to find enough men to fight three wars."

I knew he was right. "Then we are wasting time. I will take just ten men for we need eyes which can scout rather than archers who can fight battles. We will take spare horses for you and your men are mailed and your horses will be weary already."

I said little to Mary, for I did not want her worrying. I just said that we had to escort Sir Godfrey and his men to Conwy, and we would be back as soon as we could. I took Mordaf and Gwillim along with my other good scouts, but I left Hamo to continue training my men. It now seemed likely that we would be called to war once more.

Once we had left Yarpole, I confided in my scouts. Mordaf nodded.

"An English knight would be remembered, captain. Even if he is in disguise, he cannot disguise his rank. I doubt that he can speak Welsh. We need to speak to those who live on the other side of the border. If there is no evidence of his passing, then that narrows down the possibilities."

Sir Godfrey was more rattled than I had ever seen him. "But that adds time!"

"Sir Godfrey, trust my men. Why has this made you so angry, Sir Godfrey? This is not like you."

He shook his head. "Sir Thomas was once a friend. I have not had much to do with him for the last few years, but I feel guilt. I should have seen the treachery!"

I laughed. "I have learned, Sir Godfrey, that when we look back through time, we have perfect vision, and we know what we should and should not have done. Should King Edward have realised that the death of King Alexander was no accident and fetched the Maid of Norway back sooner? Looking back, we can see that he should have – but when the King of Scotland died, we all thought it a tragic accident. We will find this traitor if he has come this way."

We found evidence of their passing just thirteen miles from Yarpole. The first two places we tried had proved to be barren, but at Pencraig they remembered three Englishmen who could not speak Welsh seeking shelter. They had passed through the day before. That they had not found somewhere to stay meant that they must have pushed on and perhaps, slept in the open.

The next place was Llanfihangel-yng-Ngwynfa, and we reached that as darkness set in. We found that they had stayed there and had left that morning. They were a day ahead. The villagers were quite happy to tell us that they had headed north and west towards Rhayader, and that heartened me.

"That is rough country, Sir Godfrey, and shows that they are seeking to stay hidden. If you and your men wish to spend the night here, we will have a short break and pursue them through the night."

He shook his head. "We will rest and eat for an hour, like you. We shall leave our own horses here and ride the ones you so wisely brought. We have the scent of the traitor in our nostrils and I will not lose him in the mountains of Wales."

I did not know what kept the pursuivant and his escort going. They had endured a hard ride from London whilst we had only had the relatively short one from Yarpole. We rode through the night. The road was a good one and well used. That we saw not a soul was no surprise, and we reached Rhayader an hour after dawn. Our horses were weary, but we wasted no time. I sent my men to the two inns to discover if the traitor and his escort had stayed there. When they returned it was with the news that no Englishmen had stayed in their inns, but three men had spent the night at the home of Hywel ap Maredudd, the largest landowner in the large village. They did not know if the three had left and so I sent Gwillim and Dick to the far end of the village to keep watch and Sir Godfrey and his men went to the hall. Leaving our horses guarded I went with Mordaf and Robin over the wall to the rear of the hall. They took their bows, but I did not.

We stood in the shadows and watched. I knew my men well enough to know that I would not need any commands. They would react to my signals. I heard Sir Godfrey bang on the front door, although his words were indistinct. I heard shouts from inside and then a flash of light appeared as the rear door to the hall opened. Sir Godfrey had described Sir Thomas to me, and I recognised him as he raced out. I stepped from the shadows and shouted, "Sir Thomas, you cannot escape. I am Lord Edward's archer, Sir Gerald Warbow – and I arrest you!"

I covered the distance to him, and he drew his sword. The other two raised their weapons to defend him and two arrows slew them. Sir Thomas's sword and mine clashed but he was used to fighting knights. They had skill but I had skill and strength. My archer's arm drove down his sword and I punched him so hard in the face with my bunched left fist that he fell to the ground. As he lay there spreadeagled, I pricked his throat with my sword.

"Sir Thomas, I can maim you and cripple you and as you are a traitor I would happily do so. You do not need to be whole to be tried! Do not resist. You shall go with Sir Godfrey to London where you will be tried for treason. I will not give you the easy way out!"

I saw resignation in his eyes. He dropped his sword and his head fell back. He was defeated.

The lord who had given them shelter had been slain by an angry Sir Godfrey, who felt betrayed by his former friend. This was not the behaviour of the Sir Godfrey I had known for so many years. We stayed the night in the hall and Sir Godfrey allowed my men to ransack it for its treasures. "This will become part of King Edward's largesse and he will be grateful just to have this traitor in the tower." Sir Thomas was not only bound but shackled; Sir Godfrey was taking no chances.

The next day, as we rode back to Yarpole and with Gwillim and Dick on either side of Sir Thomas, Sir Godfrey said, "The letter means that the Scots will rebel. They never liked Balliol and they now have the chance to rise, for they believe the Welsh and the French will aid them. You will be needed."

I nodded. "The day that King Edward made me his archer I knew that our fates were irrevocably entwined. It is well."

"That day has been more providential for the king than for you. I hope and pray that he appreciates what you do for him."

I laughed. "Sir Godfrey, when does a king ever worry about a subject? I am content. I would not have the life I have and the woman

I married but for King Edward. Whatever I have to do is payment for a life I love!"

Sir Edmund Mortimer gave Sir Godfrey an escort of ten further men at arms for the journey to London. It was the start of the thawing of relations between us. Over the next months and years, my wife and I were increasingly included in social events at his castle. It was not that we needed them, but Mary deserved to be recognised for what she was, a great lady. I think the thawing came about because he recognised the service I had done for King Edward.

The new social events had little impact on my life, for I knew that war was coming again soon. King Edward was not a man to be slighted. Not only was Sir Godfrey angry about the treacherous Thomas Turbeville, so was King Edward, who knew that this had been a French plot. Worse, his appointee in Scotland had failed to win over the Scottish lords – who had taken away his power so that he was now a virtual prisoner. Almost a month after Turbeville had been captured an alliance was signed between Scotland and France.

King Edward was furious. He immediately confiscated the English property of every Scotsman. It was intended to hurt the nobles who had emasculated John Balliol. He demanded that sureties would be given that Scotland would not fight against England. These sureties were not forthcoming and in December of that year, he sent two churchmen to bring back the promises that might prevent war. We heard all this second hand and after the event, as messengers passed through the realm to inform senior lords, such as the Earl of Lincoln, Henry Lacey, of the king's decisions. My involvement with the earl and actions at the Battle of Maes Moydog meant that the messengers afforded me the courtesy of visiting my manor.

As we prepared for Christmas, I sat one evening with Mary and Hamo before a roaring fire and we speculated about what might happen.

"Will there be war, my husband?"

I nodded. "For certain. Balliol was a poor choice as king and the French have sought to exploit this. The Welsh foray also showed weaknesses in King Edward's armour. King Edward has a choice. He either ignores Scotland and risks an attack on our northern borders or he takes the reins himself and defeats Scotland."

Hamo sipped the rich red wine we were drinking. "And replace Balliol?"

"I think not. The man is barely capable of holding on to a castle, let alone a crown and country. I honestly do not know, but I fear that the king may try to take the whole country and make it part of England."

Mary looked shocked. "But how could he do that?"

"He has done so in Wales. It means building castles and appointing lords who can hold on to it. He may use the idea of Marches as he has in Wales. By giving lords special rights and privileges he uses them to control the populace. Most of Scotland is empty; it is the land around the borders that is valuable. A few judiciously placed castles could impose the king's will upon the Scots but, I confess, it is not cheap. Caernarfon cost more than twenty-seven thousand pounds thanks to the wilful destruction caused when the Welsh took it. Sir Godfrey told me that Harlech, Conwy, Beaumaris and Caernarfon, not to mention the other castles cost King Edward more than eighty thousand pounds."

My wife looked shocked. "Is there that much money in England?"

I smiled. "I believe that the Exchequer raises just one hundred and sixteen thousand pounds each year and armies must be maintained. If we are to go to war with Scotland, then the king will have to impose taxes and who knows what mischief might be caused by men like Turbeville? We know his identity, but unless those who extract such information are able to loosen his tongue, we may all be looking over our shoulders for English enemies as well as Welsh, Scottish and

French! I do not envy the king his task and I know that this will not make him popular." I raised my goblet to Hamo. "My son, I fear that you and I will be absent from Yarpole more than we will be at home."

Mary shook her head. "His sister is wed, and I would have our son wed too! I want him here and not fighting in the lands filled with barbarians!"

"Mother, I have time enough for that and father is quite right. King Edward will need his most potent weapon, the longbow and this family and manor provide the best that he has."

"And so I am expected to wait here without any word if you live or die? You have never had to experience that pain, my husband. I know you suffer hardship, but that is nothing compared with the anguish of going to bed at night and not knowing if your husband and son lives or dies. When you were in Wales, I often watched the night slowly pass – and then, you were less than a day away. It will take a week for the word to reach us from Scotland."

I had no comforting answer to assuage her fears. I merely put my hand on hers, almost devouring it with my mighty fist. "I promise that I will not be as remiss this time. I will send letters when I can. They may not be as long and loving as I would like, but they will give you news."

She smiled. "Gerald Warbow writing letters to his wife? Now *that* is something I will look forward to." She stood up and kissed me. "Go with the king when the summons comes, and end this war quickly, but both come back whole. Promise me?"

I nodded and said, "I swear!"

I knew that it was an empty promise, for in battle even the mightiest warrior could be felled from an unexpected source. I looked at Hamo, who nodded, for he too now understood the parlous nature of our profession.

Chapter 10

Yarpole, January 1296

The summons was delivered by an official from King Edward's court. I knew Walter Froissart, for I had met him both in Wales and London. He handed me the parchment which asked me to present myself in Newcastle by the first of March. Unusually, the number of men I was to bring was not specified but I was asked to bring mounted archers and to be prepared to command the archers as I had done in Wales. It was a longer letter than a mere summons and I detected, between the immaculate script of the clerk's hand, that King Edward needed me at his side.

That was something my wife could never understand. There was a bond between warriors who had fought alongside each other which transcended titles, class and status. I had been with King Edward so long that I was one of the few men left alive who remembered him as a young man. He was not only my king, but he was also my shield brother. That was an old-fashioned term and was not used by lords and nobles – but those of us who gathered around campfires on the campaign knew the meaning of the words. It meant men who would die for each other. It was a sign of a blood oath that men would not desert each other when things went ill. It meant I would follow King Edward and be with him for good or bad.

It might take two weeks to reach the Tyne and so we planned on leaving in the middle of February. That gave us just over a month to prepare. There was a great deal to do. Richard, who was now six summers old, had demanded to come to war in Wales. He did so again. I could understand his ardour but I dared not risk him, and so I gave him a challenge. If he could draw the small hunting bow I had made for him and hit a target one hundred paces away I would consider it. I knew that it was a forlorn hope, for even I could not have done that when I was his age. When he failed, he was disappointed, but he took the news with better grace than had I not issued the challenge. He now had a way to improve so that I would take him next time.

I also made the decision to take just twenty men. The king might want more, but Wales was still unsettled. The capture of their leader and their defeat had done nothing to make the Welsh accept English rule. I wanted Yarpole and Luston to be defended. The twenty I took, along with Jack and Hamo, were my best archers and I promised them all the pay of either a centenar or vintenar and they were content. This time I left Ralph and Roger at home with their father.

Jack had now seen twelve summers, and both the work and the life he led at Yarpole meant that he was unrecognisable as the diffident boy who had come to us four years earlier. He could not manage a full war bow, but he was a good archer and, because of the efforts of Hamo, only my son and I were better swordsmen. He had quick hands and reactions. Whilst he would not fight in the frontline and would still fetch arrows, if things went awry he could draw a bow and fight. The three servants we took would act as horse holders and aid Jack.

We now had very distinctive clothes and livery. We all wore the hooded, oiled, green cloak and as they were identical, when we rode they marked the company as my men. The hose and tunics were also in my colours, but we now wore a loose-fitting brigandine. Made of tough leather and studded with metal it afforded protection from some war arrows and could prevent a spear or a sword from making a mortal wound. Hamo and my men also presented me with a sallet, an open-faced helmet. I was reluctant to wear it, but they were adamant.

"Father, you are no longer a young man and have seen more than fifty summers. Our enemies will target you. The helmet will give some protection. It is no more of a discomfort than a hat and your bowstrings will remain dry beneath it."

"Then why do you not all wear one?"

Hamo grinned. "A most excellent idea, father! I shall have the smith make one for each of our men. They should be ready in four months or so!"

I had been outwitted by my son!

Scotland in March could be a cold and inhospitable land. We took furs, which we could use for bedding and also for warmth should the weather prove to be wintery. As we were leaving more men at home, we were also able to take remounts and our horses were the best that we had. The preparations were complete well before the day we were due to leave, and so my men were able to enjoy the company of their families. Margaret came to stay for a few days. My son in law, Richard, would not be going to war, of course. We had grown closer since the marriage and he promised to keep an eye on his mother-in-law for me. My wife was not getting any younger. Margaret also had an ulterior motive. She told us that she was with child. I would be a grandfather before the year was out! That, in turn, made Joan play up, for she was now sixteen summers old and she wished to be wed. Margaret showed her new maturity by inviting Joan to go with her to Ludlow – a far bigger and busier place than Yarpole. She leapt at the opportunity. I had no fears that she might do something silly, for Margaret's trip to Malton had been a revelation and she would watch her sibling closely.

The night before we left, we held a feast. It was the first time the whole family had been gathered for some time, and was one of the most joyous nights I could remember. Richard and Margaret stayed with us and we were celebrating not only the unborn grandchild, but life itself. We were a lucky family, for I knew many who had lost babies to sickness and disease. My daughters and wife took every opportunity to stroke Hamo's hand and he, in turn, paid his mother more compliments than I had given in a lifetime.

I felt detached at times as I looked at my family. It was as far away from my upbringing as one could imagine – and that was the part that made me sad. I was risking all for King Edward and his Scottish ambitions. The Great Cause, as he called it, was empire-building – and my family was more important than that.

We now had much better horses than when we first went to war, and as we headed across country to Lincoln only our hooded cloaks marked us as archers. All else about us suggested a noble and his men at arms. My new helmet hung from my cantle but, as we rode along the great highway to the east, I realised that Hamo's suggestion that I wear one was not a bad thing. I had practised with my helmet and it was no more obtrusive than my hat. Perhaps my hearing was not as good as it might have been but, in a battle, there was so much noise that it mattered not. I know that Hamo's suggestion for all my archers to wear helmets was merely a way to get me to wear one, but I had taken him at his word and the weaponsmith was already making them. They would not be sallets, but simple round-topped helmets.

Jack now rode behind Hamo and me. The servants we had brought were more than capable of leading the horses. I had planned to visit Sir John at Malton, but I had first asked Jack if he was happy with that. Margaret had told me how his life had been made a misery and I wanted no bad memories to be uncovered.

"I am happy to return. Master Edward was a bully and thought to make my life a misery. He almost succeeded. When Lady Margaret came, she was like a godsend and gave me hope. I have seen, from your home, that Master Edward was wrong. I have been to war and seen men die. Master Edward can do nothing to hurt me and I have put those bad times behind me – and I would like to go to Malton to visit the graves of my parents. I hope that their spirits can look down and see how well I have turned out. Who knows, one day I might be a vintenar!"

Hamo smiled and put his arm around Jack. "You can be, Jack of Malton, whatever you choose to be. You serve Sir Gerald, who gives hope to all of us who draw a bow that they can rise and make something of themselves!"

When we reached Lincoln, we heard of the huge army that King Edward had ordered to meet him at Newcastle. The one thousand mounted men at arms were coming from all over the land and Ireland. I did not believe that the sixty thousand foot soldiers he had summoned would be realised, but it showed his intent. If the Scots thought that France would help them then they were in for a shock. To muster an army big enough to face the English, the French would need an armada of ships thousands strong.

Malton was a convenient place to stop. We would only need one more rest before reaching Newcastle. I had guessed that Sir John of Malton would be summoned to the muster, and when we reached the manor it was confirmed by the numbers of men who were busy preparing to leave.

"This is well met, Gerald, we can travel north together!" He noticed Jack. "And how you have grown, young Jack."

He gave his former lord a chilly bow and said to me, "Sir Gerald, with your permission I should like to visit the grave of my parents."

"Of course."

When he had left us, and Sir John was alone with Hamo and me, he said, "What have I done to offend him, Gerald?"

I did not need to be delicate with my words. "He was treated badly in this house and your son was allowed to bully one who, had he defended himself, would have been severely punished."

"Edward is my son!" Sir John sounded almost petulant, as though the relationship excused all.

"And has he changed or is he still a bully?" Sir John's silence was eloquent. "I am guessing that he goes to war with you?"

"He does. He is to be my page."

I smiled. "Then I should warn him that if he tries to bully Jack or disparage him in any way, he will feel the full force of Jack's anger and he will have the backing of my son and me, not to mention our men. Jack has been to war and shown himself to be both brave and loyal. He is no longer a small boy. He has an archer's frame and fists. Your son, I can guarantee, would come off worse! What has Edward done that can compare with Jack's deeds?"

Sir John's eyes narrowed and then he nodded. "You may be right. I shall have a word and it might be better if you travel alone. I forgot that we have men who will march to war. I would not hold you up."

I knew that was not the real reason. He feared that his son would be humiliated. I doubted that we would see much of the youth before we left. Sir John was merely saving face.

The visit might have ended my friendship with Sir John, but it was good for Jack. He believed that when he stood before his parents' grave and spoke to them, that they had heard him. Belief is a powerful weapon and Jack's belief that they had heard put his mind at rest and made him stronger. I did not need the friendship of a lord like Sir John, but I did need to stand by my men.

We made the muster early and found a good place to camp on the heath north of the city. King Edward's men had left a camp for the Scots, who had been ordered to come and attend the meeting. I was not summoned to meet the king, but I did move about the camp as men arrived to speak to the archers who, if the negotiations failed, would be led by me. I found many alongside whom I had fought. Captain Geoffrey was there, and I saw that he now led twenty mounted archers. He had learned from our experience. When Sir John arrived, he camped close to King Edward's part of the camp and it meant there was little chance that Jack and Edward would meet. The king was in the castle, but Sir John knew the other knights of King Edward.

The Scots failed to appear by the first day of March as they had been ordered. The whole army had not yet mustered and the largest contingent of heavy horsemen, the Irish lords, were still to arrive. Nonetheless, the king marched us to Wark on the Tweed. Scottish warriors had raided nearby Carham but, more importantly, the Lord of Wark had recently married a Scottish lady and chosen to side with the Scots. King Edward was making a point and we would stay in the lord's castle.

The day we left I was summoned to his side. My men were breaking camp and I went alone.

"Warbow, I want your archers in the van. I know this country is not familiar to you, but your men are like hunting dogs and they have the noses for an ambush. We ride to Wark."

"Yes, King Edward. Will there be war?"

He gave me a grim smile. "If there is, then the Scots will be the ones choosing it – and if they do then we shall win! I want Balliol and the men who control him on their knees before I will be satisfied. I do like being threatened by the French with a Scottish knife in my back. I need Scotland ruled by someone I can trust. I thought it was Balliol, but now …"

The country through which we rode was a little bleaker than the English borders with Wales. This land had been Scottish and then English, and the reason was clear. It was not good land for farming. Sheep and hardy cattle, along with oats and barley, were all that could be farmed.

Even as we rode north, riders arrived to tell the king of more raids. They had foolishly attacked Carlisle in the west. That castle was like a rock, but it showed the Scottish defiance of King Edward. When we reached Wark, the Lord of Wark had fled with his bride, but we were welcomed into the castle. I thought we would simply push on and attack Berwick, but King Edward chose to honour Holy Week and the army stayed at Wark to celebrate Easter. We had with us the Bishop of Durham and we sought God's approval for our venture.

My archers had no such rest, for the king sent me to scout out the land around Berwick. Norham was nearby and was a castle of the Palatinate but King Edward wanted my eyes. I chose twenty men and while the rest of the army rested, we crossed the Tweed at Wark. I told the king that we might be away some days and my men and I took supplies. When we fought in the Clwyd and along the Welsh coast, I had been familiar with the land. It was the land of my birth – but this was almost like Gascony, a foreign country. Berwick was a mere ten miles away, but I knew that once we had taken that town, the king would wish to move deeper into Scotland. As the Scots were raiding England we were effectively at war and I felt justified in making the aggressive move.

We headed north and we were wary from the moment we stepped

onto the north bank of the Tweed. This was not Gwillim's country, but his nose and that of Dick would give us early warning of danger. The land was undulating, and our view restricted by hedges, copses as well as the rise and fall of the road. In short, it was the perfect country for an ambush. I was not worried that we would be ambushed as no one knew we had crossed the river and the border. The army would be a different matter! We spied no castles and had covered almost twenty-five miles before we saw signs both of an enemy and a defensive position.

Dunbar Castle lay on the coast and as soon as I saw it, I knew that King Edward would wish to reduce it. We found a wood close by and we camped. My aim was to get a feel for the traffic in the area. We heard no noise in the night but, as we prepared to leave in the morning, we heard hooves on the road which passed from Dunbar that lay to the east

Mordaf was the sentry at the edge of the wood and he appeared unconcerned when he reported to me. "A column of ten men at arms, captain. They were led by a knight. They paid no attention to the woods. Either they are very confident, or they are bone idle!"

Nodding, I said, "Mount up. It is time to approach Berwick."

We had a relatively short ride down the coast to the border town. We had to take cover twice as we were approached by families heading north. King Edward and his army had been seen. When we neared the border town, I was disappointed. I had expected a castle of the stature of Harlech, but it was not even as strong as Norham! An inadequate wooden wall surrounded the town and whilst the keep was made of stone it would not last long against King Edward's war machines.

That we were seen was not our fault. A column of spearmen forty or so strong, led by a mounted man at arms, came across our horses. I had gone forward with just Hamo, Mordaf and Gwillim. The others

163

had bows strung and they shouted the alarm as they sent their arrows at the spearmen who advance upon us. I suspect that we might have been able to stand and fight them but there was, it seemed to me, little to be gained.

"Mount and follow me."

I swung my leg over my horse's back and saw the man at arms ride at me. He shouted something to his men, but it was lost on the wind. Four of his men had been struck by arrows but none had been killed. The spearmen raised their shields and advanced behind the mounted man at arms. I think he thought he had a chance for glory as he galloped towards us.

"Hamo, lead the men away. I will follow." Drawing my sword, I did the one thing the Scotsman did not expect – I rode at him. He had a sword drawn and he raised his shield when he saw my intent. I was a skilled rider; I had been riding for more than twenty years and I had fought on horseback more than once. I rode as though I would meet him sword to sword but, at the last moment, I jinked my horse to his left and as he clumsily tried to raise his shield and protect himself. I swung my sword – not at his shield, but his back as I passed. He wore a gambeson and mail. Neither were any match for my sword and archer's arm. Even as the spearmen ran to aid their leader, his back arched and his arms formed a crucifix as my sword drew blood. Wheeling around the horse, which had stopped, I galloped after my men.

When I reached Hamo I said, "Well we know now that they are adding to the garrison and women and children are fleeing. That means the ones who remain will fight."

Hamo shook his head. "With the army we have brought, father, it will be like spitting in the wind."

I nodded. "It has been more than a generation since the Scots felt English steel. They have forgotten our ability. I do not think that

164

King Edward has campaigned here. Their confidence is borne of ignorance and not strength."

The king agreed with my assessment when I reported to him. "We will observe the holiday, Warbow, for it gives my ships time to get into position and then we will show them our teeth. You have done well!"

It was the end of March when riders reported our ships at the mouth of the Tweed. Crossing the river we marched along the north bank to the Scottish stronghold. King Edward was a shrewd man who knew how to show his power. He waited until the whole army was arrayed before the walls of the town before he rode, with his bishops, to demand its surrender. I was with The Earl of Warwick and we were close enough to hear the words exchanged. King Edward demanded the surrender of Berwick, promising that the garrison would be able to march out and the people would be treated well. As we awaited their response, I saw that close up, the walls were even less of a threat than they had appeared from a distance. The people of Berwick did not take long to respond. They shouted insults and many of the men bared their buttocks to him. It was a mistake. We withdrew to prepare for battle.

King Edward then did something the Berwickians were not expecting. He called forth fifty men at arms and proceeded to knight them. It was a clever move, for it made those fifty all the more determined to fight well and it added to the tension. Sadly, no one had told our captains in the estuary and they assumed the attack had begun. They sailed close to the harbour to take the ships there. When two of our vessels were set on fire, King Edward was forced to act.

"Warbow, have your archers clear the walls!"

"Aye, my lord."

"Warwick, I want a column of dismounted men at arms and knights to attack the gate once Warbow has done as I asked!"

As the men who led my archers had been chosen by me, they did not need to be told what to do. Even as I dismounted and handed the reins of my horse to Jack, the centenars and vintenars were forming lines. They each adopted a two-rank formation. The result was that by the time I had joined them and strung my bow, they were all ready. "Nock and draw!" Normally I would have paused, but speed was of the essence as there was confusion on Berwick's walls. The collective creak of yew was a reassuring sound and when I shouted, "Loose!" that crack was even more powerful. "Loose at will!" My order would suit the better archers and whilst it lacked the solid wall of arrows descending there were enough of them to knock defenders from the walls.

I sent ten flights before a rider galloped up. "Sir Gerald, the king says to desist. We will take the gate!"

I bellowed, "Archers, hold!"

Arrows, bolts, and stones were sent at the heavily mailed men as they ran at the gates, but they did little harm. When I heard the first cracks of axes as the gates were assaulted, I shouted, "Archers advance with nocked arrows!"

I already had an arrow nocked and when I saw a Scot raise a stone as large as a barrel above his head I did not hesitate. My arrow slammed into his chest and the weight of his stone and his body took him into the town. By the time we were just eighty paces from the gates, the axemen had done their job and the gates were shattered. The men at arms poured in and I raised my bow to shout, "Charge!"

Only the assault party beat us into the town. Once inside, my archers chose targets which presented a danger while the men at arms slew any who were in their path. I looked behind and saw Hamo leading eight of my archers. Jack was with them, although he just had his sword rather than a bow. I slung my bow and drew my sword. The Scots had been given the opportunity to surrender and they had spurned it. Now they would pay the price. I ran, knowing that my men would be behind me. The men at arms had cleared a path and I was looking for a suitably large house that might make us richer.

The houses with two floors were always the better houses and when I saw one with the door already opened, I ran inside. I heard a noise from the rear of the property and when I reached the kitchen, I saw a man taking a chest from beneath the floorboards. He was a well-dressed man, and I took him for a merchant. His wife and two daughters were close by. They all looked up when my shadow filled the doorway.

"Mine, I think!" The man dropped the chest and went to his short sword. Shaking my head I said, "You are no warrior and I am. Take your family and run. That is my gift to you. If you stay, then others will not only take your gold but perhaps also your wife and daughters."

Realisation dawned and his wife said, "Jamie, let us go! These are barbarians. Think of our daughters!"

I pointed my sword's tip in his direction and nodded. Sheathing his sword, he picked up his two daughters and led his wife out of the back. I guessed he had an escape route planned already. Jack and Hamo appeared behind me.

"Search the house. The man looked rich and he should have fine clothes. Take everything back to our horses. I think Berwick will be burned this night!"

Leaving my son and Jack with John, son of John, I led Gwillim, Robin and the others back into the street. Already it was a scene from hell. English soldiers are the best in the world but give them a city or town to sack and they behave like barbarians. Some had managed to broach a barrel of ale and were already showing that they could not hold their drink. "You men stay close to me. These animals cannot discriminate between a friend and foe. Let us find the king."

He was where I expected him to be, close to the castle, and he had just secured the surrender of the garrison. In contrast to the people, the soldiers of the garrison were allowed to go free, just so long as they swore an oath never to bear arms against the king again. They did so and left, by which time the wooden buildings of the town were burning.

We followed the king outside, partly to protect him and partly to see what we could salvage on the way out. We had lost barely a man in the attack, but now I saw English fighting English. It was depressing. The fire was finished by the next morning and we re-entered its smoking ruins. The fire suited King Edward and he ordered the army, which had behaved so badly, to begin to clear it and start to build his new defences. He would have a castle, but one built of stone and with a stone wall around the town. It would not fall so easily again!

The ditch around the town would be impressive. When finished it was eighty feet wide and forty feet deep. The king himself wheeled the first barrow of earth away. He knew how to make a grand gesture.

My archers and I were spared the work of digging. He had spearmen and the unskilled for that. We rode around the countryside to the north and west. We ensured that no army could approach unseen and we took every animal and sack of grain we could find. The first day, we escorted a messenger from John Balliol. I was in the king's presence when he opened the letter brought by the messenger. The letter was a message of defiance. The king was informed that Balliol renounced the former oaths of fealty, extorted by King Edward's violent pressure, and informed the king that we were at war.

The king laughed and sent back the messenger with the words, "Tell your king and those who seek to manipulate the fool that if they choose to bow the knee to me, I might let them retain some of their lands! Oh foolish knave! What folly he commits. If he will not come to us, we will go to him." When he had gone, he rubbed his hands. "I pray that the fools will choose to meet us in open battle and then we can conquer this sad little country and return to our homes. Warbow, keep a good watch. Until they meet us in battle, we will make this castle one of which we can be proud!"

Chapter 11

Dunbar, April 1296

We found the Scottish army just four weeks after Berwick had fallen. They were at Haddington, close to Dunbar and we watched them from the safety of the woods we had used when scouting out Berwick. I sent two riders back to tell the king and we waited in the woods to estimate numbers and to gather as much information as we could to help us to defeat them. We were close to the place Mordaf had seen the riders heading to Dunbar and we knew it was a good place from which to watch. I spied the dwelling of King John Balliol. It had the Scottish standard fluttering from the roof and there were knights guarding it. By my reckoning, there were, perhaps a thousand mounted men, most of them knights, and over five thousand foot soldiers. It was a large army, but I did not think that the king would be over-worried by it.

We made a camp just two miles from Haddington and later that night Hamo, whom I had left commanding the archers, accompanied by Jack, rode in.

"Sir John de Warenne, the Earl of Surrey, is fetching a large force of knights to discourage the Scots. The king will follow."

"He does not send more archers?"

Hamo shrugged. "He seemed to think that the hundred you lead, added to the thousand knights with the earl, would be sufficient. I bring another one hundred and fifty with me. The earl will threaten Dunbar and the king hopes that Balliol will leave his camp to fight the earl."

I nodded; that made sense. If he brought his whole army then Balliol might simply retreat to Edinburgh. We needed a decisive battle. "And our role?"

"The king said to watch them and aid the earl in any way you can."

Such freedom suited me, and I took it as a compliment that the king knew I would not abuse the position.

We were up and mounted the next day and, at noon, we saw the riders heading for Haddington. The edge of the wood lay just eighty paces from the road and was a perfect vantage point. We could have stopped them, but the king wished the Scottish army to be drawn east and so we waited.

I sent Dick of Luston and two other archers closer to the encampment. The Earl of Surrey would need to know when the enemy moved. In fact, the earl reached us before the Scots. His army was fully mounted and the Scottish one was not. I rode from our woods to speak to him.

"The Scots are to the west, my lord, and they have not moved in numbers."

The earl looked at the ground, which was riven with streams and rivulets. It would not suit horsemen, but all the patches of water could be jumped, even by a fully mailed man,

"We have no foot soldiers, but I dare say that your archers could cause mischief."

"Aye, my lord."

171

"Then when they are tempted and charge us, your arrows – on their flanks – will confuse them and my horsemen shall do the rest. Let me know when they come."

Dick rode in an hour after the earl and I had spoken. "They come, captain. Their advance guards are less than half a mile behind us."

"Mordaf, ride to the earl and inform him of the approach of the Scots." As my Welshman rode off, I shouted, "Tether the horses in the woods and take your positions along the edge of the wood. Await my command, for we want the head in the noose before we tighten it."

The advance guards were light horsemen on small horses. They were followed by knights and men at arms. As they passed us, I noticed that there was no royal banner; the Scottish king had not come with his army. I knew the man had little military skill, but his absence would not help the Scottish cause. Mordaf re-joined us as the foot soldiers passed. They were carrying their long spears over their shoulders. When I heard the horn from the front of the Scottish column, then I knew that the Earl of Surrey had been seen. A ripple of noise ran down the Scottish column and my command of "Nock!" went unheard.

The Scottish spearmen began to organise themselves into serried ranks, blissfully unaware that death lay in the woods. This was my kind of battle, for I was in command. Sir John de Warenne had given me permission to fight as I saw fit and I would do so.

"Draw!" The Scots were busy making their spears into the hedgehog which would defy even mounted men at arms. Such a movement took time; the long spears were awkward.

"Loose!" There were not many archers with me, but the arrows fell amongst men who had no protection whatsoever from the war arrows we loosed. We kept up a fierce rate. With two war bags each and more on the sumpters we could afford to be profligate. The rate of release was determined by the strength of the archers' arms and not ammunition.

From my right, I heard the clash of arms as the two groups of knights met and collided. I did not witness it, but I had seen enough to know what would have happened. The English had better horses and armour. Using the slope they would have ridden down to meet the Scots, boot to boot. Their lances would have been pulled back as one and the heads driven into the Scottish horsemen. The courses and destriers ridden by John de Warenne's men would have snapped and bitten at the Scottish horses, and when they flinched their riders would have been doomed.

Whoever led the foot soldiers now saw the danger they faced. The horsemen were still hidden by a rise in the land and he ordered some four hundred men to advance to the woods while the rest tried to organise a line of spears to defend against the English knights. We were in the woods and they had no idea we were there – their move was merely to afford better protection for themselves and to prevent their main body being flanked by the horsemen. I did not need to tell my men to change targets – they were all veterans – and the four hundred soon became three hundred as arrows were sent with such power that they drove through bodies. It must have been terrifying for the men in the second and third ranks, as they saw the metal heads erupt from their comrades' backs.

When the three hundred became two they broke and tumbled back towards the main body. That coincided with the appearance of the Earl of Surrey. The Scottish light horse and knights had been swept aside and were fleeing back to Haddington. The disaster was compounded with the arrival of the survivors from the abortive attack on the woods. They sought the protection of their comrades and merely disrupted its integrity. Some knights had fled, and they also ploughed into their own men. Our arrows fell on the backs of those fleeing and the spearmen in the centre of the formation. When the knights were struck, the spears were shattered, and the spearmen were ridden down. They fled.

It was now the time for swords, not bows. "Into them!" I laid my bow against the tree and drew my sword. Many of my men kept their bows and we left the cover of the trees to run over ground which was littered with Scottish bodies. Later we would retrieve arrows, but the Scottish were broken and now was the opportunity to crush them. Once more our distinctive dress identified us to the knights and men at arms, although we still had to be wary of horses that had the smell of blood in their nostrils. One spearman foolishly tried to swing his ungainly weapon around to spear me. I merely grabbed the end with my powerful left arm and then stepped towards him, driving my sword up into his ribcage. He died quickly.

The English horses were tiring and, wisely, the earl halted them. A third of the Scottish army had escaped and would, no doubt, flee to Haddington but the bulk still remained and so the knights with the better mounts prevented escape by surrounding them and we worked our way into the heart of the defeated army. As knights and lords surrendered, so the spearmen threw down their spears and dropped to their knees. They were lucky – my men were not savages and we accepted their surrender even though we gained nothing from it.

As darkness fell, we made camp and counted the cost. The earl had lost no men although one horse was so badly wounded that it had to be put down. Many hundreds of Scots were killed, and many nobles were taken prisoner: John Comyn, the Earl of Buchan, and the earls of Atholl, Ross and Menteith, together with one hundred and thirty knights and men at arms, all surrendered. They would be sent into captivity in England. None had surrendered to us, and so we would not benefit from the ransoms. We did well enough from the knights and men at arms we slew.

We soon had a fire going and food was put on to cook. The earl sent for me.

"Well done, Warbow. Tomorrow we go to Dunbar. The king's plan worked. I want you and your men to cut off the road to the north. The king will be coming from the south. Can you do it?"

"Of course, my lord!"

"I thought the Scots would have had more steel in them!"

Neither of us had experienced fighting the Scots and his words were my thoughts, too. "They were badly led, my lord."

He nodded, "Aye, my son in law is no leader, that is for sure!"

I re-joined my men at our smaller camp. All the arrows that could be salvaged had been collected and put in empty war bags. When time allowed, we would fletch them again. The knights and men at arms had yielded coins, although those taken from the dead spearmen were copper rather than silver. As was our way we pooled the coins and shared them out equitably. I took no more than a humble archer.

We rose before dawn and rode the short distance to Dunbar Castle. We positioned ourselves north of the town and waited for dawn. The Scottish flags still fluttered defiantly when the earl came to demand its surrender. They refused. However, as soon as King Edward arrived the gates were opened. Less than a month after the campaign had begun, we had taken two major towns and castles. The east coast south of the Forth was ours, and one of the towns demanded by King Edward, Berwick, was now English.

We left a garrison and then headed to Roxburgh and Jedburgh, the two other towns demanded by King Edward. They surrendered without a fight. I expected more of Edinburgh but in May, as we surrounded it, there was no army to challenge us. We prepared siege engines and my men gathered arrows to rain death upon the walls but they were not needed for after five days they surrendered, and we had not had to waste a single arrow. The war could have ended then, but King John fled before us. We headed for Stirling Castle and I was sent with three hundred mounted archers to cut it off. This was a strong castle and the king wanted it taken quickly. As we approached, I saw that there were neither flags flying nor manned walls.

When I rode up to the closed gate a porter stepped out from a sally port and bowed. He handed me a set of keys. "Here, my lord, the keys to Stirling Castle!" I cocked my head to one side and he shook his own. "I suppose I could have fought you for it but if the King of Scotland cannot be bothered, then why should I?" He chuckled. "Lock up afore ye go, my lord!"

Apart from the porter, the castle was completely empty. I could not believe that the Scots had made no attempt to defend the magnificent castle. After that, it was not so much a campaign as a royal progress. We were not hindered by the Scots in any way. King John always stayed ahead of us until July when, at Stracathro churchyard, in Montrose on the east coast of Scotland, John Balliol surrendered to King Edward. King Edward was in no mood for leniency and the first thing he did, before sending Baron Balliol back to England was to rip the royal coat of arms from his tabard. The royal appointee had failed King Edward and he would never be free again.

We headed through Scotland until we reached Elgin and there the campaign ended. Scotland was King Edward's. Scotland was not only without a king – but it also had no opposition to King Edward and the English. We spent a month returning to Berwick and we visited as many places as we could, to show the Scots their new ruler. In August he summoned all those lords, nobles, abbots and priors he had not imprisoned to Berwick, to swear an oath of fealty. Already Berwick was rising like a stone monolith from the burned wooden ruins, and it was a symbol for those who came to swear an oath that the future they faced was an English one.

Before the assembled nobles King Edward appointed the John de Warenne, 6th Earl of Surrey, as guardian of Scotland, with Hugh de Cressingham as treasurer and Walter de Amersham as chancellor. They would be King Edward's rulers in his newly-acquired northern kingdom. King Alexander's death all those years ago had been as a stone starting an avalanche – when the great Scottish king fell to his death, the result was that England gained the northern half of the island.

When the bulk of the army was released to return home, I went to speak to the king. Although the campaign had been ridiculously short, we still wished to go to our families.

I was made to wait for some time outside the hall King Edward occupied. Sir Godfrey came out to speak with me. "Sir Gerald, the king is within and he is speaking with his nephew, Thomas, Earl of Lancaster. He will see you, but begs you to be patient."

"I can return when he is free, Sir Godfrey."

Shaking his head he said, ominously, "The king requests that you stay," He inclined his head and added, "He has need of you!"

I had brought Hamo and Jack with me. "Hamo, go back to the men. I fear that we will not be returning home soon. See what horses and supplies you can acquire."

"But the war is over and most of the army has left!"

"And King Edward wishes for me to stay. That means he needs me and, I have no doubt, my archers." My Yarpole men were the only ones left at the camp. Captain Geoffrey had departed many days earlier.

It was a further hour before Sir Godfrey ushered me in. He held his hand up to prevent Jack from following. Jack grinned. "I will water the horses, my lord, they have waited long enough."

I saw that the Earl of Lancaster was within. He had recently inherited the title, for the King's brother, Edmund, had died in France during the siege of Bayonne. Thomas, Earl of Lancaster, was young, and I had not seen him during the campaign. That explained the long meeting.

"Ah, Sir Gerald, this is my nephew, Sir Thomas of Lancaster. His lands are to the west and they were attacked by the Scots whilst we were busy here and he was in London. He can explain what we require of you." He must have seen the look on my face, and he smiled. "It is little that we ask of you and you shall be paid five hundred crowns for the work that you do as well as earning the approbation of both my nephew and I."

I knew what that meant. I would have to do it, or risk the king's displeasure. I nodded.

Sir Thomas spoke. He was what I would call a typical noble. His language reflected his aristocratic upbringing, and I was a rough-hewn archer. We came from different worlds and while King Edward was an easy man to speak with, Sir Thomas was not.

"While I was in London, attending my father's funeral and dealing with the legal matters, the Scots attacked Carlisle. Whilst they were unsuccessful in their attacks on that mighty fortress, they caused great mischief in the lands around it. Many homes were destroyed, and prisoners were taken. I fear my land will not raise many taxes this year!"

I sighed. Finding such perpetrators was the job of a sheriff and not King Edward's archer.

King Edward snapped, impatiently, "Warbow, do not be petulant – listen. I am the one who has said that you can perform this task, so hear out my nephew!"

The young earl looked at me curiously and continued. "The land to which these thieves, brigands and bandits have fled belong to John Balliol, for his mother was powerful in Galloway. There is a large forest and they occupy both the forest and the villages close by. My uncle has invested Castledykes in Kirkcudbright with a garrison, but there are only twenty of them. I would have this band of bandits destroyed and, if it can be achieved, the hostages and captives returned. The bandits have asked for ransoms for the families. I believe they had fine homes and farms but they were destroyed – and that is where the value lies. It is not in gold."

I hesitated before asking, "My lord, could you not pay the ransom?"

The look he gave me told me that he had no intention of paying from his own purse, but he smiled a false smile. I knew the look well.

"I fear that my coin is all committed, or else I would happily pay."

I knew when to fight a battle and when to walk away. This was a time to walk away. It was a monumental task and could last all winter. But I was a realist and knew I had to do this. The sooner I began then the sooner I would be finished.

"Have you a map of the area, my lord?"

Sir Godfrey hurried over to a table and began examining parchments. He returned clutching one. "Here, Sir Gerald. It is not the same quality as we are used to. We shall remedy that soon."

I spread it out. "It will do." I saw that it was about twelve miles from the garrison at Castledykes to the centre of the forest, which the map-maker had identified with green ink. Just one road passed through the forest. "And where in this forest are they concentrated, my lord?"

The earl shrugged. "One man escaped their clutches and when he reached Carlisle just said that they were close to a lake – the Scots call them lochs."

As I could see at least eight blue patches, that information was of little help. "And how many men are we talking about?"

Again, the earl did not know. "The man who escaped said that there were at least two hundred and they were led by a giant!"

I could not help laughing, for this sounded like a story told by a child. "And is there a dragon, too?"

"Warbow!"

"I am sorry, King Edward, but giants!" I shook my head. "Eight lakes and two hundred men who could be anywhere ... where do I start?"

The earl said, "When I said giant, I mean he was a big man. The one who escaped said he was the biggest man he had ever seen."

The king was growing impatient; he wanted to be back in London. "Warbow. I will have Sir Godfrey give you a royal writ. It will enable you to call upon any of my officers to help you in your quest. When the bandits are gone, and you have proof for me, then your service is ended and you are discharged."

I nodded and said, "One last thing, my lord. How many captives do I seek?" The earl looked as though he was not sure. "A rough figure will do."

"The women of four families and their children were taken, along with one young man. It was he who escaped."

"Thank you, my lord." I turned to Sir Godfrey. "You know where we are camped?"

Sir Godfrey nodded. "I will not be long!"

Chapter 12

The king had not specified how many men I would need, and so I selected the thirty or so of the men from Yarpole and Luston who were young enough and had fewer attachments. I sent the rest home with the payments we had received for our service. For once those who remained with me, Hamo apart, were not happy about the new arrangement. They did not say much but their faces spoke for them. It was Jack who voiced their concerns.

"I have heard them speaking and they do not relish this prospect, which is not for England nor for their own families. The problem is, captain, that they see this as a thankless task. They may die – for brigands and bandits might get lucky, and even if they do succeed, they will be given little in the way of thanks."

They were right, of course, and King Edward was a ruthless man. Had the queen still been alive there would have been thanks from her – but now, the king was single-minded. By the time Sir Godfrey brought me the parchment and the crowns, it was too late to leave and so I questioned Sir Godfrey further. He was a man I felt I could trust.

"Are these bandits, Sir Godfrey or more?"

He gave me a searching look. "You are a clever man, Gerald, and the king is right to trust you as he does. We believe that the man who leads them is a knight or has been trained in war. Their attacks were well planned and organised. The hostages they took had rich lands and they have demanded a huge ransom. It is to be delivered to the Bishop of Glasgow, Robert Wishart."

"Then they are being ransomed?"

"Sadly, no. The bandits miscalculated and the families do not have the coins. They have valuable lands, but the lands would need to be sold to realise their worth. The heads of the families who might have raised the money were killed. There are no longer Jews who can loan the other members of the families the coin. You are their only hope."

I saw that there was no way out of this and, perhaps for the first time, thought about the people who had been taken. This could so easily have been my family. When the Welsh had come to raid Yarpole, they might have succeeded. "What are the names of the families? It might help us."

"There is the Foster family and the Wilsons, who came from Brampton. The Coggleshalls who farmed at Tindale and finally the Halls, who lived in Rickerby."

"If there is no ransom, then why do the bandits keep them?"

He sighed. "They do not yet know there is no ransom. The Bishop of Glasgow was given until All Saints to fetch the money. That will be your time limit."

I nodded. The captives would be relatively safe until then. After that, they would be used and abused as their captors saw fit. "And you return with the king?"

"Aye, unless there is another war soon, we shall not meet again for a while."

I laughed. "We said that about Wales and then along came Madog ap Llewellyn. I thank you for this."

He handed me the map I had looked at. "I brought you this. It may help."

"And the garrison at Castledykes?"

"Do not rely on them. The better garrisons are at Stirling, Jedburgh and the like. It is a place you can shelter and safely store your arrows. The parchment gives you total authority. Until a sheriff is appointed you will be the senior lord in that part of the world."

"That is something, I suppose!"

I went to the camp and saw the disconsolate faces. The rest of my men had left for Yarpole and it was like being the last people at a feast. Within a few hours, the king would have taken ship and we would be the last in Berwick, save the garrison and the labourers building the town walls and castle. I decided to bring the ill-feeling to the fore and I stood in the centre of the circle that had gathered around the comforting fire.

"I can see from your faces that many of you are unhappy that we have to ride to a faraway forest and beard bandits. You do not want to go to the aid of four families of women and children who have no hope of ransom. I can understand that. You owe these English maidens nothing and, unlike them, your mothers, wives, daughters and sisters are safely protected by Yarpole's walls." I paused and saw Hamo smile. He knew what I was doing. "I will ask no man to come with me on this venture if he does not want to. Any who think they can live with the thought of young girls being abused by Scotsmen can leave tomorrow with my blessing and there will be no hard feelings. Hamo, Jack and I will go alone if we have to. I have faced greater danger when I was sent by King Edward to find the Mongols. All I ask is that those who wish to leave come to tell me, face to face."

That was the masterstroke, for I knew that none would be able to look me in the eye and say he did not wish to follow me.

"You have until the morning. All those that follow me will do so with a smile on their face and hope in their hearts!"

I joined Hamo and Jack. The youngest member of our company asked, "Will we be going alone, then, captain?"

Hamo shook his head. "If one man takes my father's offer, then I will be surprised. The men like to grumble, it is their way, but they know that rescuing the women and children is the right thing to do. The way I look at it, Jack, is that one of those young women could be Margaret or Joan. As bad as they have had to endure it up to now, their fate when the bandits discover there will be no ransom forthcoming does not bear thinking about."

Hamo was right, and as we rode from an almost deserted camp every one of my archers followed us. Most even apologised for their sour faces. We had the king's writ and that meant we did not have to worry about food or lodgings. We stayed in Jedburgh and enjoyed fine hospitality, for it had recently become garrisoned by King Edward's men. We travelled along the English side of the old border and the parchment meant we were better fed and housed than on any other campaign that I could remember.

I intended to visit Carlisle first, even though it added to our journey. I was anxious to find out first-hand about the raid. I also needed to find out more about the families. To my great surprise, there was a new governor of Carlisle Castle and it was a Scotsman. The young Earl of Annandale I had met at Hartlepool, Robert de Brus, had been chosen by King Edward. I was not shocked so much as surprised at the speedy appointment, for the king would hope to subvert the young Scotsman who was as much English as much as Scottish thanks to his estates in England. De Brus was effusively welcoming and took us into the Great Hall. His servants brought wine and food as well as bowls of water and cloths for us to wash.

I had not expected to see him, but he was not surprised to see me. "Sir Gerald, I wondered if you might call. The Earl of Lancaster told me of your mission and if I can do anything at all then just ask."

"Thank you, my lord, I have questions, but first can I ask how you stand on the matter of Scotland? I heard that your family were claimants to the throne."

He laughed. "Sir Gerald, I heard that you were plain-speaking, and I am pleased that you are. I do not like this fencing with words and hiding behind false smiles. I have not been here for long, just two months but you are perfectly correct, my family does have claims on the crown, but as the weak Balliol discovered, it is not something which is to be cherished. There are too many enemies at home. I was honest with King Edward and I believe that his strength will allow my country to find a way through this morass. If I were to be selected by the nobles then I would accept the crown but there is, as yet, no universal support for any individual. Besides which, many of the lords are in England and captives. This will suit. Does that answer your question?"

"It does and I thank you for your honesty. These bandits – what can you tell me of them?"

His face hardened. "They are a disgrace to the name of Scotsmen. They raid both sides of the border. Their leader believes himself to be fighting for the rights of both English and Scots. It is an act, and he cares just for himself. He purports to be a knight but his behaviour is that of a savage! When you catch him then fetch him here and I will hang him myself."

"The forest he controls seems vast. Have you any clues as to which part he will be found in?"

"I fear not, for Wallace is a clever young man. They use the villages and hamlets as their base and, from what I can gather, move from place to place, like a flock of sheep grazing the fellside. He is protected by the people who have been taken in by his claims. You must know he is ruthless. When the earl first came to me I sent two men to find the whereabouts of their camps. They were found in the forest, naked and emasculated. I fear I could not persuade any other to venture into his lair."

"Wallace, what can you tell me of him?"

"Just his name, William Wallace, and his size. He is not only tall but big enough to be able to use a two-handed sword with one hand. Travellers cannot pass through the land he controls without paying him and his men a tax. He shares a little of the money with the poor of Galloway and it makes them protect him."

Hamo and Jack had not said a word, but I knew that they were listening closely and Hamo, especially, was watching the Scotsman's face.

I sipped the wine as I began to devise my strategy. "Do you have any idea yet, Sir Gerald, about how you will approach this problem?"

I shook my head for I did not trust any Scot – even one appointed by the king. "Not at the moment. What can you tell me about the families who were taken?"

"Very little for, as I told you, I have been here but a short time. Robert knows more about that sort of thing. He served the previous governor." He waved over a servant and said, "Fetch Robert of Carlisle for me."

Robert was a greybeard and when he spoke, I heard the English accent. It was one of the north and sounded different to those who lived close to Yarpole, but it was a reassuring accent.

"Robert, Sir Gerald here is being sent to hunt the families who were taken."

The Englishman smiled at me and nodded. "Thank you, my lord.

I prayed that someone would be sent to help them. They are all fine people and do not deserve this. None were from noble families as such, but the heads of their families were doughty defenders against ..." I think he was going to say *Scotsmen* but he stopped in time and said, "all enemies to England. The Foster family, the Wilsons and the Halls lived locally. The Coggleshalls who farmed at Tindale, I did not know as well. The Fosters had fine lands and Mistress Mary was good to the poor. She has a daughter, Alice, who is seventeen and two sons, James and John, aged five and six." My eyes widened at the age gap. He shook his head when he saw my look. "Two older sons were killed when a warband came south and the boys are the love of her life. Matilda Wilson was a younger mother, and her daughters were twelve and thirteen. The boy was named Edward after the king and he was ten. Eleanor Hall ..." he smiled and shook his head. "When she was younger, she was the bonniest woman in the county. I would have courted her myself, but I was just a castle guard. She is a grandmother, and it was her son, Ralph, who was killed along with her son in law, Peter. Peter's wife, Mistress Anne, was not a well woman and she died after they abducted her. There was a boy and a girl, Eleanor and Ralph, they are four and five. The Coggleshalls, as far as I can remember, were the mother, Margaret, and her two sons. I do not know their names, but they have yet to see ten summers. I hope that helps, my lord."

I was touched by his knowledge. I doubted that de Brus would ever be as familiar with the people for whom he was responsible. "That is most useful information, and you have my word that we shall do our best to get them back for you."

"Then my prayers are answered, for now I see that someone cares." He did not look directly at de Brus, but I knew that he was disappointed in the previous lack of action. I now knew why the young Earl of Lancaster had sought the king's help. His eyes pleaded with me. "If you find them, Sir Gerald, then tell Mistress Hall that I …" – I saw him struggling for words – "I have a home and I will heal her hurts."

"I swear I will bring her back if I can!"

"The houses and farms of all the families were burned. When they return it will be to blackened homes, weeds, tares and the bones of dead animals."

De Brus was irritated by Robert's words, for this meant nothing to him. "You may go now, Robert." Turning to me he said, "I have some business to attend to, but you and your son must dine with me. I should like to hear about the battle of Dunbar and the taking of Berwick. One hears rumours but I should like the truth about the shameful defeats my countrymen suffered."

"Of course, my lord."

We left the next morning and headed into what had been, until a few months earlier, Scotland. At the meal, neither Hamo nor I had revealed any plans. I had a better idea of how we would track the bandits than did Hamo. As a young archer, I had taken part in a hunt for bandits. It was not as easy as lords made out and I had seen good men die on that hunt. I would use my knowledge to save my men suffering the same fate.

We had fifty miles to go and the only safe place for us would be Castledykes. We rode as though every tree hid an enemy and all idle chatter ended. We took the road that passed by the sea. I had been told by Robert, in Carlisle, that in summer the water was almost as warm as a bath in that bay. Certainly, when we camped by the beach it was warm enough to paddle in. I wondered what made it so. All this part of the world was new to me. I had been born within one hundred and twenty miles of here, as the crow flies, but it felt and looked totally different from my homeland. There were hills rather than mountains and forests instead of fells.

It was dark when we reached the castle. Approaching from the east, we passed down the side of the River Dee. The castle was not a huge one, but it enjoyed a good position on high ground and was set apart from the village, which lay closer to the sea. The sentry who emerged from the gate asked for identification. I told him I was from the king and held out the parchment. As I had expected, he could not read, but we were allowed in and entered the outer bailey.

I knew from de Brus that Alan d'Aubigny was the constable of Castledykes. He was barely out of his twenties and even Hamo looked older than he was. The men he commanded, whom we saw as we dismounted, looked like sweepings of King Edward's army and I would not have trusted most of them. The young gentleman was glad to see us and I think part of that was that he felt so insecure. I showed him the writ and explained what we would be doing. He looked nervously at the two men who had brought us from the gate. "And do you need my men?"

I shook my head. "We may need a cell or a gaol to hold any prisoners but the work we do is well-suited to my men." I saw the relief on the faces of all three men. In d'Aubigny's case, I think it was because he feared to fail while the two spearmen did not relish a fight. "Have you room for my men? I may not take them all out at once. That might help you, as you would have extra eyes."

"We have beds, but the stabling might be a problem."

I nodded to Hamo. "Get Robin and John rig up some ropes where we can tether the animals." He left to give the orders. "If I might have a tour so that I know the lie of the land, so to speak?"

"Of course my lord, it would be a privilege. I have heard of you and I was in Wales when you fought at Maes Moydog, although I was with the king in Conwy."

I smiled and said the right thing. "Then you are an old campaigner!"

He grew before my eyes and waved over an old warrior who looked as though he could be a grandfather. "Alfred, you have served here longer than any. Walk with us and tell Sir Gerald about the castle."

"Aye, sir and it is good to have real soldiers in the castle again!"

D'Aubigny looked nervously to see if any of the others had heard him. "They are just a bit rough, Alfred! They will improve."

The old man sniffed. "Well they couldn't get any worse, that is for sure, my lord. It is a good job that the Scots have been so soundly beaten. Ah well, we shall see!"

I liked the old man, and he did know the castle. I learned more about the land to the north from the old man than ever I did from the constable. Alfred knew the bandits. He told us there had always been bandits, for the forests teemed with game and the Scottish lords who were supposed to manage the land were often in their other estates. "These new ones are just a bit better organised. It is having an effect on the game, too."

"How so, Alfred?"

"Time was you could ride down any game trail and see tracks and spoor. They are hunting so heavily now, my lord, that they have to seek their prey."

That gave me my first idea of how we might catch them.

"And how do you think they can move the prisoners around so easily?"

"The ones who live in the forest are poor, my lord. They live from hand to mouth. I daresay this bandit chief gives them food in exchange for putting up his guests. They must move them around, for the constable had houses searched and we found evidence that people had passed through, but we could not prove who. They might be unwilling hosts, but if the choice is death or starvation then you will sup with the devil."

"Yet I am told that this Wallace is popular."

"Is that his name? Aye, well, anyone who gives them food and gives a little protection will be seen as popular. It doesn't change what he is, a bandit and a brigand and he needs to be wiped off the face of the earth!"

Alfred was uncompromising and I liked that.

"Do you know where he might be found?"

"You and your men are all mounted, my lord, and there are more of you than this garrison. The bandits do not use horses but move through the forests. Their weakness, so far as I can see it, is that they have to use the roads to ambush travellers."

"Bait a trap?"

"That is what I would do. It is a risk for the bait but …"

"The potential rewards would outweigh the risks. We could take a prisoner and that would gain valuable information we could use. Thank you, Alfred, this has been a most productive conversation."

"I live here, my lord. I have one daughter and she and her husband live close by. In ridding the land of Wallace you make my life and theirs safer!"

The constable said as we headed back to the hall, "If my men can help in any way, my lord …"

"Keep the castle safe and guard the men who will stay here, and we will do the rest. I can see now why we were sent. This land may be a little less wild than that where I grew up, but I am a woodsman, and we can do this."

As we entered the hall he said, somewhat defensively, "When we heard about the captives, we did try to find them, but we saw nothing and it cost us three men killed in an ambush."

I smiled at the young man and lied to make him feel better. "When I was your age, I might have struggled to cope with such a Herculean task. You will do better when you are older."

He brightened immediately. "Then soon the woods will be safe again!"

In my mind, I knew that we could not complete the task quickly. We might still be here at Christmas.

After we had eaten with the constable, I sat with Hamo, Robin and John. It was late but we needed to act quickly. I had a rudimentary plan and I needed to refine it with their help.

"We need to know where the bandits are residing now. We cannot simply ride into the forest and look for them; it is too vast, and we might search for months and not see them." I waved them closer, for I did not wish my words to carry. "The villagers know nothing of us for we arrived in the dark. I believe that there must be someone in the village passing information to the bandits." I took out the map and spread it on the table. "It is eight miles to the place where the bandits raid. None saw us enter last night and we use that. Alfred told me that although there is a ford most travellers use the ferry. Tomorrow I will take Jack and four of our older archers. We will dress as merchants and take the ferry. We will say that we are taking spices to sell in the north. Now is the time when people are preparing food – and spices are not only valuable, but also they do not take up much space. If this Wallace is a knight, then he will know of their value. I intend to be the bait."

Hamo shook his head. "That is too risky!"

"It would be, Hamo, if you were not leading the rest of the men to get ahead of us and ambush the ambushers." I could see that he was not convinced. "Laurieston is eight miles from here and is the start of the land controlled by the bandits. It is the main way to Ayr on the west coast. We will stay the night there and that should allow you and the others you take to be in position before the bandits." I sat back. "Who do you think has more skill? My archers or deserters from a Scottish army we have beaten each time we have fought it? Do now worry, Hamo, I shall be careful. If anything happened to Jack, then Lady Mary would skin me alive. She lived amongst the Mongols and knows how to do such things!"

The humour in my voice made them smile, as did the thought of my lovely wife wielding a skinning knife. We spent the last hour of the evening refining the plan and while my men retired, I went to the constable.

After I had told him that I intended to play the part of a merchant he shook his head. "I do not believe that the villagers would betray us. They are all friendly. Since I have come here the only danger and belligerence has come from the bandits."

"In which case, Alan, when I return in a week's time, empty handed, you may mock me for a foolish old man!"

Chapter 13

Walter, Gwillim, Dick and Harry were all experienced archers and without their bows and dressed in ordinary cloaks, passed for servants. We did not ride our horses but led them, and they looked to be laden, although they were not. We could not take our bows, for that would give away our identity, but we were able to secrete our swords beneath the fake goods we carried. We waited until there were people about before we left and we played out a scene for those who were watching.

"Thank you, constable, I will be sure to tell the bishop of your hospitality." I did not name a specific bishop. "I am sorry again for our late arrival."

"Do be careful, for there are bandits north of here."

"We travelled here successfully and now that the war is over it should be easier. Farewell."

We headed for the ferry, smiling and nodding to those we passed. There were three ferrymen. One looked to be the owner while the other two were younger; I guessed they were his sons. The fee for the ferry was high, for we were merchants. It was the way of the world. Locals would pay a quarter of our cost.

The ferryman was a garrulous chap and chattered like a magpie.

I happily told him of our cargo. "That will bring you a good return. Perhaps I should charge you more!" He said it with a smile that did not deceive me.

"Any more expensive and this trip would not be worth my while. The constable said that there were bandits north of here."

His answer told me he was the spy, or one of them at least. "Oh, there were, but I think you should be safe. You travel to Laurieston and then take the Ayr Road?" I nodded. "The danger lies to the east of that road. The one built by the Romans is where they prey." As we disembarked, he said, cheerily, "Have a good journey and I will see you on your return."

"When I hope for a reduction in the fee as we are returning customers!" It was the sort of thing a merchant might say.

"We shall see!"

We led our horses on the road north. I knew that we had less than two miles on this small road before we travelled, briefly, along the Roman road. Five hundred paces from the ferry I stopped and pretended to tighten my girths. It allowed me to look back to the ferry, where I saw the younger of the three ferrymen mount a pony and head along the river. Word would soon reach the bandits.

I took the reins and began to walk again. The traffic on the road came south to Kirkcudbright and so we could talk easily and just get into character when we saw men approach.

Gwillim confirmed my suspicions. "I heard the ferryman talk to the boy as we were leaving, captain. He told him to mount his pony and leave as soon as we were far enough away."

"Good. It will take him at least half a day to get to the bandits and they cannot be ready to ambush us until the morrow. Hamo and the others will probably overtake the boy and be ready to take them."

We then chatted about other matters. The four archers all had families and their talk told me that they were hoping to be home by Christmas. Jack's conversation was about his future.

"Do you think I will be ready to be an archer in the company soon, captain?"

"You are ready now, but we have no need of another archer while there is peace. Better that you hone your skills."

"There will be war again?"

"Of course but I do not know with whom. That is why we keep training."

"You need not go to war again, captain, you have done enough, have you not?"

"I think that while King Edward draws breath, he will need me as a sort of lucky charm. Once he no longer goes to war, then perhaps."

I had not thought of retirement, but Jack's words filled my head with speculative dreams as we trudged along the Roman road and then turned off to take the Ayr road. Would I be able to enjoy retirement? I realised I would, because Margaret was with child. I would have something my father never had – grandchildren. When Hamo and Margaret were young I was absent from home. I had missed them. I smiled. Jack was right, there *was* a future after I ceased to be an archer.

I had forced my men to move at the pace of merchants and their servants rather than the fit warriors they were. We stopped frequently, for I did not know who was watching. When we reached Laurieston it was late afternoon and I sought accommodation. As it was a crossroads for a north to south and east to west road, I had expected to be able to pay for a bed for the night. There was neither inn nor abbey, but we found a farmer who had an outbuilding and for the exorbitant fee of five copper pennies he let us stay in a draughty barn. For a further five pennies, his wife watered down their evening stew and gave us some. I suspected that the farmer was in league with the bandits.

The thought neither surprised nor offended me. If I was in the same position and could not fight back, then I might well acquiesce. On the road, I had impressed upon the men and Jack that we had to play a part and unless we were on the road in the middle of nowhere, we would speak about matters unrelated to hunting bandits. I had arranged a rota so that the night was divided into five and Jack and I took the middle watch. I had thought it too soon for the bandits to risk an attack, but we watched anyway. We had a disturbed night's sleep – but that was better than waking to find men with slit throats.

I wore my sword, for I had realised that as the merchant I would have wanted some sign of my status. The others had weapons that they could draw quickly.

We adopted a defensive formation as we left the village. Jack and I led, and we walked with the horses protecting us from arrows. The others emulated us. It might cost us a horse, but we could get more animals. The first two miles were relatively easy, for the land on both sides of the road was farmed and there was no place we could be ambushed.

Then we came to the first loch; it was a small one with farmed land to our right and the water to our left. Three miles later, I spied the forest encroaching on the road. The loch was on our right and the forest almost came to touch it. I glanced left without making it obvious that I was looking for bandits. The trees were less than thirty paces from us and even a Scottish hunting bow could not have missed us. I saw nothing but when my horse neighed, I knew that there was danger of some description.

I sniffed the air and smelled man. Someone had emptied their bowels close by. Of course, it could have been a traveller – but as none had passed us going south and we were the first to leave the village, I deemed it unlikely.

The attack, when it came, was in the form of a single arrow which slammed into the saddle of my horse. The archer in me told me that while it was a well-aimed strike it was a poorly-made arrow. If it had been a better arrow, then it would have penetrated the saddle and pricked my horse. A Scottish voice shouted, "That was a warning! We could easily kill you and your wee beasties if we had a mind!"

"We are just merchants. Give us the road!"

He laughed. "This is not the king's highway, for we have no king and we rule here. You pass by our say so and we have a tax which you need to pay. The spices you carry will cover it. Now stand still while we approach and remember, there are others who watch you!"

His words confirmed that the ferryman or his men were the spies, for none other knew that we had spices. We could close that rat hole when we had finished with the ambushers. I said quietly, "Be prepared to grab your swords but let us give Hamo and the archers the opportunity to spring our trap."

The head of Jack's horse hid the drawing of my sword and I watched seven men leave the trees. They wore hide and leather. Each carried a weapon; three had swords while two had axes and the last two had spears. They were the long ones favoured by Scottish warriors and confirmed that these men were deserters or had fought in the wars.

"If you take our spices, then we will be penniless!" I tried to make my voice sound pleading.

The man who led spoke again. "Are your lives not worth more than some spices?"

I heard a whistle from behind the approaching men. It was the signal from Hamo. Our men were in position. Two of the bandits looked behind them.

"Ready!" I dropped my horse's reins and stepped out with my sword in one hand and a dagger in the other. "Without our spices we have no lives. We will fight you for them!"

The leading Scot ran at me as an arrow came from the trees. When it slammed into the back of the man at the rear of the seven, I knew it was one of my archers. The leader was oblivious to the fact that his men were falling; he was intent upon skewering me. The humour in his voice had been replaced by anger on his face. He thought he faced a merchant, and he was careless. As another of our attackers was felled by an arrow, I blocked the Scot's sword with mine and then slashed the tendons on his right arm with my dagger. The sword fell and he stared uncomprehendingly at me. I pulled back my right hand and smashed the pommel into his face. The light went from his eyes and he fell to the ground.

"Jack, watch him!" I turned to see if the others needed help, but they did not; their opponents lay dead or dying. "Gwillim, stay with Jack and bind the wound on the prisoner. Make sure he cannot escape. The rest of you, with me!"

I saw Gwillim kneel and hamstring the left leg of the Scot. He would not be able to run!

I had heard little from the trees but as I approached, I began to see bodies. All had an arrow sticking from them. Hamo loomed up from behind a tree, grinning. "You have a prisoner, father?"

I looked at the dead bodies and shook my head. "I do, and it is good that I, at least, remembered my orders."

"We tried to wound them, but when Peter was hit by an arrow in the leg, I decided that we needed whole archers. There are fourteen dead men here."

I realised he was right. "Take the bodies to the loch. Remove anything of value and recover every arrow. We will dispose of the dead in the loch and cover them with stones. This Wallace will discover that his men will not return, but by then we will be back at Castledykes.

We could be back at the castle within a couple of hours, for now we could ride as warriors and not trudge as merchants, but I made a point of stopping in Laurieston. All my archers rode behind me. The farmer who had accommodated us came out, as did others. I said, loudly and to no one in particular, "To those of you who support the bandits in the forest – know this. Their days are numbered, and I will hang any who give them succour!" I then pricked my horse to go closer to the farmer. "And if I find that you warned them, then we will warm your feet a little before we do so!" The man paled and fell back.

As we rode the eight miles to Castledykes, Hamo said, "Why warn them?"

"To put fear into their hearts. By killing their men and making their bodies disappear we put doubt in their minds, and if they think we do not care if they know then they may believe there are more of us." He nodded. "I want you and some of your men to cross the river at the ford you used. I intend to arrest the ferryman and his spies."

We parted two miles from the ferry, and I sent four men to hail it in case they were on the other shore. We arrived as the ferry was halfway across the river. I must have a memorable face, for the ferryman stopped and tried to head back. Six nocked arrows made him reconsider his decision and he came across for us.

When he reached us, I dismounted and strode aboard. He tried to brazen it out. "Back so soon? Was there a problem?"

I laughed. "You have wit, I will grant you that. Enjoy this last voyage on your ferry – for it *will* be your last." He saw the wounded Scot, draped over a saddle, brought on board and his face paled.

Leaving my men to ferry the rest of our archers across, I went back to the castle. Alan d'Aubigny stood with mouth agape as we entered. I saw Alfred nodding approvingly.

"Here are four men to be tried, constable. In lieu of a sheriff, I shall be the judge. The trial will be tomorrow. I hope you have enough ropes. Alfred, take these three to the cells and have your healer look at this man's arm. It would not do to cheat the hangman."

The Scot had recovered sufficiently to be defiant. "I will tell you nothing, Englishman! Hang me and be damned."

"The hanging will be a legal punishment. The torture we will employ will extract the information." I waved at the outer bailey. "Make the most of this daylight. It is the last you will see."

That evening as we ate, I told the constable what we had learned. "If I was on a mission from King Edward then I would be writing to the king. I will tell Earl Thomas what has happened when all is over."

"You will use torture?"

"And what do you think the captives are enduring, if not torture? I will do all that I can to save the captives and avoid any of my men dying. If that means torture, then so be it. These men chose the life they live. There are jobs for soldiers. I was a bow for hire and when I had no work, I went out to seek it. You cannot be soft on folk like this. They live their life by excuses."

Before I retired, I spoke with Gwillim and the other three scouts I considered my best and gave them a task. "You have as many days as you need, but if you will take longer than a week then send a message back to me. If you do not find what we seek then do not worry, for that eliminates somewhere we have to search later on."

As I lay in my bed that night, I prayed that the weaker elements would leave the forest. The numbers we faced would be too great for my archers. My best scouts would swing the odds in my favour, but I knew that there would be a conflict and that it would be a bloody one. I doubted that any would remember it except those who fought in the forests of Galloway but that was the way of the world. The two easiest fights I had enjoyed had been Maes Moydog and Dunbar; there were many nameless others that no one would remember, even in my lifetime.

The next day, before I began work on the Scottish bandit we had taken, I spoke with the three ferrymen. I did so in a dark cellar used for sorting meat, and I had Alfred and Alan d'Aubigny with me. The main reason was to show the young constable what he needed to do in future.

I spoke with the older man first and the intimidating darkened cellar had the effect I wanted. I kept my sword and dagger on the table between us and I made my voice as threatening as I could.

"When we left your ferry you sent one of your ferrymen to ride north. Where did he go?"

Some men can lie easily and in an instant. I am one such man, but the ferryman was not. I saw his face as he tried to come up with a legitimate reason. The man was a fool and could have come up with a believable story during his night of incarceration.

"Do not try to come up with a lie! All that I learn here will be used at your trials. If there is any hope for you and the other two ferrymen to avoid the rope, then honesty is the only way you can save your lives."

"They are my sons!" I said nothing, but my eyes bored into his. He nodded. "The ferry does not pay as well as we would like, and we were offered money to pass the information on for men taking the road to Ayr or Dumfries. The men who offered us money loaned us a pony so that we could take the message."

"Where to?"

"The last house in Laurieston. We pass on the information and the man gives us a shilling."

We had exactly the same information from the other two, which confirmed the veracity of the ferryman's words.

"So he can go free?"

Alfred gave the constable a look of disgust and I shook my head.

"The three must be punished. It is not about them; it is about others. They must see that they either support you and the garrison or they will be punished. Alfred, fetch the Scottish prisoner and Hamo, my son." After he left us, I said, "If you have no stomach for this …"

In the dim light of the cellar, Alan d'Aubigny had already looked pale, but now he looked like a spectre. He shook his head. "I will stay, for I now see that I am isolated in a sea of enemies."

I felt sorry for the young man; he came from a noble family and he must have seen this promotion as an opportunity to make his name and win his spurs. Now he realised that it was not as simple as that.

Hamo and Alfred brought in the prisoner. His right arm was freshly bandaged but when they secured his arms behind him to the chair they were not gentle and they hurt him. His eyes glared defiance and I knew that we would get nothing from him. His already gritted teeth told me that he would endure any pain and not reveal information that would hurt his comrades. I decided to use a different approach.

Leaning back in my chair I said, "What is your name?" His eyes narrowed as he sought the trick in my words. "Come, what can it hurt and I cannot just keep saying 'you'. Besides, when you are hanged and we bury the body it will need a name for the marker so that, if you have family, they can mourn your loss."

His face cracked a little. He had a family. No doubt there was a mother or wife, perhaps a sister. Whoever it was he nodded. "Angus Diarmaid." He said it with a finality that suggested I would get no more from him.

I had spoken at length to Sir Godfrey before setting off and now knew more about the politics of Scotland. The man was a highlander. His heavy accent betrayed him, as did his name. "You are a long way from your home." He gave me a sharp look. "You are a Campbell?"

Clan pride got the better of him and he nodded.

"Tell me, what is a Campbell doing fighting for a bandit like Wallace? He is not even a knight!"

I had deduced that the bandit leader must have some sort of hold over both the bandits and the people he controlled. My insult sparked an instant response.

"He is a better man than you will ever be, and he is far cleverer than a jumped-up bowman! He plans well and you will never find him. It will take an army to oust him from our forest. There we rule and we are like the will of the wisp! We know where to hide and where to shelter! You will search but wherever you search we will not be there! Do your worst! Torture me, for I care not. I will not give you one piece of information!"

I watched as he leaned forward, his face determinedly set. Then I smiled and said, "On the contrary, you have given me all the information I need, and I thank you!" I saw that I had surprised all except Hamo, who merely smiled.

"Take him back to his cell and give him food. I will try them all at noon for tomorrow I go to find Wallace!"

As his bonds were untied his face contorted and he screamed, "I told you nothing! You cannot find William! You are a trickster and I curse you."

Hamo's mighty fist slammed into the side of the Highlander's head and two teeth flew from it. "I will make the food porridge, for that will be easier to eat, but one more word from you and I will take your tongue. You do not need that to eat!"

I could see that I had them all intrigued, but I said nothing until we gathered in the hall to prepare for the trial. Alan d'Aubigny was the most confused. "I heard the same words as you did, my lord but I learned nothing!"

"I just filled in gaps and used my mind. It was you, Alfred, who gave me the information when I first spoke with you. It has lodged in my head. He said that they moved the captives around and the prisoner has confirmed that." I took the map and laid it on the table. "As far as I can see there are seven places where they can hold prisoners: Laurieston, Darngarroch, Castramont, Slogarie, Bennan, Tainotry and Cairnmore. Agreed?" The constable and Alan nodded. They must also have at least one, perhaps two camps in the forest."

The constable shook his head. "I still do not see!"

I smiled. "You know the story about the man trying to cross the river with the duck, the grain and the fox?" He nodded. That gives us our answer. The highlander said that Wallace was a clever man. I see a chess player who thinks several moves ahead. There will be at least one of his men in every settlement. We now know the one in Laurieston. There are nine places where he can hold prisoners. Two are in the forest and as he wishes to keep his captives healthy until he has received the ransom then we cut it down to seven. There are four families and each one must be kept separate. If we raid four of the settlements simultaneously then I believe we must find at least one of the families. The trick will be to get to them before they have a warning. Tomorrow we take out the one man we know to be a spy, and that leaves just six remaining places to which they can move their captives."

Alfred said, "That all makes sense my lord – but how do we find their forest fortress?"

"We will have that information in a few days." I saw the questions on their lips, but I shook my head. "Let us say that I have my best scouts seeking the trails they use to hunt. You told me, Alfred, that there are not as many animals to be hunted. Gwillim and the scouts will backtrack until they find their den." I stood and stretched. "And now, we eat before the trial. Hamo, take the map away and then speak to our men. We need four groups. I will lead one, you a second,

Robin a third and John, son of John, a fourth. Once we have secured Laurieston, then we can begin to search properly."

We had the local priest at the trial. He would have no say in the sentencing, but he would be able to hear the confession of those sentenced to death. I had been a judge at my own assizes many times, but the crimes I was about to hear were of a different order. The priest agreed to keep an account of the proceedings, but I knew that there would be no recriminations from any judgement I made. I had King Edward's backing. We had allowed any villager with an interest to attend. There were about twenty such people at the back of the hall.

The four accused men were brought in, closely guarded by the constable's men. I began proceedings by holding up the parchment. "I have here a writ from King Edward, now the lawful lord of Scotland. Herein I am given the powers of life and death. My word here is the law."

Angus snorted. "Aye, English law – but that will change!"

I nodded. "The court hears the statement of Angus Diarmaid of the Clan Campbell and it will be added to the charges brought. You are accused of rebelling against the rule of King Edward and of attacking peaceful travellers with a view to robbing and killing them. How do you plead?"

"I will not beg for my life. I am guilty and my only regret is that I did not kill any of you!"

"Then you are sentenced to be taken from this hall and hanged from the gates of Castledykes. The sentence will be carried out when the other judgements have been made. Remove the prisoner!" I did not want the bandit's glares to influence the other three.

"William MacDougall, Iain MacDougall, and Padraig MacDougall, you are all accused of aiding and abetting the bandits of the lands north of here. You are charged with conspiracy to rob and to murder. Do you wish to answer the charges collectively or individually?"

William MacDougall, the ferryman, spoke. "My sons and I will plead together, my lord. We are guilty of passing information to Angus of Laurieston, but we knew nothing of robbery and murder."

"What did you think would happen to the merchants?" He said nothing, but hung his head. "You may not have known for certain that they would be harmed but you knew that they would be robbed and that makes you guilty!"

The three looked up, shocked. The priest, Father James, said quietly, "My lord, they have families."

I nodded. "I know – but the travellers who were robbed, wounded, and in some cases killed had families too." I folded my hands together and closed my eyes. I knew that my judgement this time would be more important than when I sentenced the bandit to death. Opening my eyes I said, "I have decided. The three of you are guilty and you should be punished." I heard the gasp from behind me and saw the father put his arms around his sons. "The ditch of this castle is in disrepair and the three of you are sentenced to not only clear it now but also to maintain it as long as you live here in Kirkcudbright. You may continue to operate your ferry, but you must labour for at least four hours a day on the ditch."

When I had walked the walls with Alfred, I had seen that the ditch around the castle was neither wide enough nor deep enough, I was sentencing them to a year, at least, of hard labour. However, the looks of joy on their faces told me that in their eyes I had given them a pardon. There was a cheer from behind me.

Father James said, "That was well done, my lord. A true judgement of Solomon!"

I nodded. "Perhaps, but I hope that there are no further instances of treachery. If there are, then we shall need a ropewalk to keep pace with the hangings!"

Chapter 14

The next morning, I led my archers out of the castle under the swinging body of the bandit. Already birds had begun to peck at the eyes. My men glanced up, but there was no sympathy on their faces. The MacDougalls were already at work and they nodded and bowed as we left.

The constable rode with us, for I wanted the villagers to associate him with us. Until the new men promised by King Edward arrived, when we left the castle would be in danger. None of my scouts had come back, and that meant they were still in the woods looking for signs of the bandits.

Our target was Laurieston. I intended to flush out their man there. That there were men in the other villages and settlements did not help me, for they could be any of them and I had learned that there were too few English soldiers to make enemies of the villagers by punishing the innocent as well as the guilty.

As we rode into the south end of the village, we heard hooves from the north. There were few animals in the village, and I guessed it had to be the spy. "Hamo, take five men and take the spy."

When he had gone, I sent Robin with ten men on the road to the west and John with another ten on the road to the east. I told them to ride until noon and then return. They would be like the beaters on a hunt. They might not see game themselves, but they would flush it out and I wanted the bandits worried and moving. When we sought them the next day their signs, being more recent, would be clearer.

I reined in at the farm of the man with whom I had stayed and dismounted. I handed my reins to Jack. "Keep watch." I waved the constable over. "Let us see what we can learn."

The man looked nervously at me as he approached. Men had left Kirkcudbright to head north and I did not doubt that he had heard of the hanging. Such matters would race on the wind and he now knew that I had been serious. "Yes, my lord? Is there anything amiss?"

"There was a spy in the village. My men are chasing him now." The man hung his head. "You knew when last I spoke to you, and yet you said nothing!"

"My lord, I have a family and while the bandits help us with food, they are ruthless with any who betray them. Punish me if you will, but I dared not risk their wrath. Hang me if you must – at least my family will be safe."

I had a family and I understood. I nodded. "Know that before I leave this land, I will end the threat from the bandits. When that is done, you will have no excuse. You will either be loyal to the constable here – or I will return and bring with me the full wrath of King Edward."

The relief on his face was clear. "Thank you, my lord. I swear that once these parasites have gone then the whole village will obey the law."

As we walked our horses back to the centre of the village Alan d'Aubigny said, "Will he do as he says?"

I shrugged. "That depends upon two things: if I keep my word and rid the land of the bandits and if you can keep the land safe from bandits in the future."

209

He saw the enormity of his task. "I can see that I have much to learn."

"And this is not a bad place to do so. I do not think that the people here are real enemies, but you must use Alfred to find better men to serve you. Recruit local men who can act as scouts and archers for you need to know the mood of the land and the people. None should be able to pass through without your knowledge."

Just then I heard hooves and looked up. It was Hamo. A body was slung over the pony and Hamo looked unhappy. "You caught him, then?"

Hamo dismounted and shook his head. "The man was a poor horseman or perhaps he overestimated his ability. He tried to jump a hedge. There was a ditch on the other side, and he broke his neck when he fell. It was lucky that the pony was not hurt."

"It cannot be helped. Let us examine his home, for we may find clues."

When we reached the house, I saw the mistake I had made. I should have asked to see the inhabitants of every house. The farm was too big for one man and, as we searched it discovered that the fields had not been tended and the only grazing had been the pony. From the number of platters and cooking utensils we found, I guessed that this house had been used to hide the captives. I suspected they had not used it since my arrival.

I turned to the constable. "If you wish to return to Castledykes, we will stay here for the night."

"Do you not need me to help tomorrow?"

"I need you to ensure that your men know that it is you who command now – and that the defences are improved. It is not just the ditch that needs work, the fighting platform needs embrasures for the defenders and the mortar should be replaced. It is not only your home, constable, it is the king's castle in this part of the world."

"Then I will set the men to work. Alfred advised me to do as you have said but I did not listen."

He left, and we made ourselves comfortable as we awaited Robin and John. I left an archer at the crossroads to direct them to us. They arrived not long before sunset. We had food ready for them and we ate in the barn as it could accommodate all of us. John had made the tiny hamlet of Nine Mile Bar. He found no evidence of either the bandits or of the people being coerced. Robin made the River Cree and the hamlet of Spittal. He found the same. The negative news was good, for it narrowed the area we had to search. It also made sense, for to have control of such a large area the bandits would need to be better mounted than we had seen.

"We are still awaiting Gwillim's news. Tomorrow we ride in the four columns organised by Hamo. I will take Slogarie and Hamo, Bennan. Robin, you will take Darngarroch and John, Castramont. The other two we shall leave for the next day. They are further away and may cause us more of a problem. It is important that we do not alert the two villages which are furthest away. I hope to find at least two families in these settlements. The families are the priority. If the bandits escape, then so be it. We want the people recovered."

Hamo voiced the fears I knew others shared. "And if we find no one?"

"Then either I have got it completely wrong, or they are all hidden in the forest. As with today's patrols. The negative news is good news as it limits the places we need to search."

I had spoken to the locals in Laurieston and they had been more than helpful. I think they were trying to atone for the attack. From their words, I was not hopeful about Slogarie. It was a hamlet of four houses, one was a large, abandoned farm. From what the locals told me the farm had been owned by a prosperous farmer who had died. His wife carried on the farm for a year but when she died, the

211

two brothers had fought over the ownership. One had died and the other had disappeared. The farm had been abandoned since then. With that abandonment, the hamlet had waned and now only two families lived there, eking out a living in that desperately lonely place.

As I left with my men and, as far as the ford over the Water of Ken, Hamo, I felt that we would find an empty and dust-filled hall. It was shunned because people thought it haunted and cursed. They were superstitious hereabouts. If we did find nothing, then two of the other companies might have more success. This work was the strangest I had ever been given. It had taxed my mind as much as my body and we were still no nearer to finding the captives. Soon it would be November and then Christmas. If we did not find them in the next ten days, then we might be too late.

Although I did not expect to find anything, the fact that this settlement was the closest to the forest and on a small track made me send four of my men in a long loop through the forest. We dismounted half a mile from the settlement to string our bows and hang them from our cantles. Walking our horses on the grassed path meant we made little noise and when we emerged from the trees into the clearing that was Slogarie, we arrived as wraiths.

That we had approached silently was shown when the woman who was milking the goat suddenly started and almost knocked over her pail of milk. Her home was a simple hut with a byre and was not the one we sought. I saw that one was set apart and far larger than anything else in the hamlet. I saw smoke rising from the chimney then I knew that this was not a wasted journey.

I dropped my reins, grabbed my bow, and drew an arrow. Jack grabbed my reins and his. The other archers copied me as I ran to the house, which was just forty paces away. I heard a shout and men ran from the large, supposedly abandoned, building. I nocked, drew, and released in one motion. There were four of them and they were a big target. I knew that they were not captives and I was rewarded when one fell, clutching his thigh.

I kept running as I drew another arrow. In all, five men ran from the building. None were bowmen and they either had to run at us with swords or attempt to flee. Two more men suddenly galloped from the far side of the building. The archers who had followed me had also loosed arrows. One of the men on the ponies fell with an arrow in his back and the first four all lay writhing on the ground or were still. I thought the last horseman would escape, but when he was thrown from his saddle then I knew the archers I had sent through the woods had done their job.

"Cover me! William, come with me. There may be more left inside."

The house was a crumbling ruin and the shutters on the wind holes were still closed as I passed them. I realised that if they were opened they would simply fall apart, for the wood was rotten. The fleeing bandits had hurled the front door open and it hung from one leather hinge. Detritus and dirt had blown in from the forest and it was dark and Stygian.

"William of Ware, keep an arrow nocked."

"Aye, captain." His brother, Edward, also followed me as I entered the hall. I could understand why people shunned it, for the hairs on the back of my neck prickled.

I heard whimpering and it sounded as though it came from a room to my left. I edged along the narrow hallway aware of the smell of damp and urine. I saw a glow from the door to my left and assumed that there was a candle burning, as I could now smell tallow.

When I stepped into the room, a grim sight met me. A grey-haired lady with two whimpering children clinging to her legs had a knife held at her throat. The bandit who held her was a head taller than she was. He growled, "Back off and give me a horse, Captain Warbow – and she lives. Come closer, and she dies."

I moved into the room but kept my body between me and the door so that William could enter unseen. I knew that Edward would watch the passage to the kitchen in case another bandit waited there.

"You know my name?"

He laughed. "When our men failed to return the captain made a point of discovering who led King Edward's hunters. Now move backwards!"

The woman, I had worked out, was Eleanor Hall, the love of Robert of Carlisle's life. She said, defiantly, "Do not worry about me, Captain Warbow. Kill him and save the grandbairns!"

"Shut up, old lady, I have had enough of your cackling! I will slit your throat and then use the bairns as a shield."

I nodded and sheathed my sword. "There is no need for that!" The man relaxed his hand a little, moving his knife marginally as he thought I had obeyed him. Stepping aside I said, "William!"

The range was less than ten feet and even in the dim light of a tallow lit room, my archer could not miss. The arrow pinned the bandit's skull to the crumbling wall of the old hall.

Eleanor Hall picked up her children and rushed to my arms. I did not want the children to see the body and so, shielding them, I stepped out into the hall and then shepherded them outside. The children were shaking, and I felt the old lady sobbing against my shoulder.

"You are safe now and you will not be hurt further."

She composed herself and looked up at me. "Thank you, captain. I know not how you found us, but I thank God that he answered my prayers."

I had many questions, but now was not the time. The three of them were in no condition to answer sensibly. Now that we were outside,

I saw that their clothes were dirty and that the three were thin. They had been badly treated.

My archers were waiting for me. I picked up the little boy and handed him to Jack. "You take the boy. It is Ralph, is it not?" The boy nodded. "Well, you go with Jack and he will protect you. William, take the girl – Eleanor?" The girl nodded. "And you, Mistress Eleanor, shall ride with me." I helped her up onto my horse's back. "The rest of you put the bodies in the hall and set fire to it. The house is cursed, and this is the best way to end the curse."

I swung my leg over my horse's back and led Jack and William back in the direction of Laurieston. The old lady gripped my waist and I heard Jack joking with the boy: "Now if I fall off you shall have to pick me up. You will need to know that my horse is called Will. He is a good horse, but he needs a firm hand. I can tell that you have a firm hand from the way you grip me."

"I have never ridden before!"

"Really? Then you are a natural horseman, and I am a lucky man!"

Eleanor Hall said, quietly, "Are all your men so thoughtful?"

"I would like to think so, for all were chosen by me. They are good archers and fierce warriors, but they are kind men."

"The man who was killed should have taken longer to die. He was an evil man and the things he did …" I felt her shudder.

"Put that from your mind now. It is ended."

We rode in silence towards the river. I heard the hooves of my men as they joined us at the same time as the smell of smoke drifted over. The old hall was on fire. The woman must have turned. "Of all the places they kept us, that was the one I hated the most."

"They moved you around?"

"Every four or five days we were taken to somewhere new. Even when we were kept in their camp in the forest it was better than that old hall, for we could see the sun and stars."

"Can you tell us how to find their camp?"

"Would that I could, but no. I only know that it took half a day to reach it from the houses. One of the houses, I think it was further west, was almost a day from their camp. The bairns' feet bled after that walk. Not that those bandits cared." She was silent for a moment. "There were others held for ransom. Will you find them?"

"I will."

"There was a young man, I did not know his name for he was not from our part of the valley, but he escaped soon after we arrived."

"It was he who told us the area to search."

"Thank God! And what happens to us?"

"Tonight we stay at Laurieston, and tomorrow we will take you to Castledykes where you will be housed and protected in the castle. When we have all those who were abducted, we will take you home."

I heard the anger in her voice as she said, "Home? What home? They burned it when they took us and there is just me and the two children. We cannot rebuild and I cannot farm. What is our future?"

The old greybeard at Carlisle came to mind and I heard his words in my head once more as we rode. "Do you remember a man called Robert of Carlisle?"

She laughed. "Aye, lord, but that was so many years ago I can barely remember his face. He was a soldier in the castle. It was his smile and kind face I remember. I can see it still." She laughed. "That is it, every time I saw him, he just smiled. Even when I was wed and we went to Carlisle and I saw him, he smiled. Why do you ask?"

"When you were young, he courted you, I believe."

"I was young then, captain, and pretty enough for all the young men of the Eden Valley to come knocking at my father's door. He was one such suitor and had he been chosen I would have been happy with the choice for he smiled and seemed kind, but my father chose Ralph Hall for he had more land. I was happy with the choice."

"Robert of Carlisle has never forgotten you, Mistress Hall, and he would offer you and the children a home."

She was silent and then said, "Are you sure?"

"When I left him at Carlisle Castle, he said he had a home and if I found you, I was to tell you he would welcome all three of you."

I felt her thin and bony arms squeeze me. "God has more than answered my prayers, Captain Warbow."

We had the shortest journey, and we were the first ones back. Jack had got on well with the boy and I left him with the two children and the grandmother while I organised some food. When I heard horses I went outside and saw that Hamo had also been successful. He and his men carried a woman and two young boys. I deduced that they had to be either the Coggleshalls or the Fosters. He dismounted and said, "I am sorry, we have no prisoners. We surprised them and they either fought hard or, in the case of two of them, tried to run."

I smiled. "Do not berate yourself. We too rescued the Hall family and there the bandits died. If either John or Robin has been successful, then our work is almost done. Fetch them within. It will do all of them good to know that half of the captives have been rescued."

It was an emotional reunion. The six of them embraced and the women wept. We kept at a discreet distance and when I heard hooves approaching from the west, Hamo and I stepped out into the setting sun. Robin and John led their men towards us. There were no captives with them.

Robin dismounted and spoke. "We found where captives had been held, Captain Warbow, and both John and I questioned the other villagers. They eventually confessed that they knew what the brigands were up to but had been unable to do anything. They did tell us, in an attempt to ingratiate themselves, that none had been near the two empty dwellings for a week. Perhaps we should return to watch the two houses in case they do return."

I shook my head. "We now have two families secured. I would see them safe at Castledykes. You can both send men to watch the two houses, but I do not believe that they will use them again. I think they know of our presence and are changing how they work. Our plans have succeeded, perhaps too well. I thought to worry them and they appear to have withdrawn to the forest fortress." I looked northwest. "I am becoming concerned about Gwillim and the scouts. They should have returned by now."

Robin laughed. "Those are the best scouts we have, captain, the Scots will not find them unless they wish to be found."

We re-entered the hall and Mistress Eleanor said, "My lord, why did you not tell me that you were a knight? I would have been more deferential!"

I laughed. "It is a title and nothing more. My men will tell you that it means little to me and I am still Gerald Warbow."

I saw that the food was being brought in by my men. They gave the steaming, wooden bowls to the captives first and allowed them the seats around the table. We stood. We ate standing up and I allowed the two women to satiate their appetites before I spoke.

"The other families are alive?"

The two looked at each other. Mistress Eleanor spoke, "Margaret and I were just speaking of that. Mary Foster was not well. She tried to escape, it appears, and was badly beaten. We have not seen Matilda for some time."

I was curious. "How did this work? The movement and housing, I mean."

Margaret was the younger of the two and she spoke for the first time. "It was well organised, almost as though it had been prescribed and written down. When we were first brought from the Eden Valley, we were all gathered together in their camp. It is well defended with watchers in the trees and traps for the unwary. There is a rock upon which they keep guards the whole time. They see everything. We were only there for two days and then we were separated and escorted. We would be placed in a house with half a dozen guards for four or five days and then a messenger would arrive with different guards and we would march to another house, or, once in our case, back to the forest."

"And how were you treated?"

"Like slaves!" Mistress Eleanor was bitter. "Some of the men would touch and fondle the girls and the women. If their leader, William Wallace, was close by then the men who did so were punished – but more often than not he was away. Sometimes he would be away for a week."

I nodded. "He would be riding to Glasgow to see if the ransom had been delivered." I wondered how long the Anglophile Bishop Wishart could maintain the deception that the ransom was coming. "Tomorrow we will take you to a place of safety, and then my men and I will try to rescue the last two families."

Mistress Eleanor said, "Be careful, Sir Gerald. These are evil men. They killed many when they came to our valley and those I saw you slay were the first that they lost."

"Do not worry, Mistress Eleanor, when we enter the rat hole it will be the rats who will die and not the hounds hunting them!"

Chapter 15

The villagers of Laurieston stood and watched as we rode out of their village. The sight of the captives was a clear reminder of their complicity in the Scottish raids. We rode silently as we headed for Kirkcudbright, and my men formed a protective screen around the six of them. It was strange but no one spoke on that ride to the south. I think I know why; the captives were still unconvinced that they had escaped their captivity and my men were all determined that no more harm would come to them. They were vigilant all the way to Castledykes.

The constable had been forewarned by one of my riders and he did all that he could to make our arrival as pleasant as possible. There were no women in the castle and so he had hired two young girls to act as servants. As a single man, he had plenty of rooms he could use for them and he had also, thoughtfully, laid on water and baths for them to use. He had managed to give the two families a chamber each and they spent some time making themselves clean. It gave me the chance to speak with the constable.

"You have done well, Sir Gerald. The earl will be pleased."

"This has long since ceased to be something we do for the earl and we will not rest until this band of bandits is no more."

"Will you need my men?"

I shook my head. "I do not think so, but I am more hopeful now of securing most if not all the captives. You will need two more chambers and then we shall need wagons to return the families to Carlisle and the Eden Valley."

"Of course, and do you know how you will achieve this? I know you have slain many of the bandits, but they still outnumber you."

"You will learn, Constable Alan, that numbers are not always the deciding factor in such matters. I would far rather have quality!"

Despite my apparent confidence I had not yet worked out we would achieve this. My men were good but unless Gwillim had found the camp and knew how to approach it unseen, we were in trouble.

As we ate, Hamo discussed the problem with me. He had grown so much in the last few years that I now relied on his mind almost as much as mine. I had the experience, but he had the fresh mind of the young.

"Their camp must be close to water and a track."

I paused in my eating. "The water I can see, but the track?"

"The rescued captives told us that they had been taken from the houses to the camps and they did not mention it being a hard task. They are not warriors and anything which was not smooth would be remembered."

"Then I am more hopeful that Gwillim will have found the camp. He must be doing my work for me and coming up with a way of rescuing them."

Hamo nodded and I saw that the constable was observing us. This was as much about him developing as a leader. He may have followed lords and even distinguished himself in battle, but he had been put in a position of authority too soon.

Hamo said, "They will know, by now, that they have lost almost half of their captives. I think they will keep the rest close to hand where they can be closely guarded."

"You are right. In one way that helps us, for it means that we know where they will be but it also means they can make it harder for us. We could use night's cloak to aid us."

"We could, father, but that would negate our greatest weapon, the bow."

This was speculation and we could do nothing until Gwillim returned – but I needed a rough plan. "Then we use two methods. We have some who will get close to the prisoners while darkness hides us, and the rest prepare to attack at dawn."

Hamo became excited. "And if the advance party eliminated the sentries who are there, then the rest would be asleep and easier to take."

For the first time, Alan d'Aubigny spoke. "Kill men without warning?"

I gave him a long stare. "Constable, the moment these bandits raided and took the captives they put themselves outside the law. All civilised rules end when a man becomes an outlaw. Not all outlaws are bad men. I was once an outlaw – but when an outlaw becomes a bandit and a brigand, then he cannot expect to be treated like everyone else. He must be hunted and punished."

The constable stared at me. "*You* were an outlaw? But you are King Edward's archer!"

"And the king knows what I did and pardoned me."

"What did you do?"

"Killed the knight who had my father killed."

I saw his mouth open as though to ask another question, but Hamo gave a slight shake of his head and the constable stopped. "Will you try to take prisoners? I only ask because I would need to house them."

"I would like to take this Wallace. I do not think he is, necessarily, a bad man. From what Mistress Hall told me, he tried to stop his men from the worst privations but if he was a better leader then he would not have sheltered such men. A leader is only as good as the men he leads."

The next day we headed back to Laurieston. Until we rescued the rest, that would be our home. We took supplies and spare ponies.

The men we had left there had not seen any sign of Gwillim; but that night, Gwillim, Dick and Mordaf rode in. That they managed to do so without alerting our sentries was a testament to their skill, rather than laxity on the part of the watching archers. Of course, there would be badinage about the event and the luckless sentries would be mocked by my men – but that was always the way with warriors, and I would not have it any other way.

We had a stew cooking and Gwillim sniffed the air appreciatively. I knew they would have eaten cold rations since they had left and I said, "Eat first and then talk. Half an hour cannot harm us."

Gwillim took his bowl out and ladled some of the steaming stew into it. "I would not be too sure, captain." He sat and broke off some bread which he dunked into the bowl. "The last two days saw the camp stirred as though the fox was in the henhouse."

"Then you have found the camp?"

He had bitten off some of the stew-soaked bread and he nodded. Mordaf said, "We found it quickly, captain. There are trails through the forest which act as roads. The bandits keep a good watch on them but we moved through the empty forest and tracked the trails. It is a large camp by one of the lakes. It is not a big one, but it is protected on one side by the forest as well as a loch and on the other by a rocky crag where they can keep watch. It is six or so miles west of Bennan."

While Mordaf had been speaking, Gwillim had emptied one bowl of food and was ladling a second. "If you are going to rescue the two families, then the four men who watch from the crag will need to be silenced."

"Two families?"

Gwillim smiled. "We know that you rescued two because men who had been guarding them came to tell their leader."

"Wallace?"

"You cannot miss him, captain. He is a huge man and he *leads* his men. You know what I mean?"

I nodded. There were leaders who were there because someone had appointed them. Wallace led them because he was a natural leader, and they did as he commanded."

Dick had finished his food and he poured himself some ale; we had brought a barrel from the castle. "There was one family already in the camp and yesterday they brought the other. That was when we decided to return."

"How many are there, Dick?"

"We saw seven. There was a mother with a son and two daughters and the family which returned yesterday had a young woman and two boys."

"Not an older woman?"

"No, captain."

I turned to Hamo. "Then Mistress Foster must have died. Mistress Eleanor thought that she was unwell."

I poured myself some ale and allowed my men to finish the rest of their meal. I needed to think, and staring into the flickering flames of a fire helped me, especially when I was drinking ale.

Hamo continued to speak with the scouts. "How many bandits remain?"

Gwillim rubbed his chin. "Fewer than when we found them first. There were arguments and blood was shed. Wallace slew two of his own men with his long sword. I do not think it is a harmonious camp. Wallace looks to have a dozen or so close to him. It is an old-fashioned word these days, but I would call them oathsworn. They look to be real warriors. The two who were slain were part of the ones I would call real bandits. We were able to get close enough to hear them speak sometimes. Wallace does not like being in the forest, for he has a wife, far to the north – but he needs the ransom. That was the reason for the fight. The two he slew wanted to send the head of one of the captives to Bishop Wishart to encourage him to send the ransom. Wallace still believes that it is coming but when the two families were retaken then it upset everything. We hurried back because Wallace is planning to move."

I turned from the fire. "Where to?"

"I think, captain, to a place called Cumnock. It is closer to Glasgow and from what we heard, just as heavily forested."

"Then we need to strike quickly. How many men, exactly, do we face?"

"There are between ninety and a hundred of them. Wallace and his oathsworn are the better warriors. There are another twenty who look handy in a fight, but the majority would run if they were faced by heavy horses."

"And where are the prisoners kept?"

Gwillim wiped the froth from his mouth. "They are in the centre of the camp. The bandits have made a shelter. It was used by just one family but now both families are crammed within. They have a door which they bar at night and four men watch it day and night."

"Is it close to the fire?"

Shaking his head, Gwillim said, "No. It is closer to the crag where the sentries watch."

"And Wallace?"

"He and his oathsworn have their horses nearer to the captives and the crag than the fire."

That gave me all the information that I needed, and I nodded. "Hamo and I have spoken of this. We need to have a small group of men who will eliminate the sentries on the crag and then be ready to take out the four guards when dawn breaks. The rest of the company will attack as one when the sun begins to rise. I have seen at first hand what the bandits will do when they are cornered. Had William not been so quick with his bow, then Mistress Hall might be dead. I will take Mordaf, William, Harry, and Ralph. Jack will come with us, not to use his knife, but to take messages to Hamo if things go awry. Hamo, you, Robin and John will follow Gwillim to take our archers to the best place you can where you can kill as many bandits as possible. I will wait until your arrows begin to fall before I attack the guards."

Hamo frowned. "You have four men to attack four guards. Why not take more men?"

"Because I trust the ones I am taking, and you will need as many arrows to fall as you can. If Gwillim is right, then when the good warriors fall then the weaker ones will flee. We can hunt those who flee later, but we need to break their spirits first!" I waved Gwillim over. "I will have Mordaf with me, but I want you and Dick to tell the others the route you will be taking. The two of you will guide the men in. Hamo, you will need to tether the horses and leave two archers with them. The last thing we need is for fleeing bandits to steal them and make our task impossible."

Gwillim said, "They have six horses, Captain Warbow, and they are good ones. They are tethered close by Wallace's dwelling."

"Dwelling?"

"Aye, they have constructed a place for each of them to sleep. I would call them a hovel, but they are of sturdier construction. They have planned for the winter."

While Gwillim and Dick told the rest of the archers what to expect, I sat with the men I would take.

"Mordaf, what can we expect?"

"Wallace has chosen his campsite well. The craggy hillock is not particularly high, but it affords a good view across the whole campsite. You cannot get to it from the camp, for the rocks are too steep. We would approach from the north. The loch prevents an approach from the west and the track comes into the camp from the east." He looked at me. "Captain, I can see how we would get rid of the sentries, there were just three of them when we were there, but the sentries on the captives might notice that they are missing."

"We prop the bodies up as though they are still alive. How close are the sentries to the captives?"

The sentry post is forty feet higher than the main camp and is about forty paces from the captives' hut. Wallace's dwelling is another twenty paces from the captives."

"And the four sentries around the captives are vigilant?"

"In the main, aye. We saw Wallace beat a sleeping sentry with his fists so there are lapses but few of them."

"Then you and William will need your bows. I know that they will encumber you, but that cannot be helped. I am confident that the rest of the company will succeed, but if Wallace is so close to the captives then we cannot risk their removal from the camp and if he has horses then he can do so."

"Why not take the horses?"

The others smiled at Jack and I shook my head. "If they are tethered close to their leader and they are good horses, then they will have been trained to make a noise and to alert the camp. It is tempting, Jack, but too great a risk."

He nodded. "Why are you taking me, captain? I am not yet an

experienced archer and I doubt that my sword would avail you much help."

"You showed at Slogarie that you are good with children. There are at least three such in the camp and they will need someone to watch over them. That is why I will take you. I can trust you and know that you will do all that is necessary without me having to worry."

We left early the next morning. I had decided that all my men would approach from the north. If Wallace chose to bolt before we arrived, we would be in place to stop him. Of course, if he did then it would be likely that not only would I lose more men, but also there would be a risk that we might lose captives.

Our task was almost impossible. We had to eliminate the bandits whilst saving the captives. There was another reason, too. Wallace now knew of our existence and he would be watching the south of his domain. There was less chance of us being seen, approaching from the north.

We headed for Slogarie on a damp and misty day. The grey skies foretold rain and we were already chilled by the time we passed the tiny hamlet. The burned-out hall was no longer smoking, and its charred remains would soon be reclaimed by the grass, weeds, and shrubs. I doubted that the other two families would stay much longer. I guessed that the bandits had helped them out. As we followed the Dee north and west, I wondered if there would be any sign, ten years from now, that there had been a settlement. As the crow flies, we had fewer than six miles to go but following the river and avoiding the road made it nearer to ten, and it would feel like twenty. For part of the time, we rode in the river. It did not come to our boots, but we all felt the cold rising through our bones. The misty, now drizzly day helped us, for it largely hid us. Deer skittered out of the way as we came upon them. My three scouts were within sight, but they were spread out like an arrow and would be the first to see any enemy.

By the time it was noon we had reached the crude road which ran north to south. It was not Roman and had no stones upon its surface but the dried dung told us that it was a thoroughfare and we hurried across it. The men at the rear picked up the dung dropped by our horses and would dump it in the forest through which we passed. I reflected that the ancient Britons would have seen the same forest that we did. The only sign of man's hand was the grassy track and I guessed even that had been here then.

Gwillim, Mordaf, and Dick all halted at the same place and rode back to us. Gwillim pointed to the ground. "We have seen no fresh tracks. The bandits are still in the camp. This is where we must part."

I nodded and turned to Hamo. "You now command. If disaster strikes, then Jack will find you."

Gwillim pointed south and west. "If you head south and west you will find us where the craggy section starts. If you reach the road, then you have gone too far."

I saw Jack nod nervously and I smiled. "We are planning for the worst and I pray that we are skilled enough at what we do so that we will emerge triumphantly! God speed!"

My men nodded and Hamo clasped my arm. "Take care, father. I do not want to risk the wrath of my mother by taking your body back to Yarpole!"

"Amen to that!"

Chapter 16

We did not remount our horses and we walked them, following Mordaf through the trees. The ground was steadily rising but Mordaf picked his way unerringly along what seemed to me like an invisible path. However, as we all managed it easily, I knew that Mordaf and my other scouts had chosen the best way. He raised his hand and we all stopped. He mimed for us to tether our horses and we did so. The reins were long enough for the horses to graze on the long grass around the base of the trees. Neither Mordaf nor William had their bows. When night came, they would retrieve them, but now we needed to be hidden. Our green, oiled cloaks were useful at keeping out the cold and the west but on a misty murky day such as this, they were also a form of camouflage.

He led us to the edge of the trees, and I saw that whilst the trees had stopped there was undergrowth and weedy shrubs growing for another forty or so paces. The stone was so close to the surface that we saw outcrops of it. Fifty paces away was bare rock. Mordaf waved for us to sit behind the larger trees. We could still see the edge of the rocks, but not the sentry post. I saw smoke rising from the campfires the bandits were using. We did as Mordaf had commanded, and he took out food and began to eat. It was dried venison coated in honey – Mordaf would happily have lived off it. Back at Yarpole, he had a beehive just to supply himself with honey. I was not in the mood for food, but the others all ate.

Noon had long passed, and I knew that Mordaf was waiting for dusk so that we could spy out the sentries while there was still a little light. My scout had chosen his spot well for we were to the east of the camp and when darkness began to descend, he raised his arm and we crawled from the trees. For a man of my age, it was uncomfortable, not to say painful. While we had been sheltered in the trees the drizzle had turned to heavier rainfall and the slick ground did not help my movements. I stayed behind Mordaf until he stopped and laid flat. I did the same and then pulled myself level with him.

I saw the camp – or at least the western side of the camp. I saw smaller fires, but the smoke appeared heavier in the centre, suggesting a larger fire. I also smelled burning, which was closer to us. He began to edge nearer to the camp and, keeping just behind him, I did the same. He pulled the hood on his cloak so that it touched the ground. I copied him and then moved. We did it so slowly that it seemed to take an age, but eventually we spied, ten feet below us and thirty paces away, the fire with the three Scottish bandits. I also saw the large fire in the centre of the camp. I worked out that if we came at night, we would be able to almost walk to the edge and still remain unseen. I glanced left and right. The ground fell away. Mordaf had done well to choose this high spot. In the darkening gloom, I saw that we could make our way down the side of the rock to the sentry post.

I turned my attention to the three men. They had their backs to us; they had a good view of the whole camp for the only things I could not see were the captives' shelter and Wallace's dwelling. When I heard a horse neigh below us then I knew that they were close. The three men had cloaks about them, and I could see no sign of a shelter.

The weapons they had appeared to be daggers, a spear, an axe and a sword. Food was cooking on a pot suspended over the fire. Gwillim had told me that when they had studied the sentries, they learned that they were changed at noon each day and spent the whole time there until the next watch came. It told me much about Wallace and his organisation. He had a military mind.

Even as we watched, the sun dropped below the horizon and had the sentries not been enjoying a fire we would have been plunged into darkness. If we avoided looking at the fire when we took out the sentries, then they would be night blind and we would not. Life or death depends on such matters. I nodded and began to back away. We moved like that for twenty feet and when I stood all that I saw before me was the darkness of the trees. When we had accustomed our eyes to the darkness, we headed back to our horses.

We unsaddled them, gave them water and some oats before tethering them. We ate and this time I joined my men in eating. I did not need to, but I knew that if I did not my body would complain in the hours of darkness. A rumbling gut would be heard, and we could not afford that. The rain was now bouncing down although the canopy of leaves kept us drier than the sentries on the bare crag side. It also allowed us to talk.

"The path to the left is the easier one, captain."

I nodded. "Jack, you will bring up the rear. Mordaf, you and William and I will dispatch the sentries and Harry, you will ensure that we do so. I will take the one in the centre. Mordaf, the one on the left." He nodded. I had been in these situations before. I hoped that I would be able to slice with my dagger across the throat of one of the sentries, but we were all going to act simultaneously. We could not plan for an arm flailing and putting one of us off his stroke. Harry would ensure that any who did not die instantly would be finished off.

232

We sat in silence and waited. There was little point in going too early as there might be watchers, but we had to be close to the captives' dwelling and hidden well before dawn. It was the slight easing of the rain which made my decision for me. The sound of the rain would muffle our movements and we needed to move before it stopped completely. I rose and nodded. Sliding out my honed knife I moved towards the left side of the rocks. Mordaf hurried ahead of me to lead the way and William followed. The clouds meant that there was no moon, but our eyes were now used to the dark. Mordaf skilfully plotted his way towards the hidden route down the rocks and I just followed his footsteps. Our path meant we appeared to be going away from the three men, but then Mordaf turned as the slippery rocks flattened out and he began to head towards what I could now see was the glow of a fire. The fire in the main camp was smaller now. Men would stay in shelter rather than feed the flames.

I stepped next to Mordaf and I felt William ghost up close to me. At least two of the sentries were still awake – I heard them talking. The one in the centre threw another piece of firewood on to the fire. I saw that he took it from beneath his cloak. He was a veteran woodsman! His movements allowed me to see him more clearly. The three of us kept the same pace.

It was as I reached down to grab the sentry's head that one of them turned. I had not heard a sound and so I assumed that he had smelled us. I pulled the sentry's head back and slashed the blade across his throat; the blood hissed as it struck the fire. Although Mordaf's man had turned, he died as quickly as mine. William's, too, was dead in a flash. The three men had swords and we pulled them from their belts and then rammed them through their belts and into the rock beneath. There were enough cracks to allow that, although it would ruin the blade. It ensured that each body would remain seated. Soon the bodies would stiffen, and the swords merely ensured that the three bodies looked alive.

We had no time to waste. I placed another of the pieces of dried kindling on the fire and then followed Mordaf towards the main camp. The rain was easing more and soon it would cease. We had to be in the camp before then. As soon as it stopped, then men would begin to move if only to make water! The path we followed was easier to navigate because it was well-trodden, having been used by the sentries. As we neared the camp then we could both smell and hear. There had appeared to be silence from the craggy outcrop but now we heard the snores, flatulence and hiss of water on flames.

The path brought us out just thirty paces from the captives' shelter. I could not see the four sentries, but I knew they would be there, sheltering from the rain. It gave us the opportunity to find shelter ourselves – not from the elements but from the prying eyes of sentries. We found some elder trees and bramble bushes, which were close to the rock wall behind the dwellings. A few berries hung from both of them and as they were behind the captive's shelter then we would be hidden.

We had barely managed to secrete ourselves when one of the sentries rose from beneath the overhanging logs of the roof of the shelter. I heard him say something and a second guard rose, laughing. We were just twenty paces from them but we were behind them and hidden. Our part of the plan had gone as well as it could and now, we waited.

I heard the horses which were to our right but we were far enough away that I knew they had not smelled us. I saw men walking to the fire to feed it. It became clear that the camp was waking but it was not yet dawn. I frowned. There was more movement than we had anticipated. I had counted on killing the ones who were awake and then slaying men who had just awoken. When one of the horses was led close to the fire and saddled then I knew what this meant; the brigands were moving. They were heading north. Our plan might still succeed but there was now a very real danger that some of the enemy might escape and that I would lose some of my men. The latter worried me more than the former. I could do nothing, and was reliant upon Hamo to make the right decision.

The rain had ceased, but the clouds still remained and would delay the dawn. When I saw men putting a cooking pot close to the fire, I knew that although the camp would be awake they would not be leaving before the sun rose. Wallace was a good leader, and he was feeding his men before they left. Gwillim had told me that as well as sentries on the crag, there were two other groups of watchers. They were placed at the ends of the two tracks which passed through the camp. Hamo would have men eliminating the sentries close to him but if the camp was breaking then they might be relieved to be fed. My carefully made plans were unravelling and when I heard the door of the captives' dwelling unbarred and then opened, they appeared to be in tatters – for the women were brought out and headed directly for us. When the boy captives made water close to the dwelling, then I knew what was going to happen. The four females were also going to make water.

I watched the older woman – I took it to be Mistress Wilson – with her arms around her daughters. The young woman, Alice Foster, was slightly ahead of them. This must have been a regular event, for the sentries did not watch them but stood with their backs to them affording some privacy. The young woman kept coming. She was heading directly for me while the other three were to my left. I saw her lift her skirt and squat; I prayed that she would not look up. She was just eight feet from me, and she could not fail to see me if her head came up. She finished and I was just breathing a sigh of relief when her head jerked up and her eyes met mine. I put my finger to my lips, and I smiled. I watched her mouth open and then close. She nodded.

Turning, she said – I think for my benefit – "Mistress Matilda, I think we had better bind the children's feet, for today we have a long walk ahead of us."

Mistress Wilson had finished and said, "Aye, when will our ordeal end? Why could we not have been rescued like Eleanor and Margaret?"

The young woman said, "I pray to God that he will send someone to our aid."

One of the sentries turned as they spoke. He laughed. "That will not happen! The men they sent will come and find an empty camp and the next time they seek us we shall be waiting – for we have friends to avenge!" They headed back to the other side of their dwelling.

Now that attention had been moved from the rear of the captives' dwelling, I tapped Mordaf on the shoulder and nodded to our left. It was time to move from our vantage point and find somewhere we could be ready to strike. It was obvious to me that we should hide between our present hiding place and the back of the wooden structure. Our green cloaks and the darkness allowed us to move out from behind the bushes and scrubby trees. We were helped when someone threw a piece of resinous pine onto the fire and it suddenly flared. One of those feeding the fire leapt back screaming, and the others not only looked but also laughed at his discomfort. With everyone's attention there, we were able to move safely behind the wooden shelter.

I could now see where Wallace's horses were tethered. That was something to think about once we had the captives. As I looked in that direction, I saw a lightening of the sky. It was what men called false dawn, but I knew that soon light would rise from the east – and my son would start the attack.

The plans were going to have to be changed for, although I could not see the man, I heard a voice shout, "Iain, can you see aught in the east?"

I knew that someone was shouting up to the dead men.

"Iain, Angus, Alan, are you all asleep?"

There was no answer. I worked out that the man who was speaking was Wallace, for he shouted, "I like not this. Robbie, come with me and we will see what is happening. Rouse the camp! There is something amiss! Sound the horn!"

As the horn sounded, I drew my sword and pressed myself into the back of the wooden shelter. I tapped Mordaf and pointed to the left. He tapped Harry to join him. I gestured to William and Jack and prepared to head to the right. I had often witnessed the sound of arrows being loosed and, at Evesham, I had endured arrows coming back at me, but this was the first time I had heard the sound of arrows when all that I had was a sword in my hand. I suppose having a bowstring next to your ear affected your hearing, for the sound of my archer's arrows as they were sent towards the bandit camp was terrifying. We all knew to wait until at least three flights were sent. My men were trained to send three almost without aiming. I heard arrows thudding into wood and bodies. The sound of the arrows plunging into bodies was followed by a scream or a shout, sometimes a curse. The poor light would lessen the casualties, but men had been hurt and each wounded or dead man evened up the odds.

I said, "Now and raced around the side!" I saw my archers had already accounted for twenty men, including one of the guards. As we ran around, one who looked almost as big as Wallace had been described as whirled with a long sword in his hand. It was not a two-handed sword but a hand and a half sword. It was almost a handspan longer than mine.

Even as I drew my dagger to aid me, I heard a voice from above me shout, "Treachery! Kill the prisoners!"

I knew that it had to be Wallace and it gave urgency to our task. I could see the door to the shelter and one of the surviving guards went to open it. Jack and William were racing to get to him before he could do so. I concentrated on defeating the huge man before me. He swung his sword at my head, and I did the only thing I could, I used my own sword to deflect the blade up. I was not wearing my helmet and the strike was so close that it took the top of the hood of my cloak. I lunged with my dagger, but he was wearing a leather brigandine studded with metal. All I succeeded in doing was slashing his face.

As he swung again, I stepped back and to the side. It afforded me a view of the shelter and I saw that those within were holding the door shut. William's sword bit into the Scottish bandit's neck and Jack's was rammed up under his arm. My opponent and I danced around each other. My flashing dagger had taught him respect and I was wary of his sword. I saw that many of the bandits were heeding the orders of their leaders and moving towards us. Of course, they were also moving towards the horses and an escape route. I saw men fall to the arrows of my archers. As I blocked the next blow which came down towards my head using my sword and dagger together, I shouted, "Get the captives to Hamo!"

As sparks flew from the three colliding blades, Jack shouted, "He and the archers are coming here, captain. We can defend them better if we stay!"

I nodded. Jack had a better view than I did. I had to do something to end this conflict. Wallace would be returning soon, and I doubted that I would be able to best him.

As the Scottish warrior raised his sword, I did the unexpected and, putting my right shoulder down, ran at him. I struck him just as he began his downward swing and my shoulder hit his chest. He began to topple back. Holding my sword and dagger like a cross I fell upon him. His head rolled from his body as the two blades and my weight decapitated him. Before I could move, I heard a roar and saw the giant that was Wallace racing towards me. The sun had risen but the light was still poor, and the arrows sent at the quick-moving Scottish leader all missed. I saw that Mordaf and Harry had been wounded and the door to the shelter was guarded by William and Jack. This would be a coming of age for Jack – if he survived. When Wallace's sword came down to hack my body in two, I rolled to my right. His sword missed me but hit the body of his sentry. He pulled back the sword and I made my feet. I had to draw him away from the shelter. I could see Hamo and my men streaming across the increasingly brighter campsite. Arrows struck the bandits who were coming to obey Wallace's orders, but some were running towards Hamo and the archers. All that I had planned had been undone. Not only might we fail to rescue the captives, but there was also an ever-increasing likelihood that we might lose our lives.

I turned and ran towards the horses. Wallace thought I feared him. "Come back here you timorous coward! I thought Warbow was a worthy opponent!"

I reached the horses, which were still tethered but were now becoming agitated. I laughed. "Wallace, put a bow in my hand and you would be a dead man!" I sliced down to cut one end of the rope which held the horses.

"Get the horses!" Wallace was struggling to get at me. The slippery and slick ground did not suit the big man. As I ran to cut the other end of the tethering rope his men came to get the horses and eliminate me. A sword was thrust at my side from a lithe little bandit who had raced ahead of the others. I barely fended it off with my dagger and, aware that Wallace was closing with me, I slashed almost blindly at the bandit. The sword hit the small man in the side of the skull, and I brought up my dagger to saw through the rope. It was not easy as the horses, now thoroughly terrified, were rearing and pulling at the rope. I sensed rather than saw the two-handed sword which came down towards me and I just managed to evade it. Wallace's sword finished the job for me, and the rope was severed. As the horses, now free, tried to flee, the bandit leader had a dilemma. I could see, for the campsite was before me, that my archers were winning the battle. Wallace had a choice, escape or kill me. He chose the former.

He grabbed one end to the rope, and he hauled himself into the saddle. He was remarkably agile for a big man. Others were running to get at the horses, and I had to turn to defend myself. I do not know if Wallace was aiming at me or the rope again, but the long weapon came within a handspan of ending my career as an archer.

"We will meet again, Warbow! William Wallace does not forget!"

I had no time to answer, as I had to fight off two men. The horses were the target, and I was in the way. As one sword cut along my cheek, I gutted the bandit but the other raised his axe to finish me an arrowhead came through his body, As Wallace and the men who had gained the horses galloped off the other bandits who had sought the horses now took to their heels and raced towards the loch which lay to the north of us.

"Stop as many as you can!"

Hamo ran up to me. "You take too many risks, father!"

For once, I agreed with him. We had saved the captives and my attempt to capture Wallace was unnecessary. He was a danger, but we had broken his power in this part of the world. I should have let him go.

"We need to pursue him. You and the rest of my men need to clear the camp. I will go to speak to the captives and to thank Jack."

Hamo grinned. "Aye, the young man did remarkably well and kept his head." I nodded and, sheathing my weapons, headed back towards them.

The captives were all huddled together. They were outside the shelter but beneath the canopy of the trees. The rain had stopped but droplets of water still splashed into the puddles which had formed. The older woman, I took it to be Matilda, took my hand and kissed it. "Thank you, Sir Gerald! Your men told us what you did! We are beholden to you."

"I am just glad that we made it before we left." I nodded to the young woman. "You must be Alice." She nodded. "Thank you for not giving us away and having the wit to warn us of the departure."

She smiled and I saw that beneath the dirt, grime and lack of food, she was a bonny girl. "I have had more than enough Scottish hospitality, and I have no wish to be their neighbour again. When we return to the Eden Valley, I will take my brothers to my uncle who lives in Chester. Mayhap now that my mother is dead, he will forgive her."

Her words confirmed that Mary Foster was dead. "Forgive?"

"Her elder brother did not approve of her marriage. My mother and father eloped to the valley to make a new start."

Now I saw why at least one of the ransoms was not forthcoming. I turned to William. "You and Jack fetch our horses." They hurried off and I saw that Mordaf and Harry had been tended to, but they would be of no use to me for a while. "You two did well. Are you able to walk and ride or do you need a wagon?"

Mordaf snorted. "We can ride, captain!"

"Good – then until Hamo returns I would have you watch over these people."

"Where are you going, captain?"

241

"It may be a waste of time, but I would find this Wallace if I can. He has shown that he is capable of mischief."

Alice said, "I think he would go home to his wife. I do not think he will be a bandit once more."

I heard hooves as Jack and William returned. "I might believe you, but if I had a wife to return to, I would not have continued as a bandit here."

Matilda said, "He did not consider himself a bandit but a leader of warriors fighting the English. He tried to make these men into an army." She shook her head. "He failed, but at least he stopped his men from hurting us when he could. The ransoms were to pay for arms and equipment. They were not for him." She suddenly looked at me, as Jack and William reached us. "There were no ransoms, were there?"

"None of your families could afford them and I do not think the Earl of Lancaster was going to pay them."

She looked down. "Then we have nothing!"

I took the reins of my horse and swung up onto his back. My bow was still hanging from it, safely stored in its case and a war bag of arrows hung from it. If I met Wallace, then I could show him where my true skill lay! I saw Gwillim and Dick hurrying over to us. I shouted, "Take Mordaf's and Harry's horses. We have a bandit to find!" They slung their bows and vaulted onto the backs of the horses. "Mordaf, tell my son to head back to Laurieston and thence Castledykes. I will join you all there."

Jack said, "I found a leg of mutton, captain. We have a little food!"

I laughed. "Jack, the best thing we ever did was to give you a home. Let us ride!"

Chapter 17

There were two ways around the patch of water we later learned was called Loch Skerrow. The one which was longer but afforded more cover was the western side. The eastern side bordered the craggy land and had patches of cover. I pointed to the eastern trail. "We will take that one!" There were just five of us and, by my estimate, more than seven men had horses in addition to which there were many others afoot and ahead of us. I wondered as we saw grey rain clouds forming ahead of us if I should have left Jack behind. He had already done more than most of my archers, but he seemed like a lucky charm and over the years I had learned not to discount such things.

Suddenly Dick shouted, "Captain! I spy horsemen ahead!"

They were a mile away and had just cleared the end of the water, but I saw eight horsemen and the distinctive Wallace was one of them. We were now on their trail. This would be a test of horseflesh and horsemanship! Dick and Gwillim had their scent and would keep following no matter what the bandits did. That it would not be an easy chase was made manifestly clear when we reached the end of the loch. Some of the bandits who were on foot saw us and ran at us with an idea that they might take our horses. They were between us and the trail which Wallace had taken. My bow was in its case, but William, Gwillim and Dick had theirs. We rarely used a bow from a saddle as it was impossible to make a full draw. At Yarpole I had the Mongol bow which I could use from the back of a horse – I had shown my men how the Mongols used them and as the range was short, just forty paces, the three of them held their bows horizontally and sent three arrows into the first three bandits, who looked in shock as the fletch blossomed from their chests.

I dug my heels into my horse's flanks as I drew my sword and, as three more arrows found flesh, rode directly at the closest bandit. He turned, but it was too late, and my sword split his skull. It was too much for the others, who fled.

"We have wasted too much time! On with the chase!" We had been forced to stop and that would allow Wallace to increase his already substantial lead.

When we reached the road which led to Balmaclellan we were forced to stop again. Gwillim leapt from his horse and while Dick rode along the road to the signposted settlement, Gwillim examined the ground.

"They have gone across country! They are not heading along the road."

That showed me Wallace had a plan. He was not fleeing blindly. If he wished to simply evade us, he would use the roads where he would make greater speed. Gwillim mounted and led us north. Our pace was much slower as we did not wish to lose the signs.

It was well after noon when we spied them again. We were on the flanks of a mountain. It was not a large one, but it afforded us a good view to the north and east, despite the relatively poor visibility, we spied six riders. I wondered if something had happened to the others. Perhaps they had split off or rode ahead. Wallace was with the six ahead of us and that was all that mattered.

In the distance, I saw something which looked like a man-made structure. I guessed that they were heading there, but as we had them in our sights, we could afford to try closing with them. They might outnumber us, but we had four bows and that more than evened up the odds. Even at that range I saw their faces as they turned to look at us.

We descended the trail, which wound down the slope, and gradually the settlement and stone castle came into view. It was not a huge castle but if they reached its walls then we would have lost them.

"We must push our horses; if they make the safety of the gates, then we have failed."

Gwillim said as we spurred our horses, "Perhaps it is held by those loyal to King Edward!"

I shook my head. "The fact that he is approaching it makes me think it is an ally, but we will keep going in the hope that you are right!"

It became clear that the bandits were going to escape. We were less than half a mile behind them when they entered the castle. We crossed the River Nith, for it was just a few paces wide, and reined in. William of Ware said, "All for nothing, captain."

"Not true, William. We are tired and our horses are tired, but Wallace now knows that he has an enemy in England. He ran from us and I am guessing his pride will be dented. Let us dismount and let the animals drink."

I did not know it, but the Scottish warriors inside the castle we later learned was called Sanquhar, must have thought we were deliberately insulting them – for suddenly the gates opened and I saw Wallace leading twenty wild warriors towards us.

"Jack, hold the horses and be ready to take them across the river."

I grabbed my bow case and arrow bag. The other three had already nocked an arrow each. They loosed as soon as the first eager Scottish warriors were less than two hundred paces from us. I sent my first arrow a heartbeat later. By the time they had covered another one hundred paces, half their number had been struck. I aimed an arrow at Wallace who was now within range. He should have died, but a precocious puff of wind struck the arrow and it landed not in his chest but his thigh. He was forced to stop. I decided to finish it and I nocked another arrow but two of his men who had brought shields held them aloft and my arrow was wasted. Dick and William managed to hit both of his protectors, but the three men stayed on their feet. They began to edge back. The wounded were helped back too so that only the dead remained. We sent more arrows until they were out of range. We waited until they were back inside the castle and then mounted our horses. We rode to the dead men and retrieved not only our arrows but also their weapons. On the walls, the Scottish jeered at us.

I raised my bow as my men headed back to the river and holding it above my head I shouted, "Wallace, my arrows have tasted your blood and the next time we meet they shall drink deeply. Now you know who it is that you face: Sir Gerald Warbow! I am King Edward's man and if you are his enemy then you are mine! You have been warned!"

I turned and rode away. I heard the crack of crossbow bolts but knew that they were wasted. I was well beyond their range.

We camped that night on the slopes of the mountain where we had seen Wallace. We did not light a fire, for the leg of mutton Jack had found was cooked already and we had filled our waterskins at the river.

"Do we go home now, captain?"

"Our work is not yet done, Gwillim, and we have captives to return home. I do not relish that task. Mistress Eleanor has hope, for Robert of Carlisle will care for her and her family – but the others? They have nothing in the Eden Valley. It may be that they have neighbours who will aid them, but I doubt it."

Jack said, "Why not, captain?"

"Robert of Carlisle told us that the four families were the ones who were well off and that they were targeted by the bandits. I would like to think that they would be helped, but sometimes people are envious of those who are richer and revel in disaster when it strikes them. I pray that I am wrong, but I doubt it. Alice Foster has no wish to stay close to the Scottish border and she is our responsibility."

Jack frowned and I heard the disbelief in his voice. "Surely the Earl of Lancaster will give them succour?"

I laughed. "I do not think so. You have had little to do with those who have everything. It is a rare lord who worries about the likes of Alice and her brothers."

We headed back to Castledykes, for I knew that Hamo would have taken the captives there as soon as possible. It was a slow journey, for our horses had been pushed hard the day before. We reached it just before dark and we were weary beyond words. The only food we had eaten in two days was the leg of mutton. We had drunk beck water and our horses were almost broken.

The constable and Hamo greeted us. Sentries had spied us as we approached. "Did you get him, Sir Gerald?"

I smiled and shook my head. "He now has a wound and knows who gave it to him. He took refuge in a castle well to the north of here." I turned to Hamo. "And the captives?"

"They are pleased to be safe, but all wish to return to Carlisle as soon as they can."

The constable laughed. "I think that one of the captives wishes to travel further south than that."

I saw Hamo blush, but I was too tired and hungry to think straight. "We are desperate for food and ale."

"I am sorry, Sir Gerald, I should have thought. Come with me and we shall feed the heroes of the hour."

"Hamo, take some men and see to the horses. My men are as weary as me."

Hamo put his hand on my shoulder. "Father, you do too much. Do you not trust me? I could have followed Wallace and his men."

"I know, but while I can still draw a bow and lead my company I shall do so. Do not worry, you will soon lead this company and I shall enjoy Yarpole but until then …"

The only people dining were my men. The constable and Hamo sat with us and we told them all that had happened on the chase. "Someone will need to scour the forests north of here or others, like the four families we take back, will suffer a worse fate for Wallace will not be with them."

The constable nodded. "Sir Gerald, if I write a letter, would you see that it reaches Earl Thomas?"

"Of course, but if you do two copies then I shall ensure that King Edward receives one, too. He thinks the war here is over, but it is not!"

I could feel my eyes closing. Getting old meant I could no longer keep awake for days on end. I needed sleep. I knew I had to be sharp for the last part of the journey. Although it was not a long one, we would be passing through land which would contain those who wished us harm. Only when I reached Yarpole would I be able to relax my vigilance.

I saw that the constable was torn between the politeness of keeping me company and the need to write the letters. "Go, my friend, and write the letters. I shall soon retire, for I wish to be up early. You have been a good host, but we must get home."

He nodded and rose. "And I thank you, Sir Gerald, for the lesson in leadership. I wish that I could follow your banner just to learn from you, but I now see the enormity of my task!"

He would do. I turned to Hamo, Jack and the others were still eating but I had satiated my appetite. "Did you secure wagons?"

"Aye, William MacDougall was more than happy to let us have his two. They are not the best, but we have a cover to shelter the captives if the weather continues to be unpleasant. We have horses although they are not draught ones. I have found men amongst our archers who can drive them. It will be cosy, but the women are just grateful that they have their families safe and that only one lost her life."

I nodded and drank down the last of the ale. "Aye, it is a shame one was lost. That family is one we may have to care for. I cannot see de Brus rushing to take on the three of them."

He leaned forward, earnestly. "Alice is strong, father, and she knows her own mind. She does not wish to stay close to the border. I thought we could take the three of them to Yarpole."

Something the constable had said came to mind and I studied my son's face. "And how does she feel about travelling to somewhere she knows no one?"

He said, easily, "Oh, she knows us. We got to know each other on the journey back."

"*We?*"

He flushed. "The archers and I." He hurriedly went on. "I described the land and she seemed happy. I am sure my mother would find employment for her."

"Your mother is a kind woman, but do not make work for her. Have you told Alice about the danger from Wales?"

He looked confused. "That war is over!"

"That is what King Edward thought until Madog ap Llewelyn rose in revolt. You should tell her. You need honesty in such matters."

He tried to look innocent. "Such matters?"

I laughed. "I am tired, and it is some days to Carlisle."

"We did the journey quickly enough."

"We took the direct route and did not have wagons and women. The sixty miles will take at least two days." I rose. "I shall see you in the morning." Turning to Jack and the others I said, "You all did well and I could not have done what we did with any others." I gave a small bow. It was little enough, and it was true.

My bladder woke me well before dawn, but once awake then I could not go back to sleep. I rose and went to the kitchens where the cooks were already preparing breakfast. I took some food and went to the empty great hall.

As I ate, I pondered the journey. Once we left Carlisle, we would have two hundred miles to travel. Without Alice and her brothers then the journey would take just five days but with them ... I missed my family and I yearned to see them. Margaret would be due to give birth, if she had not done so already. I might be a grandfather and not know it.

I heard a buzz of noise and the captives came into the great hall. I suppose I should not have been surprised. They knew that we were leaving for home and they would be desperate to leave the place which had caused them all such grief. They were all still thin, but they were now clean, and the laughter from the six young children was a joy to my ears. When they saw me eating, they stopped.

"I pray you enter, ladies. I do not mind sharing the hall with you. There is food prepared in the kitchens."

It was Eleanor who smiled and spoke. "Aye, Sir Gerald, I can see that you are not one of those nobles who wishes to see only other nobles. Eleanor, Ralph, wipe a table and sit down. Maud and Ann, watch over the little ones. Do not let them bother Sir Gerald!"

The four women left and I said, "Maud, is it?" The elder of the two daughters of Matilda nodded. "Come and join me at my table.

I promise that I will not eat you." They hesitated. "Come, I would get to know you. We have a two day ride to Carlisle."

Maud nodded. "Organise yourselves on the benches, children. Ralph, do not tease your sister! You are her big brother and should watch over her!"

I smiled. I had been away when Hamo and Margaret were growing up. My wife must have had such issues. I had missed them but, perhaps, as a grandfather I might see them. Edward, Maud's brother, was the eldest boy and I saw him looking surreptitiously at my sword.

"Would you like to see the sword, Edward?"

His grin answered me, and the other five boys all leaned forward eagerly. I took the sword and scabbard from my belt and laid it on the table. "Now, leave the blade in the scabbard. It is sharp enough for me to shave with and it is not a toy." They nodded. Although a simply-made sword with a plain pommel, there was a single blue stone as the pommel stone. It was not a precious jewel, but when I had found the stone in the Holy Land it attracted my eye and on the voyage home, I had polished it so that it became bluer. The scabbard was also finely decorated. I had made the scabbard using wool and wood, but the leather cover had been decorated by Mary.

Edward's fingers touched the pommel, and it was as though he had put them in icy water. He started. "It feels alive, Sir Gerald."

"If a weapon is well made then it *is* alive. It is the same with a bow."

He nodded and moved his hands so that the others could also touch it. "I saw you fight William Wallace. Were you not afraid?"

"Afraid?"

"He had a longer sword, and he was bigger than you."

I nodded and answered him seriously. "I can see what you mean. Fear is something every warrior lives with, for no one wishes to die, but you put it to the back of your mind. Fear is a weapon that can

251

kill you. You need just enough fear that it keeps you alert, but not so much that you cannot fight. I fear no man – and certainly not Wallace." I leaned forward. "When last I met him, I showed him my skill as an archer. There is a wound in his leg which will remind him of me and the next time we fight, he may be the fearful one!"

The noise of the four women bringing in the food made me take the sword and hang it from my belt. Eleanor frowned. "I thought I said not to bother Sir Gerald."

I smiled. "I invited them, if that is all right with you, Mistress Hall?"

"Of course, I meant no harm!"

The women busied themselves dividing up the food and I waited until they were eating before I spoke. "We will leave as soon as we can. It will be a long journey, but I hope to be in Carlisle in a couple of days."

They nodded and Alice said, quietly, "Your son, Lord Hamo, said we might travel to Yarpole with you."

I saw the smiles exchanged between the other women and nodded. "If that is what you wish – but he is not a lord. Did he tell you that?"

"No, Sir Gerald, I just assumed …"

"I was like Hamo, just an ordinary archer, but Queen Eleanor chose to ask the king to knight me. I am just the same as you. I think my background was so humble that you might be surprised. Yarpole is just a simple home and we live a life uncluttered by titles. My son will inherit my title, but only when I die."

She nodded.

I said, "I know that Mistress Eleanor and her grandchildren will be cared for – but what of you Mistress Matilda, and you, Mistress Margaret?"

"We have spoken of this. We both have land and good neighbours. We shall start again. The Scots shall not drive us from our homes.

This time, when we build, we will make strong walls! Our husbands paid the price for failing to defend what we had. God rest their souls. Thanks to you we have the opportunity to begin again!" Margaret Coggleshall looked determined, as did Matilda Wilson.

I did not say anything, but my men had taken some coins from the Scottish bandits. They had given me my share. I would give the purse to the ladies. It was the least I could do.

We headed first for Dumfries, which had good walls and a garrison. It meant we would have a longer second day but that was worth it, and I used King Edward's writ. What I learned was that there was an increased presence of bandits to the north, east and south of the castle. That would be our fault. Having destroyed their home some would have gravitated south to take the richer pickings there.

With that news we left for the last part of our journey as though we were going to war. My best scouts were well ahead of us. Mordaf and Harry had insisted upon riding with us, but I did not allow them to be the advanced scouts. I noticed now what both the constable and the other ladies had alluded to. Hamo spent as much time as he could riding next to Alice. It made sense. There were just a few years between them and apart from his sisters, Hamo had not seen many young ladies his own age. And I could see that Alice saw him as the young hero who had saved her. It was a passing phase, but it would not harm either of them.

We were not far from Gretna when Dick rode back. "My lord, half a mile up the road and down a side track there appears to be some sort of conflict."

"Bandits?"

"I would guess so."

I turned and dismounted "Hamo, keep the wagons closely guarded." I strung my bow. "William, Robert, come with me!"

As I mounted my horse again Hamo said, "Five men will not be enough. Take more!"

"No, my son, these captives need the best of my men to watch them. Five should be enough to deter them. They know me now and will not relish a length of ash in their bodies."

I spurred my horse and headed up the road to Gwillim. I saw the smoke rising from the farm. "Gwillim, the five of us must do what I would normally expect half a company to do. We dismount a hundred paces from them and use our bows. Let us see if we can discourage them."

"I have counted at least twelve bandits. The people in the farm have barred the door. All those who are outside must be bandits, captain! The fire is from the barn fire. I think the brigands thought to draw them hence."

The smoke was blowing towards us from the barn fire and hid our approach. We dismounted and I nocked an arrow. The five of us spread out and moved like a net towards them. Gwillim was the first to find flesh. He was next to me and I heard the twang of his bow and the cry as the man was hit. I saw nothing, for the wind blew some noxious smoke into my face. I heard a Scottish shout, "Where did the arrow come from?"

I knew their dilemma. Although Gwillim must have sent it into the bandit's back an arrow could easily spin a man around. The smoke cleared and I saw myself looking at a range of less than twenty paces, at two bandits. I sent one into the chest of one and as the other ran at me drew another arrow. It was a race, but I won. He was one pace away and my arm was half drawn back. Even with a half pull, the man would be dead.

"You have until I have finished this sentence to decide if you wish to live or die. Drop to your knees and release your weapon or meet

254

your maker." As I pulled back a little the bow creaked, and he obeyed. I eased my bow and then swung around as I saw a bandit running at William wielding a war hammer. He was fifteen paces away when my arrow slammed into him so hard that he was knocked to the side. I saw, now that we were closer to the farm, that my archers had slain eight men. Nocking another arrow, I shouted, "Throw down your weapons or die!" The man I had made to lie on the ground began to rise and I sent the arrow through his hand to pin him down. "When I say you can rise then you can move!"

Those in the farm had realised that aid had come to them and they burst out. It was too much for the remaining bandits. They fled, or they tried to flee. I swung my bow into the mouth of one man who tried to pass me. He fell unconscious at my feet. The rest died.

The farmer and his sons were bleeding, but they were defiant. "Let us hang the bastards now, archer!"

I shook my head. "They must be taken to Carlisle. The constable there has a responsibility to keep this land safe. They will be tried there."

He nodded. "You are right. We have been left abandoned for too long. I did not get your name, archer."

"I am Sir Gerald Warbow, King Edward's archer."

He dropped to his knee. "Forgive me being so forward, my lord. We are grateful to you."

I pointed to the wagons, now passing the end of the lane. "We have just been north of the border rescuing families taken from the Eden Valley. You are luckier than they were. Can you manage now?"

He nodded. "We will burn their bodies, if only to stop the carrion!"

I walked over to the man whose hand had been pinned to the ground. I pulled the arrow carefully. I was not concerned with the man, but I wanted to preserve the arrow. When I managed to remove it with the head still intact, I beamed.

"You had better find the other arrows." My archers were already doing so. "You," I pointed to the wounded archer, sling your comrade over your back and walk down the lane to the wagons!"

"But my hand!"

I tore a piece of material from his kyrtle and tied it around the wound. "*Now* pick him up!" The tone of my voice brooked no argument and he obeyed. We had spare horses and I said, "Put your friend over the back of the horse until he wakes."

It was as he did so that Alice screamed: "It is him! He is the violator of girls!"

The other three women saw him, and their reaction shocked me. They spat and cursed at him. Hamo said, "He violated you?"

I saw then that Matilda's two daughters, Maud and Ann, were cowering together. Alice shook her head and said, "He tried, but he valued his manhood too much – but he made their lives a misery." She pointed at the two girls.

The man cowered as Hamo leapt from his horse and ran towards him. I shouted, "Hamo, stop!"

"But he should be punished!"

"And he will be but not here on this road to nowhere! He shall be tried and then hanged in Carlisle. His head will be displayed on the gates and then all the world will know of his crime. Jack, bind him and tie him to the cantle of the horse with the other captive. Bind him also and guard them both." I looked at Hamo. "I would not have them harmed further. The hangman will not be cheated." Hamo's hands bunched into fists and I knew that he was angry. Was it just with the captive, or had I made him so?

Eleanor said, as she helped Matilda to comfort her daughters, "Sir Gerald is right and the other was from the band too, my lord."

"Then the ones we just slew have also been served justice." Jack had finished. "We have wasted enough time with this scum. Let us ride. Hamo, ride with me at the fore! Mordaf and Harry, help Jack." I knew that they would ensure there was no mischief.

Once we began to ride, I spoke quietly but firmly to him. "Hamo, until today I could not find fault with you, but I saw anger with a command which I gave, and I did not like it."

"He violated girls!"

"And he will be punished – but it is more than that, is it not?"

His head hung and he said, "It is Alice." I nodded and waited for him to continue. "Father, when you met my mother did you know that she was the one?"

I laughed. "When I met your mother, I was just trying to stay alive, as was your mother." I saw that he wanted a genuine answer and so I made a straight face and said, "It was Queen Eleanor who put us together, for I did not think that your mother would even look at me. Do not make a hasty decision, Hamo. You are young and have your whole life ahead of you." He nodded. Is this why you suggested she and her brothers come to Yarpole?"

"It seemed a perfect solution."

"Then behave as though she was your sister until we reach Yarpole. If this is meant to be, then all will be well."

We continued in silence for the last ten miles. I sent Gwillim and Dick ahead to warn de Brus but when we reached the castle it was Robert of Carlisle who greeted us. "Sir Gerald, the Constable left a week ago to visit his lands in Guisborough. He left me in command!"

"We managed to rescue the captives – all save one, who died before we even left for the rescue." I saw his face pale and cursed my choice of words. I gestured to the prisoners. The second had awoken. "We found bandits close to Gretna. I would have riders scour the woods. I shifted Wallace but his bandits remain a danger."

He nodded and, as he raised his head, the wagons entered the outer bailey and he saw Eleanor Hall. I have never seen such a transformation. It was as though he had been told that a sentence of death had been lifted. He ran from me and held out his arms to lift her down.

"It has been many years, Eleanor."

When she reached the ground, she hugged him. "Too many, Robert, but we can start again eh? There are two young people who will need your wisdom!"

"And that they shall have!"

Epilogue

We stayed to see the men hanged, and that was just to give the women and girls a sense of peace. The two bodies – which jerked and twisted as they were hauled up to the battlements – were now consigned to the past. The farewells were emotional, for the women and children had endured much together. Alice, James and John were given horses and we headed south, through England to the comparative safety of the Welsh border. We delivered one letter to the castle at Lancaster, but the earl was not at home. Hamo heeded my words and was a true gentleman all the way south – although he was never more than a pace from the side of Alice.

When we reached Chester, I told the Earl of Lincoln what had happened, and he took the letter. "De Brus was a claimant to the throne. I hope that King Edward was right to put such faith in him. If Carlisle fell into Scottish hands …"

I thought about Eleanor and Robert, not to mention the others, and replied, "It does not bear thinking about!"

I sent William and Gwillim on ahead to warn my wife of our imminent arrival so that when, on a cold December morning, we entered my courtyard, my whole family was there to greet us. I saw the faces of Joan and Margaret behind Mary. I jumped from my horse and threw myself in her arms.

"It is good that you are home, husband. Gwillim told me all." She kissed me and pulled back. "We both have news, it seems. Hamo has discovered ladies – and you," she stepped aside, "are now a grandfather. Meet your grandson, Gerald Launceston."

Margaret held up the babe for me to hold. I reached for the bairn, knowing that I stank of horses and needed a good wash but joyous that there would be another Gerald to carry on the tradition. Would he become a Gerald Warbow too?

That was in the future and as the door was closed behind me, I put the problems of Scottish and Welsh behind me. I had served King Edward well, and now I would serve myself and my family.

Historical Note

The Great Cause was the term used for the problem of Scottish succession. King Alexander's death, at the time, was put down to a freak accident and a reflection on the character of the king who was happy to take risks. I have put a more sinister interpretation on the events, and in light of the suspicious death of Margaret of Norway may not be far from the truth. We shall never know.

The battles were all real but the details, after so many years, are a little vague. The loss of the baggage train in Wales is documented, as is the fact that the storms were the worst in living memory. Edward's conquest of Scotland appears to have been as easy as I describe it. According to one chronicler, 10,000 Scots died at Dunbar. I find that hard to believe, but the scale of the victory was so great that there was no more opposition to the English. A porter was, indeed, the only person in Stirling castle and appears to have waited to give the keys to someone. The whole conquest took mere months. Robert de Brus was made governor of Carlisle in 1295.

The William Wallace segment is fiction, but fiction based on facts. Before he became the leader of the Scottish rebellion he was a bandit, a sort of Scottish Robin Hood. Little is known about his early life or, indeed, anything until he killed the English lord who had Wallace's wife murdered. That was the act that triggered the revolt against Edward's rule. Therein lies a future book!